WHAT READERS HAVE SAID:

"I loved this book, it is just the type of book I like to read, very exciting, I did not want to put it down."

"I had to get up early the next morning and was sleepy, so I went to bed early and thought I would just read a few pages before I went to sleep. I finished the book at 2:00AM."

SURVIVAL
AT STARVATION LAKE

GARY P. HANSEN

COVER DESIGN BY: SARAH B. MILLER

WESTBOW
PRESS

The author can be contacted at garyphansen@juno.com

WestBow Press books may be ordered through booksellers or by contacting:

WestBow Press
A Division of Thomas Nelson
1663 Liberty Drive
Bloomington, IN 47403
www.westbowpress.com
1-(866) 928-1240

ISBN: 978-1-4497-0347-9 (sc)
ISBN: 978-1-4497-0348-6 (hc)
ISBN: 978-1-4497-0346-2 (e)

Library of Congress Control Number: 2010931016

Printed in the United States of America

WestBow Press rev. date: 10/7/2010

I would like to dedicate this book to my late mother, Polly Hansen to whom I owe my Christian faith, and to my father Laurin Hansen who unselfishly took care of my mother for almost ten years as she suffered with cancer. I was truly blessed to be their son.

CONTENTS

ACKNOWLEDGEMENTS

I would like to thank the following people for their help with this book. Alfred L. Brady, Joan Kruithoff, Gayle Preston, Julie Hansen, Laurin Hansen, Carol Sniadowski, Janet Fabiszak, Diane Kuhlman, Virginia McCarthy, Sarah Miller and Pastor Rick Mavis.

CHAPTER I

The Perfect Storm

From the outside, the ill-destined plane looked perfectly all right, just like all the other planes in the airport that day.

Paul Sinhuna boarded the small commuter plane and made his way down the aisle. He was surprised by the size of the plane because the one he had arrived on only a week ago had been much larger. He was hoping for a window seat, but the seat number on the ticket they had given him at the terminal appeared to be an aisle seat. Almost all the aisle seats were full. Paul found the seat that corresponded to his ticket and said to the woman sitting in it, "Excuse me, madam. I believe you're sitting in my seat."

"Do you mind taking the window seat? I prefer the aisle," she replied.

"That is fine with me, madam," Paul said as he waited for her to step into the aisle, so he could squeeze his six-foot-four-inch, 350-pound frame into the window seat. *I may have just made two mistakes,* Paul thought after he sat down. *I would have had more room on the aisle seat, and also, I am already overheated.* Paul laughed to himself and thought, *Sometimes when I get what I want, I find that I don't actually want it.*

It had been below zero degrees that morning when he left camp. His outfitter had driven him to the airport in a truck that had a less-than-perfect heater. He had been grateful that he was wearing a T-shirt, quilted shirt, hooded sweatshirt, and winter hunting jacket, but now, in the heated plane, he was already becoming too warm. *I should have taken off my coat and sweatshirt before I sat down,* he thought. *Now, in these tight quarters, I am not going to be able to take them off without disturbing the person in the seat next to me.* He unzipped his coat and sweatshirt and figured he would just make do.

Sally McPhearson sat back down in the aisle seat. *Just my luck*, she thought. *I get Santa Claus for a seatmate.* Except for his height, with his white beard, bald head, and plump appearance from his extra clothing, Paul did look remarkably like the good saint. Two of Sally's college friends had married men they had met on planes, but here she was, almost forty and only married to her career. Now she was sitting beside a man who was at least ten years her senior and someone she could never have the slightest interest in. Besides, out of reflex, she had already noticed the wedding band on his finger.

Maybe I should buy a corporate jet, she thought. She found herself on a plane an average of two times per week and could not remember the last time she sat with anyone she could remotely have thought of as marriage material. She had just about resigned herself to the fact that she would never marry. Her career had virtually used up all her time for the last sixteen years. She had taken over running her father's newspaper when he suffered a heart attack. He recovered from his heart attack in a year, but by that time, Sally had been doing so well running the newspaper that he just decided to retire.

In the fifteen years since her father retired, she had acquired seven other major newspapers, three magazines, and a television broadcasting network. She was now the CEO of one of the largest corporations in Canada. She would have already owned a corporate jet, except that three years ago, one of her competitor's magazines had named her Businesswoman of the Year. The accompanying magazine article had mentioned how Sally always flew commercial to save her corporation money and keep in direct contact with the people of Canada. Now how could she buy a jet after that?

Paul had barely noticed his attractive seatmate. He was lost in thought. For years, Paul had wanted to hunt the massive whitetail bucks of northern Saskatchewan but never dreamed he would actually have a chance to do it. The weather on the hunt had been unseasonably warm, in the fifties, and the outfitter had blamed the warm weather for the lack of deer sightings. Only on the last day of the hunt did the weather turn cold. There had been so few deer seen that out of six hunters in camp, Paul was the only one to harvest a buck. The buck was the only deer Paul had seen on the whole hunt. It was a nice buck by anyone's standards and the second largest Paul had ever taken, but somehow he was disappointed. Maybe it was just that now that the hunt was over, he was going to have to figure out what he was going to do with the rest of his life.

Paul's thoughts turned to the last ten years. They were years full of sorrow and loss for him. Thirty years before, he had married his high school sweetheart and started his business as a builder and contractor. In the first twenty years of marriage, he and his wife had raised two fine daughters, and his business had flourished. Then, ten years ago, it seemed that everything in his life began a slow, but sure, downhill spiral. The economy in Michigan, where he made his home, slowed down because of the auto industry's problems. Paul's business suffered because of no fault of his own, even though he never really figured that out. His company had gone from employing a dozen people and many subcontractors and building twenty-five to thirty-five custom homes per year, to nothing. Ten years ago, Paul's sister had been murdered by a serial killer, and his beloved wife, Joan, began her long, heroic fight with cancer. His business failure and Joan's medical bills had eaten up all their life savings and retirement accounts. In order to keep his financial head above water, he sold practically everything he or his business owned, yet he was still broke.

The only bright spot in the last ten years of his life was that both of his daughters had met and married fine young men. His sons-in-law were both pastors, but they were called to small churches at far ends of the country. One was in Florida and the other in Oregon, so even his daughters were somewhat lost to him. Last year, Paul's parents had been killed in a car accident caused by a drunk driver. Then, early that spring, his wife lost her long battle with cancer. Over the course of his ten years of loss, his faith in God had remained strong. He had prayed long and hard for many things, and anyone looking at his life from the outside would have said that his prayers had gone unanswered. However, Paul knew that his prayers had been answered; the answers just were not the ones that he wanted.

The loss of his wife, Joan, was the hardest answer for him to accept. It was very difficult for him to watch as Joan, the mother of his children, changed from a kind, beautiful, and outgoing woman to a shadow of her former self. There were times in her ten-year fight with cancer when it looked like she had turned a corner and was on her way back to health, but alas, that was just an illusion. He had prayed very hard for Joan and would have happily taken her place if that had been an option. In the end, the end came quickly. Her death hit him hard, and he sank into deep despair and depression. Paul's prayers had turned to pleas to God to make his mental pain go away. "God, please just take me home!" Paul prayed. He would have welcomed his own death.

For two weeks after his wife's death and memorial service, Paul never left his house. He could not even bring himself to go to church. He did not want to be around other people as he mourned her loss. Even the stormy weather fit his dark mood, with thunderstorms for a solid two weeks, but then the skies began to clear. Paul's best friend, Randy, had been worried about Paul. Randy had also been worried about himself, as he was a real estate agent and had not sold a house in many months. He had listed Paul's parents' house for Paul after their car accident, and after months on the market, someone finally made an offer. The offer was an answer to Randy's prayers.

Randy knocked on Paul's door early in the morning on the first sunny day after Joan's death. In fact, Paul had to get out of bed to let Randy in. Randy laid some leaflets on the kitchen table about hunting in Saskatchewan and said, "Paul, I have been worried about you, and I think you need to do something to get your mind off all the problems that have been plaguing you. I want you to promise me that you will look these over, pick an outfitter, and book a hunt."

"Randy, I don't have two nickels to rub together. I don't even know how I am going to pay this month's electric bill," Paul replied.

"Well, you will not have to worry about that after you sign the papers I have brought with me. I received an offer for the full asking price on your folks' house." That was how Paul came to be sitting on this plane.

The pilot's voice brought Paul's mind back to the here and now. "Good morning, everyone. My name is Captain Ron Miller, and I am going to be your pilot today. We will be taking off in a few minutes and will be flying nonstop to Detroit Metro Airport, and then, after a brief layover, we will be continuing on to Toronto. There is no doubt that many of you were expecting a larger aircraft when you booked your flight, so I feel I owe you an explanation. Last night, the airline had ninety-two cancellations for this flight; most of them were from a local high school whose students were taking a field trip to Toronto. Evidently, there is a flu outbreak at the school." The pilot then went on to explain all the common safety measures in case of an emergency. Apparently, the plane was so small that it did not warrant a flight attendant. "Sorry for any inconvenience, folks. Hope you enjoy your flight." A few minutes after the pilot finished his speech, they were in the air.

From his window seat Paul watched as the airport they just left grew smaller but in a matter of minutes the cloud cover put the ground out of sight. Well at least I can lean my head against the window frame and try to get some sleep, he thought. Paul often had trouble sleeping unless of course he was on a deer stand or in a church pew. In this case, being slightly overheated and listening to the drone of the plane's engines had him fast asleep in only a few minutes. Shortly, he began slightly snoring; much to the annoyance of Sally who, true to her mode of operation, was trying to get some work done on her lap top. I just have to look into getting a corporate jet, Sally thought.

Modern commercial aviation has a very fine safety record. Aviation regulations, redundancy of critical aircraft systems, and global positioning navigation equipment are all designed to safely deliver the passengers to their destination. Pilots rely on their training, aircraft systems, and standard operating procedures to provide for their passengers' safety. However, sometimes in the course of human events, problems can come up that cannot be foreseen or engineered away. Normally, these problems are of little concern. The redundancy of systems and the prescribed operating procedures keeps these problems from becoming anything but a minor inconvenience to the flight crew. In other words, when only one of many possible problems occurs it is really no problem at all and the odds of more than one of these problems occurring in the same flight are remote. It is highly unlikely that a group of unrelated problems would cascade out of control and cause the loss of an aircraft, but that was what was about to happen.

The Pilot choose a longer more remote route to avoid some heavy weather and filed a flight plan electronically, but an undocumented bug in the software garbled some of the information and no one noticed. Ground controllers hand off monitoring a flight from one controlled air space to another. In this case an inconveniently timed shift change combined with a waste paper basket fire in the control room at precisely the same time the plane's transponder stopped sending, meant that no one on the ground noticed the plane was heading off course. Had the flight taken place under clear weather and VFR (Visual Flight Rules) instead of IFR (Instrument Flight Rules) the pilots would have noticed that a glitch in their navigation computer had taken them off course. None of these things would have mattered. The pilots would have eventually noticed they were off course and would have corrected course with the only effect being a longer flight. However, a cascading electrical fault along with an unrelated mechanical failure meant that the flight was doomed, a perfect storm of unrelated problems, and technology failures.

After a couple hours of uneventful flight, some bumps from air turbulence woke Paul up. He turned and looked out the window. Still nothing to look at, just clouds , Paul thought. He glanced over at Sally, thought about saying something to her, but decided against it when he saw she was hard at work. He was thinking about how uncomfortable he was and how he would like to stretch out when a loud bang came from the aircraft.

The pilot immediately knew they had lost an engine and came on the intercom. With a calm voice he said, "We are experiencing some problems, please fasten your safety belts and store any loose objects in the seat back in front of you." As soon as the pilot had shut off the intercom the co-pilot tried to make a distress call but found the radio was dead. By now both the pilot and the co-pilot knew they were in the worst type of trouble and that they were going to go down. It should have been possible to control the plane and even land it safely with only one engine, but there was something else wrong. Their flight controls were mushy and it took both of them to keep the plane under what little control they had. The plane and the passengers were violently being bounced around.

When they dropped below the cloud cover they were expecting to find themselves over Lake Superior near Sault Ste. Marie, Canada but were surprise to find themselves over the waters of a long narrow lake. Fortunately, although, flying the length of the lake. They would never know they were almost five hundred miles off course. The pilots knew they were not where they were supposed to be but did not have time to even think about how, why, or what had happened. Many people in the cabin of the plane were screaming or crying. People who had not prayed in years or had never prayed were praying. Again the pilot's voice cracked over the intercom but this time he could not hide the panic in his voice. "We are going down. Everyone put your head between your knees and brace for impact against the seat back in front of you." Everyone complied with the pilot's orders, everyone that is, except Paul.

Paul calmly turned and looked out the window again. Unlike everyone else in the plane, no extra adrenalin surged through his veins. Surprisingly, for a man who was always praying he did not even offer up an extra prayer. No need to make his peace with God because he was already at peace with Him. The thought that ran through his mind was, it looks like I am going to die shortly so I might as well watch what is going on.

The pilots knew that ditching in the lake offered no hope for survival for anyone. To survive being in that cold water they would need to be rescued within minutes. They did not know where they were but could tell they were in a wilderness area with no hope of immediate rescue. They were now only a hundred feet above the water and ground effect was helping keep the plane in the air but they would shortly be running out of lake. They could see a river coming up and that the terrain turned into a marsh down the river a ways. Without saying anything to each other, they both knew that setting the plane down in that marsh was the only hope for anyone on board and they were fighting to keep the plane in the air until they reached the marsh.

Paul looked at the whitecap waves on the lake below him and causally thought it must be really windy. Normally by this time of year, early December, the lake's surface would have been frozen solid. As the plane entered the river valley Paul noticed a small cabin flash by his window at the convergence of the lake and the river. The plane was now just above the tops of the trees that lined the river bank and the pilots were desperately trying to thread a needle by keeping the plane centered over the river below. Suddenly it occurred to Paul that placing his head between his knees and bracing for impact would not be such a bad idea after all! Seconds after he did, the tip of the wing clipped a large white pine tree lining the river. This caused the plane to turn into a group of several other pines that were along the edge of the river.

Instantly, Sally had the sensation that she was flying through the air without the benefit of being surrounded by a plane. Debris was hitting her all over and she kept her eyes closed. How could this be happening to her? She was not ready to die. This must be a bad dream. Did her panic cause her to black out? Did the concussion from impact knock her out? How long had she been unconscious? Was she even conscious now? Was she even still alive? She did not know how much time had passed. The next thing she knew she was on her back looking up at the sky, disoriented and in shock.

Paul was asking, "Are you alright? Are you alright?". She was still in her plane seat which was now laying on its back in a marsh. Very cold water from the marsh was seeping into her coat and up the back of her blouse as Paul was unfastening her seat belt.

"Where's my laptop? Where's my laptop? I have important work on my laptop, I can't lose it!"

"That is the least of your worries lady." Paul coldly replied as he helped her up from the inverted plane seat. He did not realize she was talking out of shock and disorientation because he was in shock and disoriented himself. He helped her to the edge of the marsh and sat her down on the bank. "Stay here." he ordered and returned to the plane's debris field to help other people. There was another plane seat about a hundred feet from where his plane seat had come to rest with a woman in it. She was still alive. Paul could see that her leg was broken and he carried her to the nearest bank which was separated from but within sight of where he had left Sally. Paul could tell the lady with the broken leg was somewhat incoherent but she was imploring him to leave her alone and go find her son. He returned to the debris field, looked under a piece of sheet metal and found a small boy who was also still alive. Then Paul carried him to her side. He was hoping for her sake that the boy was her son but he would never find out, because by the time he laid the boy next to the woman they were both dead. Paul carried five more bodies that had spilled out of the plane to the bank. He laid each of them next to the bodies of the woman and boy.

Where the other people who had been in the plane were, Paul did not know. Perhaps they were in the wreckage of the large part of the tail section that was mostly submerged in the river. If that was the case Paul knew there was no hope for them. He could see the cockpit of the plane farther into the marsh and it was mangled so badly he knew there would be no survivors there either.

Sally had sat on the bank where Paul had left her and had watched as he carried people out of the marsh. She was not used to taking orders from anyone and under different circumstances, ordering her to do something would have been a sure way to keep her from doing it. However, she knew she could be of no help. Somewhere along the line she had twisted her ankle and it would have been throbbing except for the fact her feet were soaked, and numbed from the cold. So she just sat there struggling to wrap her mind around what had just happened. My cell phone, she thought, where is it? In my purse? Where is my purse? No, it is in my coat pocket. She retrieved it, but it had no bars. By now she should have been in her hotel room putting the finishing touches on a presentation she was making to her corporate board about another possible acquisition. She was still trying to make her mind focus on the circumstances she found herself in when Paul walked back to her.

"I am afraid that we are the only survivors." Paul said. "Can you walk?" Paul asked and continued without giving her a chance to reply.

"We need to take shelter. There is a cabin up this way and we need to get there while there is still light." It was raining hard now and the wind was bone chilling.

"We need to stay here and wait for rescuers." Sally replied as she thought how could he possibly know there is a cabin up there?

"The wind is too strong and the weather is getting worse; we will not be rescued tonight. If we stay here out in the open we will die. I am soaked to my knees from stepping in holes in the marsh and I can't feel my feet. We need to get moving now!" Paul demanded as he helped her to her feet.

"I can't feel my feet either and, I think I twisted my right ankle." she said through chattering teeth. Paul moved to her right side, and to help support her, he placed his arm around her.

"Lean on me." he ordered, as they started along the bank.

As they made their way along the marsh bank back towards the river, Sally kept protesting "We are making a mistake. We should have stayed where we were and waited for rescue." but Paul just ignored her objections and encouraged her to move faster.

When they reached the river they found themselves on some type of trail. Was it an old overgrown logging road, a snowmobile trail, or just a game trail? Paul could not tell. It was getting darker and he kept trying to spur his companion on. Every time they went around a slight bend in the trail he was expecting to see the cabin. Had he just imagined the cabin? He questioned himself. The distance to the cabin was proving to be a lot farther than he thought and it was getting dark. Paul did not know what time it was. He had a watch but because he did not know where they were, he did not know what time zone they were in. Also, he could not remember for sure if he had changed the setting of his watch to reflect the time it was going to be at Detroit when they landed. With the gathering storm it was getting darker faster than it normally would for that time of day. The cold front that had dropped the temperatures back in Saskatchewan had reached this place. He was greatly relieved when they rounded a bend in the trail and he spotted the outhouse that went with the cabin.

They reached the outhouse first and Paul opened the door to check it out to be sure it was safe. Even after exerting themselves getting here, both of them had chattering teeth. "You had better use the outhouse before we go into the cabin." Paul said. Sally went in and shut the door without saying anything. While she was in there Paul relieved himself behind a bush, then he turned and looked at the cabin. Somehow, he was not sure that this was the same cabin he had seen from the plane. It did not matter;

it was getting dark and they were going to have to stay here for the night. The metal roof of the front porch had collapsed on one end and the front door was behind it. A pile of firewood was holding up the other end of the porch. They would not be able to enter by the front door and from the size of the cabin it was doubtful there would be another door. A large maple branch was laying on the roof. It had knocked over the stove pipe chimney flue, collapsed the porch and also broke a pane in the side window. That side window would need to be their entry point and the flue laying on the roof would mean there could be no fire until it could be fixed and he determined if a fire would be safe. Just then the outhouse door opened and Paul helped Sally up the hill to the log cabin.

The broken window pane was in the lower sash of a twelve-paned-double hung window. Paul easily broke off the branch that had broken the window pane. He then carefully removed the broken shards of glass with his numbed fingers, and pushed up on the sash. The latch on the sash was not locked. Behind the window inside the darkening cabin there was a kitchen counter. That will making getting in easier, he thought. "I will help you through the window." Paul said.

" No, you go first, I can get in easier than you can." Sally replied. Paul realized she was right and hoisted his 350 pound frame through the window. He would not have made it without Sally's help. Somehow giving an order to the man who had been ordering her around made her feel a little better. Paul slid over the counter, turned around, regained his footing, and helped pull Sally through the window.

The cabin was only about twelve feet by sixteen feet. There were only three windows; the one they had crawled through, one in the door, and another in the gable above the porch. In one front corner there was a stone hearth with a wood stove made from a 55 gallon oil drum. The hearth and stove took up a lot of space along the 16 foot wall. There was a stack of firewood between the barrel stove and the outside wall. The other front corner contained a small table and two chairs. In between the table and the hearth was the front door that had been blocked by the downed porch roof. In one back corner there was a double bed with a steamer trunk at the foot of the bed. The other back corner contained some cabinets and the kitchen counter with a sink and pitcher pump. In almost the center of the room there was a log ladder that went up to a half loft. There was only about four feet of clearance between the floor of the loft and the ridge log of the roof in the center and no space at all near the outside walls. Not much room up there for anything but storage. On the floor beside the bed was a homemade rag rug.

By now it was too dark to see any real detail, and Paul retrieved a pen light that was attached to his key ring. The bed was covered by a canvas and Paul uncovered it. Below the canvas was just a bare mattress. Paul then tried to open the steamer trunk hoping there would be warm blankets inside but he found it was locked. Next he opened several cupboards and in one he found an extra large heavy sleeping bag and a couple of pillows all stored in plastic garbage bags. He laid the pillows and sleeping bag out on the bed and unzipped the bag. He then pulled the canvas back up to act as an extra blanket. Next he bent over to pick up the rag rug to use as another blanket but found that he could not. It was nailed down.

By now Sally was now shaking uncontrollably from the cold. All her clothes were soaking wet from the rain. Paul's pants were soaked from the knees down and the outside of his hunting coat was wet but it was designed not to absorb water so all his clothing under it was dry. Paul turned to her and said, "Take off your clothes and get into the sleeping bag."

Sally could not believe what she was hearing and began to cry. "I survived a plane crash and now you are going to rape me!"

"Lady! I am not going to rape you! I am trying to save your life, err our lives. We are both going into hypothermia and we will die if we do not warm up. I am so cold I could not possibly rape you, even if I was so inclined, and believe me I am not. Your clothes are soaked clear through and you are not going to warm up with them on. Now take off your clothes or I will do it for you." Then, as a panicked after thought he added, "I did not mean all of your clothes; it is OK to leave on your underwear." Sally complied and took off her clothes down to her underwear. She was having trouble because she was shaking so hard and her stiff fingers did not want to work. While she was taking off her clothes, Paul was hanging their wet clothing over the backs of the chairs and stripping himself down to his T-shirt. Sally was getting into the sleeping bag when Paul handed her his dry quilted shirt. and said, "Put this on." Paul also gave her a dry ski mask he pulled from the pocket of his hunting jacket and helped her pull it on over her head.. He then put his dry sweatshirt back on, pulled the hood over his bald head and pulled the drawstrings tight so only his nose, eyes, and beard were visible.

" Lay facing me." was the last order Paul barked out that night. Then he crawled into the sleeping bag after her, zipped it up, turned over, and wrapped his arms around her. The sleeping bag was a very large one but only meant for one person, so it was a tight fit. There they laid, shivering with their teeth chattering for what seem like hours. Then, slowly their bodies began to warm up. Paul stopped shivering first, as he was much larger and was not as cold to start with. Paul normally prayed silently but without even realizing he was talking out loud he prayed a simple prayer of thanks "Lord Jesus, please be with the families of the dead and thank you for seeing us through this trying day." Sally thought, "Great, I am trapped in this situation with some type of Christian nut." A half an hour later Sally also quit shivering and within a few minutes was fast asleep and snoring softly. Paul was exhausted but laid awake half the night listening to the wind howl in what had turned into a blizzard outside, or perhaps some of it was from the howls of wolves.

By this time, their flight was long over due, and literally hundreds of people were franticly trying to figure out what had happened to them. Coast Guard planes from both the U.S.A. and Canada were out flying a search pattern grid over Lake Superior listening for pings from the missing plane's black boxes on their radios. The electronically filed but garbled flight plan had been retrieved and found to be useless. There were two search areas; one over Eastern Lake Superior and the other near the edge of the Saskatchewan air traffic control area. Both areas were hundreds of miles from where the plane really went down. The search would take thousands of man hours and last another two weeks before it would eventually be called off. The missing plane would receive world wide news attention but with nothing new to report, interest would dwindle. News announcers would talk about the 19 missing people being presumed dead but would only mentioned Sally McPhearson by name.

After Paul finally fell asleep he had a fitful night. He kept having nightmares about the people he tried to save at the crash site and kept waking up every few minutes. Each time he woke up it sounded like the storm outside was louder. Paul normally was a restless sleeper and would toss and turn all night. However, this night he never moved. Sally's face was nestled into his beard and she was fast asleep. He did not want to disturb her, and besides even though he had quit shivering he was still cold and she was his only source of heat.

Paul was an early riser and woke at first light. He ached all over from the activities of the day before and remaining motionless all night. His feet were still numb but he could wiggle his toes and he took that as a good sign that they were not frost bit. He got out of bed and within a few minutes he was shivering again.

He pulled on his pants which were stiff because the moisture in them had frozen. The good news was that his socks were dry. He had paid $30 for his socks and they were made of some super duper, special fiber. He thought to himself, his special socks had sure paid for themselves this morning. He had a hard time getting his boots on because they were frozen also.

Paul knew they would be in bad trouble if he could not fix the stove flue and get a fire going. Paul looked through the cabinets until he found a mason jar with a box of kitchen matches inside. At least I've got matches, he thought. He unscrewed the lid of the jar and got out the box of matches while his hands were still warm. Next, he opened the door to the barrel stove and found that someone had left wood in it arranged to make a fire easy to start. Further inspection revealed that the stove pipe on the inside of the cabin was in good shape.

Sally woke up when Paul got out of bed but she did not stir and had kept her eyes closed. She did not want Paul to know she was awake. She was not totally sure, but she did not think she much liked the man she was trapped in this adventure with. He had been demanding and gruff and ordered her around like she was in the Army. She was used to giving orders in her corporation; not taking them. Actually, she was a even a little afraid of him and thought it best not to let him know she was awake. Maybe she would be lucky and they would be rescued before she was forced to talk to him again. She just laid there wondering what he was doing and did not open her eyes until it sounded like he went out the window.

Paul had found an ax in the cabin and had taken it with him when he went out the window. He had worried that he would have trouble getting up on the roof, but he was able to climb the branch that had knocked down the porch and the flue when it fell from the tree. He was able to reattach the stove pipe without too much of a problem. Then he slid off the main roof and down the porch roof, taking as much snow with him as he could. He needed to make the roof as light as possible if he was going to be able to put the porch roof back up. Using the ax Paul chopped the branch into three pieces in a few minutes. The branch was now in manageable pieces and he was able to pull them off the porch roof, then he was able to raise the porch roof and prop it up with the original post. Paul leaned the pieces of the branch against the cabin so they would not become covered with snow because he had a feeling he would need them as firewood.

He was plenty cold by then and anxious to get a fire started but Paul discovered the front door was latched from the inside. However, there was a note taped in the window of the door that read "Pull the latch string." Paul's eyes followed the arrow on the note to a string that was hanging out of a hole in the wall by the edge of the door. When he pulled it the latch and the door opened. He went in, closed and re-latched the door behind him. Paul was glad that he had the foresight to get the matches out of the jar while his fingers were still working because now they were very cold and stiff. He opened the stove door and lit a piece of birch bark and held it up inside the stove near the flue opening to get a draft started. Soon he had a fire blazing away, however, it would be a few hours before the air inside the cabin warmed up. Paul took off his frozen boots and put one of the chairs on the rag rug near the stove so he could prop his feet up on the hearth and thaw out his feet and hands.

Once his hands and feet warmed up, Paul got to work. He closed the window, and found a rag to stuff in the hole left by the broken window pane. Then he cleaned up the snow drift that had blown through the open window over night. The snow drift was on the counter and the floor. Paul packed the snow from the inside snow drifts into five pans he found in the cupboards and put them on the stove to melt. There was a piece of U channel steel laying on the top of the barrel stove to provide a flat cooking surface. After the snow in the pans melted, he poured all the water over to one pan and used it to prime the pitcher pump. It takes melting a lot of snow to make a little water. After priming the pump, he pumped water for several minutes to make sure he was getting fresh water and not water that had been setting in the pipe. Then he filled the pans with water and put them on the stove to warm up. He took Sally's frozen and still wet clothes and hung them from nails in a log cross tie over the stove. With the stove blazing away they would thaw and dry quickly.

Paul was hungry and found a few mason jars full of rice in the cupboards and was planning on cooking some of it when he realized he did not really remember how. He had cooked lots of rice during his wife's illness but that was with a microwave. Maybe he should ask for advice from his companion who he suspected was pretending to be asleep but then thought better of it. It is just rice; how far could he go wrong? He dumped about a cup of rice in one of the larger pans of boiling water and decided to wait until it was ready to wake her. The boiling water in the other pans was used to rinse out a couple of bowls from the cupboards and sterilize some silverware. He had not found any dish soap in the cupboards but had found that some rodent had been using the silverware drawer as a seed warehouse. While he was doing this he made sure to stir the rice he was cooking every few minutes.

Sally had been pretending to sleep but as the cabin warmed up and she became more comfortable she had fallen back to sleep. When the rice was almost ready, Paul checked Sally's clothes and found they were dry so he took them down and laid them on the bed beside her. Then he woke her up. "Time to wake up, it is almost noon and lunch is almost ready." he said. Paul then turned and walked to the door and looked out the window while she got dressed. Sally had trouble putting her boot on her right foot because of the swelling in her sprained ankle. Her foot fit in it as long as she did not zip it up. She really needed to use the outhouse but knew she would need help getting there because of the pain in her ankle. So she swallowed her pride and asked, "Could you help me to the outhouse?"

"Sure thing." Paul replied.

He helped her down to the outhouse and then back up the hill to the cabin and sat her down at the kitchen table. Paul could feel some type of tension in the air between them and his late mother had always told him you should be quick to apologize even if you feel you have done nothing wrong. So he said, "I want to apologize, if I did or said anything that offended you in any way yesterday, I am truly sorry. Please forgive me". That simple apology greatly changed the way Sally felt about him, and she also said, "I want to apologize to you also."

Paul dished up half the rice for Sally and then took the rest for himself. He sat down, bowed his head and said a simple prayer out loud. "Thank you Lord Jesus for providing this cabin, this heat and this food at our time of true need. Be with the families of those who lost their lives in the crash and those who are searching for us now. Amen." Sally was more amused than offended at the prayer. How odd she thought that in this day and age there were still people who superstitiously prayed to a make believe supreme being, but she did not say anything. The rice was edible but not very good. It was kind of stale. Who knew how old it was?

"When do you think we will be rescued and where are we?" Sally asked.

"We might be rescued this afternoon if this storm quits and I think we are in Northern Ontario but we could be somewhere in Minnesota." Paul replied. This reply surprised Sally. Somehow she thought by some strange manner of fate Paul had been here before.

"If you do not know where we are, how did you know there was a cabin here?" Sally asked.

"I saw it out the window of the plane just before we crashed." Paul replied.

Well that explains it Sally thought. "But why were you looking out the window just before we crashed?"

Paul just replied, "Divine providence."

"I have been thinking." Paul said. "I do not think that the rescuers would miss the smoke coming from the chimney of this cabin, but I do not want to take any chances. There is some fluorescent orange surveying tape in the pocket of my hunting coat and I think I should go back to the crash site to mark a tree with it and leave a note so they know where we are. Do you have anything to write with?"

Sally smiled, "I think I have a permanent marker in the pocket of my coat if it did not freeze."

"Don't get up, I will check." Paul said as he got up and stepped to the door where Sally had hung her coat on a hook, when she returned from the outhouse. He found the marker in her pocket and removed the latch string note from the door. Sitting back down at the table he wrote on the back of the note, TWO SURVIVORS AT THE CABIN, PAUL SINHUNA &... he stopped and said, "I do not know your name."

Sally laughed, "It is Sally McPhearson."

"Well Miss McPhearson, let me introduce myself I am Paul Sinhuna." He added her name to the note and put it in a plastic bag he pulled from his pocket.

"Where did you get the cardboard you wrote the note on?" Sally asked. Paul told her about the latch string note, and she asked "Why would anyone put a note like that on the door?"

Paul explained that in wilderness areas people often left cabins unlocked in case someone needed shelter in a survival situation, and besides a lock is not going to keep anyone out if they really wanted to gain entry and leaving the door unlocked kept someone from damaging the cabin by breaking down the door.

"McPhearson is obviously Scottish." Sally stated, "but what nationality is Sinhuna?"

"I think it is Ottawa Indian." Paul replied.

"You do not look Indian." Sally said with surprise.

"I am not Indian. The story goes something like this. A group of Ottawa or perhaps Chippewa Indians found my Great, Great Grandfather who was only a small boy at the time in a cabin. His family had died from small pox and he was all alone. So the tribe adopted him and raised him until he was a young man. He was too young to know his name so the Indians gave him a name. I have been told that Sinhuna means survivor!"

"Are you kidding? I guess it runs in your family." Sally said.

"No, I am not kidding." Paul replied. "It may be just a family legend. I once tried to confirm the meaning of Sinhuna with some Ottawa Indians and they could not tell me for sure. It seems that Ottawa for the most part is almost a dead language in Michigan and I could not get in contact with anyone who could still speak more than a few words or phrases. The language sounds kind of "sing song" or almost musical. No one could tell me how to say survivor so I do not know for sure. Who knows, maybe Sinhuna mean something like "stupid little kid." and no one wanted to tell me.

Before he left for the crash site Paul filled the stove with firewood, and said "There is no insulation in the roof of this cabin, and it will take a lot of wood to keep it warm until it gets a few feet of snow on the roof. Hopefully we will not be here long enough for it to matter". Paul left the cabin carrying the ax but before he started down the trail he went over to a small storage building with a collapsed roof. The roof had collapsed in a prior year from the weight of snow or rot; Paul could not really tell which.

He was looking for a loose board and a couple of nails he could use to nail the note to a tree. Paul found the board he was looking for, and a broken canoe paddle that he thought would make a good crutch for Sally. There was also an old snowmobile with an empty gas tank and some other junk that might come in handy if they were not rescued soon and the snow did not cover it up. He dropped the paddle off for Sally at the cabin and started down the trail.

On his way down the trail he thought "Sally McPhearson." That name sounds familiar but he never gave it another thought. When he got near the crash sight, he noticed the broken tops of the trees that the plane had hit and sheared off. Paul was amused that the distance between the crash site and the cabin was a lot shorter than it seemed yesterday. Everything looked different than it did the day before. Yesterday there had been no snow but now there was a foot of it on the ground. When Paul reached the edge of the marsh where he had deposited Sally the day before, he cut a large blaze on the side of a two foot diameter white pine with the ax. Then he flagged it with plenty of orange surveyors tape and nailed his note and plastic bag to the tree through the board he had brought. It was good planning, as anyone in the area would notice it, and the note being in a plastic bag would remain legible for a long time. It was just too bad no one would ever see or read it to aide in their rescue, but Paul would not have ever guessed that.

After he finished his task of posting the note Paul thought about trying to retrieve anything that could be of use in the debris field. It was now covered with snow and he could not see anything he wanted to go after. Then the thought occurred to him that trying to salvage anything would be a waste of effort. After all, they were sure to be rescued as soon as the storm stopped and besides he did not want to wade out into the marsh and freeze his feet again.

Then a solemn thought crossed his mind. He should cover the bodies of the dead, so that crows and ravens did not scavenge them. There were some pieces of sheet metal that had been part of the outside skin of the plane laying on the bank that he could use. Paul walked to the edge of the marsh where he had left the bodies and made a terrible discovery. They were gone!

The thought that instantly jumped through Paul's mind was that the rescuers had already been there, recovered the bodies and left. Sally was right, they should have stayed there. Wait, how could that be with the storm? Paul turned and looked at the river. The tail section was still there. It had moved down stream a little and was now more submerged, but it was still there. The crumpled cock pit cabin was still in the marsh where it had been yesterday. Maybe this is not the spot I left the bodies he thought. Everything looks different with the snow. He looked back again to where he had been standing. I am sure this is the spot but the bodies are gone, he thought. Then he noticed a mound under the snow and thought, I don't remember that rock. Before and without thinking, he walked to it and kicked it. It was not a rock! It was the head of the woman with the broken leg.

CHAPTER 2

Crash Diet

The surprise and shock of this gruesome discovery caused Paul to throw up. The bodies were gone because something had eaten them bones and all. Something had eaten them yesterday before the snow and the snow was now covering what little evidence remained. Seconds later a wolf howled on the ridge just two hundred yards away, along the bank of the marsh. Paul looked up and spotted the wolf just as it was joined by several companions. Paul knew that wolves were responsible for very few human deaths in North America, but that thought was of little comfort to him right then.

Paul fought the urge to run away. He knew running could trigger the predator/prey response and that the wolves could run along the marsh bank and be on him before he could make fifty feet. He also knew that wolves like to surround their prey and attack from all sides and that a wolf's reflexes are much faster than that of a man's. The ax he held in his hand would be almost useless. Normally wolves are afraid of humans, but these had already scavenged the bodies from the crash. That fact might overcome their normal fear. This was bad; very bad!

Would a bluff work? Paul raised his hands and ax above his head to make himself look larger, let out a loud scream and began running along the marsh bank towards the wolves, waving his arms and the ax. For brief seconds it appeared that his bluff was not going to work. The wolves just stood there as if at a loss on what to do, but then they turned and quickly disappeared one by one, over the other side of the ridge. This was Paul's chance to retreat and he began hiking back up the trail. As he hiked he kept glancing back on his back trail checking to make sure he was not being followed. Each time he looked back he could see nothing.

A memory of a story he had read as a child replayed through his mind. In the story a man had temporarily escaped a pack of wolves by climbing a tree. Only to have the wolves camp out under the tree waiting for their victim to come down. Paul did not know if the story had been based on fact or if it was fiction but the thought of being trapped in a tree in this weather by a pack of wolves was not appealing to him at all. Still, as he hiked up the trail he was assessing the trees for ease of climbing. That is when he spotted a piece of luggage hanging from a branch about ten feet above the ground. As he reached the tree, with one fluid movement he swung his ax, he hit the branch holding the luggage and down it came. Without losing stride Paul scooped up the luggage with his free hand and swung it over his back. The luggage would protect his back if the wolves made a surprise attack.

Sally had sat with her ankle elevated for most of the time that she waited for Paul to return. Her ankle had not hurt during the night because it had been numbed by the cold but now that she had warmed up it was throbbing. She realized it was important to keep her foot up to keep the swelling down but she was restless and kept trying to think of ways to improve their situation. What a difference a few hours had made. Just twenty or so hours before she had been consumed by thoughts about her business. How the profit margins on her newspapers were evaporating and how her possible new magazine acquisition would hopefully make up for it. Worrying about her business had been her norm for years but now her thoughts were on survival. She glanced around the cabin. The amenities were certainly not close to her comfort zone, but she thought that perhaps staying in such a cabin under different circumstances for a few days could be fun. The kitchen window provided a beautiful view of the lake framed by picturesque white birch trees. She could see the waves lapping on the shore.

Sally wondered if this was a fishing cabin. There was a fishing pole over the door but there was also a pair of snowshoes hanging from the ceiling by a shoelace over the corner of the bed. So it appeared someone had spent time here in the winter. Did they live here year round? From the layer of dust on everything along with the numerous mouse droppings it was obvious no one had lived here for a long time. As her eyes looked around the room they stopped on the steamer trunk. She saw Paul try to open it and knew it was locked, but there would surely be something it it that could prove useful. Now where would I hide a key? She thought. Maybe on a ledge above one of the logs in the wall, but as she looked around she noticed the logs fit together tightly and there were not any ledges. Maybe on top of the cabinets? She climbed on top of the counter and felt around on top of the cabinet and found a key!

Sally excitedly stuck the key in the steamer trunk's lock and turned it. The trunk unlocked. She found another sleeping bag, blankets, sheets and pillow cases all wrapped in plastic garbage bags. Sally used them to make up the bed. First she moved the sleeping bag, they had used to the edge of the bed. It was the biggest one, so that would be Paul's. Then she opened the second bag and put up against the wall. That one would be hers. Finally she put the pillow cases on the pillows and spread the blankets over the sleeping bags. Let's see what else is in the trunk she thought, when she put the sheets back. She found more garbage bags but this time there were clothes in them and to her surprise and delight she found they were women's clothes and they were her size. Then she thought, a women had lived here? Alone! Sally quickly took off Paul's quilted shirt. It had, helped save her life but it was way too big and she knew Paul would need it back. She then put on a long underwear top and a quilted shirt she found in the trunk. It looked like there were four or five sets of womens clothes in the trunk but she left the rest in their garbage bags and in the trunk. Then she pondered just what type of woman could live in this wilderness all alone.

Just as Paul reached the porch of the cabin he heard another wolf howl and it sent a shiver down his spine. Fortunately, the howl sounded a long ways off. He had seen wolves before but he had either been in a car or had a rifle in his hand. Those encounters had pleased him and he had never felt endangered. However this encounter was different. This time he felt he had been in real danger. He was out of breath from the speed he had hiked up the trail through the foot of snow. The weight of the luggage he was carrying had not made the hike any easier. Paul pulled the latch string, opened the door and sat the luggage on the table. He was greeted with the exclamation, "You found my luggage."

Paul looked at the name tag and sure enough there was Sally's name on the tag "How did you find my bag?" Sally asked.

"It was hanging in the branches of a tree I was thinking about climbing." Paul replied.

"Why would you climb a tree?" Sally asked.

Paul then told her about the pack of wolves he had encountered but he did not say anything about them eating the bodies. He did not feel the need to upset her with the mental image of what had happened. It was bad enough that he could not get the image out of his own mind. He had a feeling that he would relive the last two days in nightmares for years to come. Sally was ecstatic about Paul finding her luggage but realized that the clothing she had found in the steamer trunk would be far more practical in this cabin than the designer clothes she had packed in her bag.

Paul did not notice that Sally was wearing different clothes or that she had made up the bed. Daylight does not last long in the winter in the far north, and it was already getting dark. They had no lights inside the cabin so he needed to work fast while he could still see. Paul filled the stove with wood and went to pump more water to boil some more rice. He discovered that the pump had already lost its prime and had to re-prime it. "We are going to need to always keep some water by the sink to prime the pump." he said as much to himself as to Sally. Paul was hungry. The earlier meal of rice would not have been enough to hold him over and he had lost half of that when he thew up. After he had pumped some more water he put the large pan on the stove and waited for it to boil before adding the rice.

Sally was a little disappointed that he had not noticed anything she had done while he was gone. So she said, "I hung the quilted shirt you loaned me by the door."

By this time the water was boiling and Paul was stirring in the rice. Without looking up from what he was doing, Paul replied. "You might want to wear it to bed. Your blouse will not keep you very warm."

"Oh, I am not wearing the blouse I had on in the plane and I think the clothes I have on will keep me warm." Sally said.

This confused Paul. Had Sally already retrieved clothes from her luggage and put them on? That could not be. She was setting on the bed and had not crossed the room to where her luggage was sitting on the table. Paul looked up from what he was doing but it was already too dark to see what she had on. "So where did you get what you are wearing?" Paul asked. Then Sally told him about finding the key, the blankets and the womens clothes.

"Do you think this is a fishing cabin?" Sally asked.
"No, it is a trapping cabin." Paul replied.
"You seem sure of that." Sally said.

"I am. Earlier I noticed there are a bunch of nails in the log cross ties that run from the top of the one outside wall to the other. They were used to hang skin stretchers. Under the sink is a pile of boards. They are stretchers used to stretch and dry the skins."

"You mean the woman who lived here was a trapper? How could a woman be involved with cruelly trapping defenseless animals?" Sally questioned.

"The wolves I ran into today did not seem defenseless to me." Paul said. He wanted to explain that it is a cold, cruel world in the wilderness. Animals are often attacked and are partially eaten even before they are dead, and trapping is a more humane way of controlling animal populations than starvation, disease, and predication. However, this woman was a city gal and she would not understand, so he just dropped it.

Paul dished up the rice and asked a blessing over it and gave thanks for escaping the wolves. This meal was not any better than the rice they had earlier and by the time they finished eating it was too dark to see much inside the cabin. Paul filled the stove with wood again and asked, "Do you want me to spend the night in a kitchen chair?"

"That doesn't sound very comfortable or very fair. I will share the bed with you if you promise to mind your manners and not try anything funny." Sally replied. "There is just one thing. What is your wife going to say, if she finds out you shared a bed with another woman?"

"My wife would be grateful to you for allowing me to be warm and comfortable." Paul replied.

Sally laughed, and stated. "There is no woman on earth that is that trusting of their husband."

"Maybe you're right but my wife in not on earth. She is in heaven. She passed away last spring after a long illness."

"Oh, I am very sorry to hear that." Sally replied.

Paul asked. "What about you? Is your jealous husband likely to shoot me?"

"No, there is no need to worry about my husband. I am only married to my job." Sally responded. "Oh, by the way, I also found another sleeping bag in the trunk, so now we can each have our own. With that conversation concluded and because it was dark , they crawled into bed .

Paul was on the tired side from his strenuous activities but Sally was wide awake because even though it was dark, it was still early in the evening. Sally told Paul about her family and some things about her work. She did not however let on that she ran a major Canadian company. Sally then asked Paul about his wife and Paul told her about their thirty years of marriage. He spoke of happier times, funny things that happened early in their marriage, and the birth and raising of their two daughters. Then he spoke about the last ten years of sorrow, his wife's cancer, holding her hand as she slipped away, and how much he missed her. The story brought a tear to Sally's eye and put a lump in her throat.

Surprisingly, wolves did not stalk Paul's dreams that night. In fact he did not even toss or turn much. He slept like he was dead to the world and was up at the crack of dawn. It was cold in the cabin. The fire in the stove had burned to just a bed of coals. Paul filled the stove again and frowned when he noticed that most of the firewood that was stored inside the cabin had already been used up. He did some mental calculations and figured there was enough firewood on the porch to last about two weeks at the present rate of consumption. However, the storm had broken and it looked like it was going to be a nice day, so surely the rescuers would find them today.

While Sally was still sleeping, he decided to take an inventory of the cupboards. The upper cabinets appeared to have been mouse free, but the former resident had put everything in mason jars just to be safe. There were a bunch of mason jars with lids but most were empty. He found one that held about a pound of salt and another that held a container of pepper. Two other jars held kitchen matches and one was full of cooking oil. Some jars looked like they had once contained flour but were now empty. There were four full quart jars of rice and one partial jar they had been using. He did more mental calculations and figured if they restricted themselves to eating a cup of rice a day, they had enough for about eighteen days.

There was one more mason jar of interest. It contained about three hundred .22 Long Rifle cartridges. These could come in real handy if there were also a rifle in this cabin but were useless if there was not, he thought. Paul already knew there was no rifle in the cabin, unless, he thought maybe Sally had found one in the trunk and forgot to mention it.

When Sally woke up Paul said, "I have been doing some calculating and I figure we have about eighteen days of rice if we only cook a cup a day. The weather has broke and we are likely to be rescued today or at least soon. Whoever owns this cabin might arrive sometime depending on having this rice, and could be in a bad way if we eat it all. So, I think we should limit ourselves to a cup a day to make it last."

"That is fine with me, I could stand to lose a few pounds anyway. I guess we could call it our crash diet." Sally said with a smile. "Besides, I do not much care for rice and no offense to your cooking, but this rice is not very good."

"That is for sure." Paul agreed. Paul asked, "Did you by any chance find a .22 rifle in the trunk?"

"No, there is nothing more in the trunk except womens clothes some sheets and a towel." Sally replied. Then Sally said, "My ankle is a little better but it still hurts. Do you think you could help me to the outhouse again?"

"No problem." Paul replied. As he helped her, he thought about her comment about standing to lose a few pounds. Why do women always think they weigh too much? I, on the other hand, could lose seventy five pounds and I would still be too fat.

When they returned to the cabin, Sally told Paul, "The broken canoe paddle you gave me yesterday is a little too long to work as a good crutch.

"Well, then let's cut it off. How long should it be?" Paul asked.

Sally held it up to her shoulder and they marked it where it needed to be cut off. Then Paul got a Case sheath knife out of the silverware drawer. He laid the broken paddle on the table, sat down and scribed a line around the shank of the paddle where it was to be cut off. Then Paul pared off the paddle below the line and as he handed it back to her said, "You may need this if I am not around to help you."

"Where are you going?" Sally asked with surprise.

"I need to look for some dead trees I can cut down for firewood." Paul said as he put the knife and sheath on his belt. He usually carried a pocket knife but because of flight regulations he did not have it with him. "However, I was thinking I would try a little fishing first." Paul said. "That is, if you promise not to tell on me. I don't have a Canadian fishing license and don't know if the season is open."

Sally laughed and said, "I promise."

Paul retrieved the spinning rod from the pegs over the door. There was a Mepps spinner tied to the end of the line. He did not realize it at the time but would later discover that the Mepps spinner was the only lure in the cabin. He pulled on the line and it easily snapped, as it was rotten. He kept stripping off line and testing it until he found sound line and then tied the spinner back on. "Hopefully I will be back in a little while with breakfast," Paul said as he went out the door.

The lake was now frozen but there was still open water where the lake and river met. There was a deep hole where the water flowed out of the lake into the river. At the confluence of the lake and river, the river was about a hundred yards wide, shallow, rocky, and fast. Downstream, where the tail portion of the plane was, the river was more narrow, deeper, and slower. As Paul walked down to the water he thought what a beautiful, clear and calm day God has given us today. Surely, we will be rescued by this afternoon.

As he made his first cast into the deep hole he was not expecting much. He let the spinner sink for a few seconds and started retrieving it. He had only taken a few cranks of the reel when a fish slammed into his bait and he set the hook. The fish made a run and the drag of the reel screamed. For a few seconds Paul though he had a walleye on but when he saw it, he knew it was a brook trout and what a brook trout it was, about three and a half pounds. Paul played the fish until it was spent and as he slid it up on the sandy beach, he realized he had just landed the largest brook trout of his life. Paul grabbed the fish with one hand and reached for the knife on his belt with his other. Seconds later the fish was gutted and laying on the snow bank. With his hands shaking from excitement Paul deposited the fish guts in a knot hole of a tree, thinking he may need them for bait later.

Paul's second cast was uneventful, but the third cast hooked an even bigger brook trout. When he got a look at it, he figured it would go five pounds; a real trophy. Sadly the line parted with a snap and the fish returned to the unseen depths, taking the only lure with him. It was a terrible situation for an angler to be in. The fish appeared to be really biting and now there was no tackle to fish with. Well, at least we now have breakfast, and maybe we will find more lures in the cabin, Paul thought. As Paul trudged up the hill back to the cabin he said a silent fisherman's prayer, thanking God for the fish, the beautiful day, and nicer weather.

Sally was surprised when the door of the cabin opened and in a cheery voice, Paul said, "I got breakfast." because he had only been gone a few minutes. Paul told her about losing the bigger fish and the lure and asked if she could look around the cabin for more lures or even just some hooks.

Sally told him that she had already pretty much looked around and had not seen any fishing tackle but that she would keep on looking. This was a disappointment to Paul, who was really hoping to be able to catch some more fish.

Paul was hungry and wasted no time getting down a cast iron frying pan from the cupboard. He also got down the mason jar of cooking oil and unscrewed the lid. Paul smelled it to make sure it was not rancid before adding some to the pan. After putting the pan on the stove to heat up, he added some more wood to the stove. While he waited for the cooking oil in the pan to heat up, Paul prepared the fish to cook. Normally he would have just put the whole fish in the pan to fry it, because brook trout are usually a lot smaller. However this one would not even fit in the pan and was so thick he would have had trouble getting it all cooked without burning the thinner portions. There was no need to scale it, because brook trout do not have scales, and he planned to cook it with the skin on. Paul cut the fish into steaks about an inch thick and when the oil in the pan had come up to temperature he added all the steaks and the fish head to the pan.

"Why did you put the head in the frying pan?" Sally exclaimed! Paul explained that there was a small hunk of meat on the fish's cheek. "Well, that is really gross, and I am not eating its the head." Sally replied.

"Don't worry, I will eat the meat off the head." Paul replied. He thought about telling her how he had read that the Inuit would bury fish heads under sand in the Fall and then dig them up in the Spring and eat them, but he decided against it. When the fish had finished cooking, Paul divided it evenly except he also took the head. Neither Paul nor Sally realized that when they would finish their meal it would be the last time either of them would be full for a very long time.

After Paul dished up their plates, he bowed his head, folded his hands and asked a blessing over it. This was a longer more complete prayer than Sally had heard him say before. He once again thanked God for sparing their lives in the plane crash, providing this cabin for them, the supplies in the cupboards, the wood stove and the firewood. He thanked the Lord for saving him from the pack of wolves. He also gave thanks for the ax, fishing pole, and the fish they were about to eat. Then he asked the Lord to be with the families of the dead and asked for safety for those who were searching for them. Paul then thanked God for being with Sally and him and asked for continued guidance and help.

The whole prayer annoyed Sally. She was hungry and did not see a good reason to wait to eat. Besides, hadn't Paul already prayed about most of this stuff before? She decided that she was going to have to talk to him about this praying thing. She would need to do this diplomatically, because of the situation they were in, as she was being forced to depend on him for a lot. She could not afford to offend him, but after all she was a CEO of a large company, and she could be very diplomatic if she needed to be.

After the prayer, Paul showed Sally how pulling on the back bone of the cooked trout would remove all the rib bones also. Then they ate until they were both stuffed and all the fish was gone. It was very good. Paul cleaned up after the meal by throwing the bones and what was left of the head in the stove and rinsing off the plates with boiling water.

As Paul was cleaning up Sally said, "My cousin Beth is a Christian and she is the only one I ever knew before I met you."

Paul replied. "I think you might be surprised to find that you know a lot more Christians than that. There are a lot of closet Christians out there. I know that there are more churches per percentage of population in the U.S. than there are in Canada, but there are still a lot of Christians in Canada. In fact I have known a lot of Canadian Christians."

"When I was a little girl, my family use to go to church. I think it was just sort of a social thing. Then when I went to University and took a philosophy class, I was taught that modern science had pretty much proven that most of the Bible is false. We now know that the dinosaurs died out millions of years before man evolved, yet the Bible teaches that man was created within the first few days and the Bible doesn't even mention dinosaurs. So the Bible could not possibly be true." Sally said.

"It is too bad they taught you so much wrong information in college." Paul replied. "The Bible actually does mention dinosaurs. Of course, since the word dinosaur was not invented until the 1800's the Bible does not call them that. By simple reasoning, the Bible tells us the dinosaurs and humans shared the earth at one time. Modern science claims that the dinosaurs died out long before man came along but it ignores lots of evidence to the contrary." Paul replied.

Paul's reply surprised Sally, and she asked, "Where does the Bible talk about dinosaurs and what evidence are you talking about?"

Paul stated, "The book of Job talks about two creatures that sound like dinosaurs called the behemoth and the leviathan. The book of Isaiah also talks about the leviathan. The Bible's description of the behemoth sounds like what we would call a brontosaurus and the leviathan sounds like a plesiosaur." In the book of Job, God says "Look now at the Behemoth, which I made along with you. He eats grass like an ox. Now see, his strength is in his hips, and his power is in his stomach muscles. He moves his tail like a cedar; the sinews of his thighs are tightly knit. His bones are like beams of bronze, his ribs like bars of iron." Some have suggested that this refers to an elephant or a hippopotamus. but "tail like a cedar" does not describe those animals. Also the Bible describes both the behemoth and the leviathan as being too powerful to be slain by man and we know that primitive people were able to hunt and kill both elephants and hippos.

"There is a lot of evidence that dinosaurs and humans co-existed but some of the most indisputable are fossilized tracks of dinosaurs and humans side by side. There are multiple places that show this evidence, but I saw a place in Texas with my own eyes. I saw a place where human tracks cross dinosaur tracks imprinted in the rock strata. How did that happen if they were not living at the same time? Could the dinosaurs have walked across a mud flat, then the mud turned into rock only to turn back into mud a million years later and have a man walk across it and then turn back into rock? Not likely! Some scientists explained it by hypothesizing that early Indians saw all the tracks made by animals they had never seen and for some reason chiseled human tracks into the rock. That sounded plausible but the tracks disappeared into a rock face. When they air chiseled the overburden rock away they found that the tracks continued under the rock face." Paul said, "I can tell you a lot more about this type of thing later if you want, but I better get out and work on some firewood. We will likely be rescued soon and I don't want to leave the owner of this cabin short on firewood."

Sally asked Paul if he could take her cell phone to the top of the hill and use it to call for help.

Paul said that he doubted that it would pick up a signal, but he promised to try. Of course they were far out of range of any cell phone towers, and whenever they tried the phone it would prove useless, and the batteries would eventually die.

Paul left to get more firewood, leaving Sally to think about what he said. Could what he said be true? He did not seem like a person that would lie, and he did say that he saw dinosaurs tracks and human tracks in the same rock strata. Why isn't this common knowledge? If that is true then what she was taught at University was wrong. Of course that did not prove that the Bible was true. Even if part of the Bible could be proven true, that would not mean that the whole Bible is true. I know, I know, Sally thought, I will ask him about the story of Noah. That story is so wild it couldn't possibly be true. Let's see what he has to say about that.

Paul was out looking for dead trees he could cut down for firewood, but not just any dead tree would do. He was hoping to find some small dead maples; small enough that he could cut them down and drag them back to the cabin. Paul wanted to get as much wood back to the cabin as possible. Once it was back there, he could cut it up as he needed it, but the snow would likely only get deeper and that would make dragging the trees back much harder. Paul not only wanted to re-supply the cabin with firewood for the owner, but he wanted to make sure there was no chance they would run out if they were not rescued soon. Whoever had cut the firewood back at the cabin had used a chain saw but all he had was this ax, and the ax was not as sharp as it could be. Yet he was able to find and cut several small maples and drag them back to the cabin that afternoon. When he got them back to the cabin, he leaned each small tree against the large maple whose fallen limb had knocked down the porch and the flue. This was to prevent the possibility of them becoming covered up with snow and lost. Unknown to Paul at the time, the wood he dragged back that day would prove to be very important to their survival.

CHAPTER 3

Dear Diary

While Paul was out cutting firewood Sally had made herself busy cleaning up the place. She did not have any soap, but thanks to the pump and wood stove she did have plenty of hot water. After a couple of hours, there were not any mouse droppings or dust in sight. As she was working, she was thinking about something that puzzled her. If the porch roof had not collapsed, they could have just pulled the latch string to get in. The latch on the window was unlocked so the woman who had lived here must have latched the door and left by the window. That made sense to her, but if you were going to leave the cabin unlocked, why lock the steamer trunk? It would seem that the pots and pans or even the ax would be far more valuable to someone that wanted to steal them than some woman's clothes. After all, just how likely would it be that someone who happened upon this cabin would have a use for womens clothes?

After she finished cleaning the cabin, Sally unpacked her luggage and laid everything out on the bed. The clothing that she was not likely to use because it just was not practical in this cabin went back in the luggage. She just could not see herself wearing a formal dress or high heels in this cabin. One thing she laid aside was her over- sized wool sweater with a scooped neck that had belonged to her favorite aunt. It was way, way too big for her but she always took it on winter business trips to wear at night in her hotel room because it was warm and comfortable and reminded her of her late aunt. With the clothes she had found in the steamer trunk and some of the clothes in her luggage she had an ample supply. However,

Paul only had what he was wearing. She wondered if the sweater could possibly be big enough to fit Paul and the thought of Paul wearing it made her laugh out loud.

Sally also removed all the clothing from the trunk and took inventory of it. She was thinking about packing all the useful clothing back in the trunk and using it as a dresser when a plan occurred to her. When they were rescued, she would leave all her practical clothing behind, packed in the trunk, sort of a "Thank You" for the use of the cabin. After all she could easily afford to buy new clothing and whoever owned this cabin might really need her clothing. She folded all the clothing up and was about to pack it away when she noticed something. The floor of the trunk was about fourteen centimeters above the floor of the cabin. Could this be the reason the trunk had been locked?

There was a layer of brown shelving paper on the bottom of the trunk and when Sally pulled it up she discovered finger holes in the false bottom. Removing the false bottom revealed a locked diary and some sewing thread and needles, along with paper and pencils. This little book was why the steamer trunk was locked! Sally could not have been more excited if she had found a treasure. However, now Sally had a moral dilemma. Should she open it and read it? She looked again in the bottom of the trunk hoping to find the key, but it was not there. Under normal circumstances Sally would never have considered reading another woman's diary but she was as curious as a cat about this woman who lived in this wilderness all alone. She could easily break the lock but not without leaving evidence. What should she do? Maybe Paul could unlock it, but what would he say? Would he think that opening it and reading it would be OK? She could hardly contain herself! She decided to wait and see what Paul had to say about it.

Sally thought, it is getting dark and Paul should be home soon. Home soon? Why was she thinking like that? The thought amused her. She had noticed Paul through the window, leaning small trees against the great maple several times during the day. Now she was thinking, I just can't wait until he gets home so I can tell him about my discovery. Home? There I go again. Just then she noticed him out the window. He was carrying a load of firewood in his arms and Sally went and opened the door for him.

Paul stepped through the open door and thanked Sally for opening it for him. He laid his wood between the wall and the stove. He wanted the snow to melt off it and dry up before he needed to burn it. As Paul filled the stove with the last of the wood that had been in the cabin Sally was excitedly telling him about finding the diary. "Do you think we should open it and read it?" Sally asked.

Paul replied, "My feet are frozen. Let me sit by the fire and thaw them out, and think about your question for a few minutes."

What type of answer was that, Sally thought. Maybe I should have just opened it and not told him about it. Why is he making me wait? It sounded like he was going to pass some type of judgment!

Paul sat there silently, thinking and warming up for what seemed like hours to Sally but it was really only a few minutes. Finally he began to speak. "First I want to say that you found it, so the decision on whether or not to open it and read it is yours and yours alone. However, these are my thoughts on it. We have been using this cabin, firewood, and food like they belonged to us. That is OK because we have only the choice to do this or perish. This cabin may have been permanently abandoned or the owner may have even died, but there is a good chance that the cabin has not been abandoned. Trappers often have a number of cabins like this and only use one every few years. This gives the populations of the targeted animals a chance to recover. If that is the case, the trapper might show up tomorrow or next fall. There is just no way to tell. We may be rescued soon and if that was the case, I would feel bad about invading someone's privacy. On the other hand, there could be information in that book that could be very useful to us and there is no way to know without reading it."

Paul continued, "Only because the information it may contain could be a matter of life or death to us, would I be tempted to read it. If we had a key, we could open it and skim through it to see if it says anything we need to know. Then we could put it back where you found it, and the owner would never need to know that anyone had read it. Because we don't have a key, the owner would know that their privacy had been violated. If it were my diary I would not care if anyone read it, but then again, I have never kept a diary. What about you? If it was yours, would you care if someone read it?"

"No, I would not want anyone to read mine." Sally replied. Paul's statements had quenched Sally's burning desire to read it, and she was now glad she had asked his advice instead of impulsively breaking the lock and reading it. How could she explain the broken diary lock if the owner just showed up? Paul had used the words "A matter of life and death." Did that mean he thought they may still die from this situation? Sally said, "Thank you for your thoughts. They have helped me make a decision. I have decided to put it back where I found it and not open it. At least for now; I might change my mind later, especially if we find a key." She then put it back where she found it and packed her clothes in the trunk.

Paul said, "Sally, I thought about not telling you this but I do not want to hold anything back from you. As you know, today was a clear day and I expected that we would be rescued. As I was gathering firewood, I kept my eyes on the sky and did not see a plane all day; not even a high flying jet. Also, when I took a break on the top of the hill behind us, I was listening. On a calm day like this in the winter, traffic noise can sometimes carry up to ten miles, but I heard nothing. Also, the top of that hill looks like the highest point around here and there was no signal for your cell phone.

When I was a kid my dad took me on a fly-in fishing trip to Northern Ontario. I can remember seeing hundreds of lakes, streams and rivers from the air and my dad saying, "If someone was lost, the only way they could ever walk out would be to wait for the lakes to freeze so they could walk in a straight line." Of course he was just kidding but what he said was true. However, I think that civilization is a multipliable days hike from here in who knows what direction. With this type of weather and with your bad ankle trying to walk out would be suicide. Hopefully, we will be rescued soon but not seeing any planes today, not even in the distance was very discouraging. I just wanted you to know how serious I believe our situation is."

Paul's statements were very sobering to Sally. For the first time since their first night in the cabin she realized that there was a good possibility they would not be found, and that Paul's suggestion that they ration the rice was out of at least as much concern for their welfare as it was for the owner of the cabin. She just sat there in the darkening cabin and pondered Paul's comments as he carried in more firewood to dry beside the wood stove. When he had finished carrying in several loads of wood Paul sat back down. They just sat in the darkness and silence until Sally remembered her scooped neck sweater.

"Paul, because you found my luggage and I found the clothes in the trunk I have plenty of clothes. You, on the other hand, have only the ones you have on, and I was thinking of giving you my old wool sweater."

Paul laughed at the thought of trying to wear a sweater that would fit Sally. He said, "Thank you for the offer but I do not think that there is any way I could squeeze into one of your sweaters."

"The style is extra floppy on me." Sally replied as she retrieved the sweater from the bed and handed it to Paul. After taking off his sweatshirt and quilted shirt Paul tried to put it on but it just would not quite fit. Paul took it back off and said, "Thank you but it looks like I will need to wait until our crash diet kicks in before I wear it."

Sally said, "Earlier you said you would tell me more about evidence that men and dinosaurs shared the earth at one time." Sally really just wanted to have an opportunity to ask about Noah and the ark, figuring there was no way Paul could explain that.

. "Well, like I said before, finding human and dinosaur tracks in the same rock strata is probably the best evidence but it is far from the only evidence. Drawings of dinosaurs from antiquity have been found all over the world. How would the people who drew them have known what they looked like?"

"Many engraved burial stones have been recovered from Inca tombs in Peru. About a third of these stones have images of people interacting with dinosaurs. I have seen photos of some, I remember one showed a man riding a triceratops and another showed a man fighting with a meat eating dinosaur that stood on two legs and had short "arms" like a small Tyrannosaurs Rex. The convincing part is that the dinosaurs are depicted anatomically correct based on our current understanding. You must remember that early palaeontologists thought that dinosaurs walked with their legs splayed out to the side and with their belly close to the ground like a modern lizard or alligator. It was not until sometime in the 1900's that they realized that they had been depicting dinosaurs incorrectly. If the ancient Incas had been depicting dinosaurs based on fossil finds they most likely would have illustrated them incorrectly also."

"These Inca burial stones are not without controversy." Paul continued. "Some have claimed that at least some of the stones are forgeries. However one scientist studied some samples and found that there was a natural occurring varnish on the stones. If I remember correctly he said the varnish build-up was caused by algae, bacteria and time. He found that the varnish build-up was thinner in the engraved parts of the stone than the parts that had not been engraved. He believed that his findings were consistent with the stones being genuine. He felt that if they were recent forgeries there would not have been sufficient time for the varnish to build up over the engraved areas."

"I am not sure I buy all that." Sally said.

"Well you can look it up on the Internet and decide for yourself; that is, if we ever get out of here." Paul replied. "While you are looking that up, I have more evidence for you to check out." Paul said. "I believe that you and I may be or at least were contemporaries of the plesiosaur."

Paul continued, "I have read several accounts of dead animals that washed up on shore and were identified as some type of plesiosaur. Most of these events occurred long ago and only a written account still exists. In 1925 one was washed up in Santa Cruz and was identified by the president of the Natural History Society of British Columbia but the photo evidence is not all that clear. However, a more recent event happened in 1977. A Japanese fishing ship off the coast of New Zealand pulled aboard in their nets what appeared to be a plesiosaur. It was dead and in an advanced state of decomposition. Fearing that it would contaminate their catch, they returned it to the sea, but not before taking photos and samples of its flesh.

This was a well publicized event in Japan but not well known in the West. I think the Japanese even put an image celebrating it on a postage stamp. Western scientists claimed that it was the carcass of a Basking shark that only looked like a plesiosaur because of the advance decay. However, the fishermen reported that there was no ammonia smell that is present in a decomposing shark. Sharks, unlike other fish, eliminate urine through their blood circulatory systems, and that is what causes their flesh to smell like ammonia. The fishermen said it smelled like a rotting mammal and not a fish. Also the fishermen said it had hard bone and sharks' skeletons are made up of cartilage and not bone.

Now if this corpse was a plesiosaur, where did it come from? There are only two choices. One is that it had been frozen in an iceberg or the second possibility would be that it had been recently alive. If it had been recently alive, what is the chance that it was the last one?" Paul said.

"What is the chance that we would walk away from a plane crash where everyone else died?" Sally replied.

"Likely about the same as the only piece of luggage that also survived, belonging to you. I believe that God has reasons for every thing that happens." Paul answered.

As Paul filled the stove for the night, he stated, "I am really whipped, and it is dark. Do you mind if we just go to bed?"

Sally replied, "That is fine, I am tired too." Then she thought, I can just wait until tomorrow to ask him about Noah. That night hunger keep both of them from getting a good night's sleep. Hunger was a feeling that both of them would become better acquainted with in the days to come

Another big storm blew in overnight, bringing with it another foot of snow, high winds and a below zero wind chill factor. Paul was up with first light, and built up a fire in the stove. Looking out the window, he was glad that he had spent yesterday afternoon dragging as many small trees to camp as he could. The two feet of snow they now had meant that he would need to wear snowshoes for any distant wood gathering forays. The small trees he had gathered were smaller in diameter than the wood already stacked on the porch. That would mean that it would burn faster and not last as long. He decided he would keep the wood already stacked on the porch in reserve as long as possible. Hopefully he could keep enough of the wood he gathered, chopped that there would always be some drying between the stove and the wall. Since there was less than a day's worth drying now, he would need to chop more no matter what the weather.

Paul was hungry. His last meal had been the fish breakfast the day before. He put another cup of rice on the stove to cook and seasoned it with salt and pepper. While he was waiting he thought maybe I could touch up the edge of the ax, I should be able to sharpen it on the stone hearth. That is when he noticed just how unusual the hearth was. It was just one piece of stone. One part of it was parallel to and about a foot above the floor and another part ran up the wall. The person who had built this cabin had found this natural rock formation and had built the cabin around it. Paul was surprised that he had not noticed this before. Being a builder he had noticed the craftsmanship in the construction of the building. Whoever built the cabin had certainly known what they were doing. The logs fit together tightly, with no need for chinking. The bottom of each log was coped to fit the top of the log below it. This is sometimes called the Swedish Cope Style.

The kitchen table, chairs, log bed frame and cabinets all showed signs of quality hand craftsmanship. Paul could imagine a lonely trapper working on building these things to pass the time in between running the trap line. He found a flat spot on the hearth where he intended to rub the ax head edge to sharpen it. In the early morning light he noticed that this spot on the hearth was already stained. The owner of the cabin had sharpened the ax on this spot before.

Sally awoke to the sound of the ax head being rubbed on the hearth. Paul heard her stretching and said, "Madam, may I take your breakfast order?"

"Sure, I will take two eggs over easy, a slice of toast, hash browns, and a glass of orange juice." Sally replied.

"That order just made me at least twice as hungry as I was just a minute ago." Paul said.

"Sorry, but you are the one that asked for my order." Sally smiled.

"Breakfast is almost ready but I am afraid all we have is rice and our ration will just be enough to take the edge off our hunger for a few hours." Sally got up as Paul dished up their rice. After she sat down, Paul asked a brief blessing and they soon finished their meager meal.

Sally had already noticed there was another storm raging outside, and asked, "What are the plans for today?"

"Well, with that wind and storm it will be too cold to spend much time outdoors, but I will need to chop at least a days worth of firewood." Paul answered. "I also would like to find a board and fit it to where the window pane is missing. The rag I have stuck in there lets too much cold air in." Then he asked, "Have you checked the loft for fishing tackle or a rifle?"

"I looked up there and it appears that the only things up there are some more of the skin stretcher boards like under the sink and a bunch of hoop things in the back." Sally replied.

"Are the hoop things made of metal? They may be Conibear traps. I know how you feel about trapping but if there are any traps up there, I might be able to trap something to supplement our diet." Paul stated.

Sally said, "No, the hoops things are made of wood. The only way I could tell if there is anything else up there is to take everything down. Do you want me to?" Sally asked.

"That would be great, if standing on the log ladder would not hurt your ankle too much." Paul replied.

"Well, I was thinking that I could crawl up into the loft and pass things back to you while you stand on the ladder and you could carry it down. Then we could burn it in the stove." Sally said.

"I could do that, but I only want to burn the stuff as a last resort. After all we are just guests here and I do not want to destroy anything the cabin's owner needs to earn a living." Paul said.

"OK, we should be able to stow every thing that is up there under the bed. That way if we are ever forced to burn the stuff it will be easy to get at." Sally said.

"That is a good idea." Paul agreed.

That is exactly what they did. Sally crawled into the loft, and handed things back to Paul. He would then carry them down the ladder and store them under the bed. Sally was surprised to find it was actually hot up in the loft. Heat goes up! When Paul saw the wood hoop things he recognized them as beaver skin stretchers and told Sally. They did not find any fishing tackle, a .22 rifle or any traps. All Sally found was just skin stretchers. All that is, except she did notice a small gold cross hanging on a gold chain from the back side of a log rafter on the far end of the loft. She was not interested in it, and it was on the far end and not worth the extra effort to crawl there and retrieve it. She also did not think to mention it to Paul.

After they finished their task Sally complained that she had never gone a week before in her life without taking a bath. "You still have not." Paul replied, "This is only the morning of the fourth day after the crash."

"Really, I guess you are right. It seems much longer." Sally replied after she thought about it. "I am sure I would feel better if I could even just wash my hair. Ugh it is just terrible."

"Your hair does not look so bad to me. Do you have any shampoo in your luggage?" Paul asked.

"Yes, I have a small travel bottle." Sally replied. Paul, then offered to help her wash her hair that evening.

Paul ventured out into the storm four times that day, to chop firewood. The cold wind made him so uncomfortable he was only able to chop four arms full of firewood; not even twenty four hours worth. He also retrieved a board from the storage building with the collapsed roof. to use to fill in the broken window pane. While rooting around looking for a board he also found a large wash tub and retrieved that also. When Paul opened the door to the cabin he said, "I have brought you a bathtub." Sally came over to look at the wash tub and right away noticed that there was a small hole in the bottom. The tub was made out of galvanized steel; maybe there had been a defect in the galvanized coating and that had caused a small rust hole. When she pointed the hole out, Paul just shrugged and said, " I guess I will just have to fix it."

"How are you going to do that?" Sally asked.

"You will see because I am going to need your help." Paul said and he turned and went back out the door. He walked down to the river and picked out a couple of hard flat rocks and brought them back to the cabin. Sally looked at the rocks Paul laid on the table and puzzled over their purpose. Paul then turned and went back out the door and selected a large log with square chainsaw cut ends from the original pile of firewood and brought it into the cabin. Paul set the log on end on top of the hearth and began searching the pockets of his hunting coat.

"What are you looking for?" Sally asked.

"I am looking for the extra nails I took with me when I posted our note at the crash site." Paul replied. Paul found the galvanized 16 penny nail he was looking for and laid it on the end of the log. Next he laid another piece of firewood over the head end of the nail and asked Sally to hold it down and she complied. Paul said, "I hope this doesn't put a big dent in the blade." Then he swung the ax slicing part of the head end off the rest of the nail. The head end that Sally was holding down with the piece of firewood stayed where it was and the other piece went flying to parts unknown.

Paul drove the shank of the head end of the nail through the hole in the bottom of the wash tub from the inside. Then he turned the wash tub upside down and asked Sally to hold the rock on the head of the nail as he peened the shank of the nail with the head of the ax. When he was finished, Paul poured in some water from one of the pans on the stove and checked the bottom. Then he pronounced it water tight.

Sally was amazed, "Where did you learn to do that?" she asked.

Paul explained that one time out in the woods he came across a junk pile by the ruins of an old house, and that he had noticed that many of the old pans in the junk pile had rivets in them to repair holes.

Then Sally asked, " Why did you bring up two rocks?"

"I brought two rocks up from the river because my feet have been cold ever since the crash." Paul enjoyed the questioning look of Sally's face. Then he laid the rocks by the side of the stove to heat up, and said tonight, I plan to put these under the foot end of our sleeping bags to keep our feet warm. They used to do that back in the colonial days and I do not know why I had not thought about doing it before now. Really, I just brought two rocks up from the river so I would have a second one if the first one did not work for riveting the nail but when you asked, I had the idea to use them for bed warmers. The rock bed warmers would prove to be a good idea and would help keep them warm every night from then on.

Paul took the board he had retrieved from the shed over to the window. He used the sheath knife to mark the board where he would need to cut it, in order to fit it to the broken window pane opening. Then he sat down at the table and began whittling on the board because he lacked a saw. While he worked he said, "I was thinking when I was out chopping wood, that the shampoo you have is the only soap we have. It likely froze while your luggage was hanging in that tree so it may or may not lather up like you expect. In any case, I think we should collect the rinse water from washing your hair in the wash tub so we can reuse it for washing clothes."

"That is a good idea, and if you help me wash my hair I will wash your clothes for you. I want to wash up some things myself," Sally said. She had already changed into clothes she had found in the trunk and her dirty clothes were stored in one of garbage bag she had found in the trunk.

Sally retrieved her shampoo from her luggage. Paul pulled out a kitchen chair for her to sit on and laid the wash tub on the floor. He then pumped some more water into the pans he had taken from the stove so the water they held would cool. He checked the temperature to make sure the water was not too hot then poured a little over Sally's head as she leaned over the wash tub. The shampoo did not lather up as good as it would have if it had not frozen and thawed but it was still much better than nothing. Sally worked the lather through her hair and then asked Paul to rinse it. After the rinse, she dried her hair with the towel and put it up in a ponytail; the first ponytail that she had worn in twenty years. She was shivering by the time was finished because the fire in the stove had died down. When Paul noticed her shivering, he added more wood to the stove.

Sally pumped some water to refill the pans and put them back on the stove to heat up. Then she went and retrieved her dirty clothes and put them in the wash tub. "I need your dirty clothes to soak before I scrub them." she told Paul. He tool off his sweat shirt, quilted shirt and T-shirt and then put his sweat shirt back on and added the others to the tub.

Paul then asked Sally to turn around and face the other way, please! Sally was amused because she perceived that Paul was embarrassed. Paul removed his pants and underwear and put his pants back on. Then he added his underwear to the wash tub and told Sally she could turn back around.

After the water on the stove had heated up, Sally added more to the wash tub and scrubbed the clothes. There really was not much lather but when she was finished washing them she used some more hot water and rinsed them out in the sink. Then Sally wrung them out and hung them from nails in the log cross tie over the stove to dry. While Sally had been doing the laundry, Paul was sitting at the table carving the board to fit the window pane. When she had finished hanging everything up to dry she moved her chair back to the table and sat down. It was already getting dark but she knew they would need to sit up until the clothes dried because Paul would need to wear his to bed.

This was a perfect opportunity to ask about Noah and the ark. Paul seemed like a reasonable guy. Perhaps if she asked her questions just right, he would realize just how impossible some of the things in the Bible really were. She opened the conversation, by saying, "I watched a television program about Noah's ark and it gave scientific reasons that the story could not possibly be true. They listed several reasons but their biggest reason was there is not enough water to flood the whole earth. The top of Mount Everest could not possibly be covered. What do you think about it?"

Paul laid the board aside. It was getting too dark to work on it anyway. "I think I saw that same program, and I will be happy to tell you what I think about it, but first I would like to tell you what I believe about the Bible."

"There are a lot of Christians who believe the stories in the Old Testament are just morality tales given to us to help us understand how we should live. Some of them may believe that the New Testament is true, at least as long as what it has to say is not too inconvenient. There are other Christians who believe that most of the Bible is true but not necessarily every line. I on the other hand, belong to the school of Christians who believe that the Bible in the original text is the inerrant word of God. Parts of the Bible were written in three different languages Greek, Hebrew, and Biblical Aramaic and I am not fluent in any of them so I have to rely on a translation. We currently have a number of versions of the Bible and plain logic would indicate that some would be better translations than others. I have done a line by line comparative study of a few popular versions and can tell you that I have found some differences in some places. Most of these differences are minor, often things like numbers and do not really make a difference in the overall meaning. Also, languages change over time. In the Old King James version David says he has been making roads into the surrounding territories. At the time of the translation people would have realized that he was making war but someone reading it now might mistakenly think he was building roads. Also when the King James version, used the word gay it was talking about being happy. Now the word gay has a whole different meaning. The point I am making is I believe the Bible but I realize that my understanding of it is very likely not always correct."

Paul continued, "The TV program I saw said water could not possibly cover the surface of the earth because of the heights of the mountain ranges. However, that assumes the earth has always had the same topography as it does now, and even modern science agrees that it has not. If you leveled out the surface and filled in the ocean trenches, the water would be hundreds of feet deep over the entire surface. Modern science believes that there was once just one major land mass and that the continents were formed by continental drift through plate tectonics. Surprisingly that theory totally agrees with what it says in the Book of Genesis. We know that the Himalayan mountains are the the highest mountain range on earth and that they are getting higher, Yet, I have read that there are clam fossils on the very top of Mount Everest and that shows that the rock was once the ocean floor. "

"The show I saw said Noah could not have built an Ark the size that the Bible claims because it would collapse under it own weight because Noah did not have iron nails. I laughed at that and wondered how the producers of the show knew that Noah did not have iron nails because it says nothing about it in the Bible. Maybe they thought that Noah did not have iron nails because it was before the iron age. However, there have been many cases of technology being developed, forgotten and rediscovered in history. Tubal-Cane who came before Noah was listed by the Bible as an instructor of every craftsman in bronze and iron. So it is likely that Noah did have iron nails even though the Bible does not talk about it.

There is no doubt from the dimensions given in the Bible that the ark was a very large ship, likely the largest wood ship ever built. However, we do not know the exact size of the ark because the dimensions are given in cubits. One cubit is thought to be the length from the elbow to the tip of the fingers so obviously the actual size of the ark would depend on the size of Noah's arms. However, it is interesting to note the ratio of width to length matches that of a modern ship. It is often thought that Moses was the author of the Book of Genesis. How would he have known the proper proportions of a large ship if he was not getting the information from God?"

"The show I saw also said that if there had been a world wide flood there would be evidence of it found all over the world, and there is none." Sally stated.

Paul laughed. "That is the problem with people, when the evidence does not support what they believe they ignore it. Everyone is susceptible to this, even me. If you asked me, I would say that there is all kinds of evidence of a world wide flood and that it has been found all over the world."

"Oh, what kind of evidence is that?" Sally asked.

"Surely, you are familiar with the Canadian fossil beds in Alberta?" Paul asked.

"Why yes I am." Sally replied.

"Good." Paul continued. "Those fossil beds show that thousands of dinosaurs of different types were buried together in mass graves. I would say that is evidence of a catastrophic flood, wouldn't you?"

"Well, yes, but not a world wide flood." Sally replied.

"Yes, however there are also coal beds found all over the world. Modern science teaches that these coal beds were formed by burying vast amounts of organic material, and because of pressure and large amounts of time it turned into coal. Science also believes that oil deposits were formed in a similar manner, by burying large amounts of once living things. Now what would be a better explanation of vast coal and oil deposits buried all over the world than a catastrophic world wide flood also know as the Great Flood of Noah."

"Remember when I said that when people find evidence that does not support their conclusions, they tend to ignore it?" Paul asked. He continued, "Whenever modern science comes across an anomaly that contradicts their world view they tend to ignore it, thinking that the anomaly is a hoax or just somehow does not apply because it happened through a process we do not understand. Currently modern science believes that coal is about 300 million years old or older and that man appeared on the earth seven million years ago or less. So the fact that man made artifacts have been found in coal seams all over the world is a problem for them. It is just an anomaly, and they believe it to be a bunch of hoaxes and so just ignore it. To me the artifacts found in coal seams are evidence of civilizations that existed prior to the Great Flood. I have seen photos of some metal artifacts found in West Virginia coal seams, which appear to have been made with technology that is presently still unknown to modern man."

"What did you mean when you used the terms 'current modern science beliefs'." Sally asked.

"I was tying to imply that what science believe as facts are constantly changing." Paul said.

"Care to offer any examples?" Sally asked.

"Sure, I am fifty years old and in just my lifetime the scientific thoughts on the age of the earth has gotten billions and billions of years older. Another example would be the make up of the sun. About 100 years ago scientists mostly agreed that the sun was a big ball of burning gas. Then some scientist realized that if it was a ball of burning gas it would have consumed itself. When WWII and the atomic bomb came along science switched their ideas about the sun to nuclear fission, until someone realized that idea did not really work either. Their latest idea I believe is that the sun is some type of nuclear fusion. That will be the standard belief until someone else comes up with a better theory."

Sally said, "You sound a little cynical about modern science."

"Not at all," replied Paul, "I just recognize that modern science thought does not always follow its own scientific method."

Sally knew all about the scientific method but she asked Paul to explain it to her anyway because she wanted to use it to judge whether or not he knew what he was talking about. After all a lot of what he was saying contradicted much of what she thought she knew.

Paul answered, "There are variations, but the steps to the scientific method usually go something like this. 1. State a problem, 2. Do research, 3. Form a hypothesis, 4. Perform an experiment, and 5. Accept or Reject the hypothesis. In order to prove a hypothesis the experiment must be designed to eliminate variables and the results must be repeatable." Sally thought, he pretty much nailed that. Paul went on, "Sadly, many things that pass for fact in the minds of many scientists do not conform to those rules."

By now it had grown very dark inside the cabin. Usually, because snow reflects light so well it does not get very dark in the far North. However, the heavy snow storm outside made it much darker than it normally would have been. Paul opened the stove door for light and checked the clothes and they were now dry. Then he said, "I will leave the stove door open so you can find your way to bed. I need to fill the stove with wood anyway. Sally got in bed while Paul filled the stove, then he closed the stove door. He washed up and changed back into his newly washed clothes. There was no need to ask Sally to turn her head because the cabin was too dark to see across the room. It felt good to be clean even though he had not had any soap.

CHAPTER: 4

The Birthday Gift

The next morning Paul finished the board he was making for the window and installed it. Then a routine set in that would last for almost two weeks . Paul would get up at first light, check and see that the storm was still raging outside, fill the stove with wood and cook a cup of rice. The remainder of the day he would chop firewood in a valiant but futile attempt to keep the firewood on the porch in reserve. After his initial supply of small trees he had dragged to camp ran out he was forced to put on snowshoes and retrieve more small trees. This was exhausting work. The snow was already over three feet deep and the snowshoes were made for a smaller person. This meant that Paul would sink in deeper than he would have with the proper size snowshoes.

Paul was worried, not so much for himself but for Sally. Each day there would be one cup less of rice in the cupboard and a little less firewood in reserve. The question in his mind was whether they would starve to death or freeze to death. He had not given up hope and was still praying that their situation would change for the better. The only good thing was that they were using a little less firewood. There was a constant Northwest wind and it had drifted snow to the height of the eaves on the west and part of the north sides of the cabin. That and the three feet of snow on the roof added to the insulation value. Paul was a little concerned about the weight of the snow on the roof and had closely examined the roof construction. There was a ridge pole running the length of the cabin and it was a foot in diameter at it smallest point. One of the log side supports for the ladder to the loft ran all the way to the ridge pole. This cut the ridge span down to only eight feet. He decided that there was no real cause for concern about the strength of the roof.

Hunger was their constant companion. Cooking one cup of rice yields three cups of cooked rice so they were each living off one and a half cups of rice a day. That is only about 300 calories and is truly a starvation diet. Paul had much more body fat than Sally in the beginning but surprisingly she was actually doing the best health wise. Paul had lost a lot of weight and now could easily fit into Sally's scooped necked sweater. While he was out exhausting himself trying to keep up chopping firewood he would often feel faint and would have to stop to rest.

While out cutting firewood in the mornings Paul would often notice a red squirrel run along the trunks of several cedar trees that had partially tipped over and were leaning into other cedar trees along the bank by the river. This seemed to be a squirrel highway from one group of thick cedars to another. That gave him an idea. When he was a kid in the Boy Scouts he had went on a number of weekend survival camps. Once, one of his camping buddies had successfully snared a red squirrel with a piece of wire. He remembered the meat was tough, and there was not much of it when shared with three Boy Scouts but at least it was food. If he could find some suitable wire he was sure he could snare a squirrel.

Paul knew there was no wire in the cabin and so he searched the storage shed but ended up empty handed. Then he thought about the possibility of salvaging some wire from the old snowmobile. He took off the cowling but found no suitable wire under the hood. Next, he thought about the wreckage of the plane. Surely there would be some wire there. In the end he decided that searching the debris field would be just too much effort for too little possible reward.

One day at breakfast Sally said. "My gums are getting soft and are bleeding."

Paul replied, "Now that you mention it, I am having trouble with mine also. That can only mean one thing. We are both coming down with scurvy."

"SCURVY!" Sally cried, "That sounds terrible! Do people even still get it?"

"Yes, I believe we have it so people can still get it." Paul replied. "It is uncommon in our modern world because so much of our food is vitamin fortified." Paul added.

"What will happen to us now?" Sally asked.

"Well the next thing that would happen is our teeth would fall out, but do not worry I know of a cure. All we need is some vitamin C and we will be as good as new." Paul answered.

"I have never taken vitamins, and don't have any in my luggage so where are we going to get vitamin C?" Sally asked.

Paul replied, "I once read that there is a lot of Vitamin C in spruce needles so while I am out gathering firewood today I will chop a spruce tree down and drag it back. We will use the needles to make tea. I should have thought of that before."

"It is almost Christmas so we need a Christmas tree anyway, and we can use the needles for making tea." Paul stated.

"Christmas!" Sally exclaimed. " What is the date today?"

Paul looked at his watch and said, "It is December 23rd" "Tomorrow is my birthday." Sally said.

"Your birthday, how old are you? Paul asked.

"Mr. Sinhuna, don't you know that it is impolite to ask a woman how old she is?" Sally replied.

"Sorry, but if I did not ask, how would I know how many candles to put on your cake?" Paul asked, and they both laughed. "Well, I guess it's OK to tell you how old I am, just as long as you promise not to tell anyone. I will be 40." Sally said.

"You are kidding, I would have sooner guessed that you were going to turn 30." Paul replied.

Sally laughed. "Now I think you are the one who is kidding Mr. Sinhuna."

Sally had a scare while Paul was out gathering firewood and retrieving a spruce tree. There was a path of packed down snow from the cabin to the outhouse. Sally's ankle was much better but it still hurt and she was still using the canoe paddle crutch. She had just finished using the outhouse and when she opened the door she found herself staring practically face to face with a large wolf standing in the path between the outhouse and the cabin. She stepped back into the outhouse and slammed the door.

A couple thoughts shot through her mind simultaneously. One was that she did not know that wolves were so big. She thought of them as just big dogs but that wolf was at least one hundred and fifty pounds! The other thought was even with her leaning into the door with all her strength she would not be able to keep it out. Then she remembered her crutch, and wedged it between the door and the back wall. After awhile, she regained enough composure to turn around and look through the vent in the door. The wolf was gone, but she still waited until she was very cold before she hobbled up the path to the cabin. She was much relieved when she reached the cabin, went inside and latched the door, but then she was worried about Paul.

She need not have worried, the only trace of a wolf Paul saw, were its tracks when he returned to the cabin. Paul pulled the spruce tree through the door and propped it in the corner while Sally told him about her wolf encounter. He reassured her that there had been only a couple of recorded wolf attacks on humans in North America.

"Is that because they eat all the evidence?" Sally asked, as Paul stripped spruce needles off a branch into a pan.

Paul just replied, "Maybe." as he thought about the wolves having devoured at least seven bodies within hours of their crash.

He put the pan on the stove to simmer and soon the wonderful smell of spruce filled the cabin. After the water came up to boil, Paul poured some of the tea into two coffee cups from the cupboard. He was careful to just transfer liquid and not needles. After handing a cup to Sally, she exclaimed "Oh, how can something that smells so good taste so horrible?"

"It does taste awful." Paul agreed, but added that Doctor Paul's scurvy prescription calls for drinking as much of this stuff as you can stand. Spruce tea would become a staple of their diet and after awhile they would even grow to like it.

The next morning was much like the previous few. Paul awoke at first light , got up, filled the stove, cooked a cup of rice, and woke up Sally when it was ready. Only this day the weather had much improved. As Sally got up, Paul said. "Happy birthday! And in honor of your birthday I have placed an order for some nicer weather. It is a clear day and maybe we will even be rescued today."

"Don't get my hopes up," Sally replied, "But for some reason, maybe the nice day, I do feel better than I have in awhile."

"You owe that to Dr. Paul's magic spruce tea elixir, Madam" Paul said with a smile.

When Paul left the cabin, Sally said. "Don't forget to stop at the Department Store and get me a birthday present."

As Paul strapped on the snowshoes he had other problems on his mind than a birthday present. There were only two days of rice left and he had depleted all the small maple trees from the area he had been working in. The trees to the North along the lake and West of the cabin were white birch. They are pretty to look at, and their bark makes an excellent fire starter even when wet, but they do not make good firewood. The trees to the East down bank from the outhouse were mostly white cedar. When burned for firewood cedar burns quickly and does not last. If he had a chainsaw both the white birch and the white cedar would have been worth cutting but with only an ax neither lasted long enough to be worth the effort.

There was an elevated food cache that was made of cedar logs. It looked like a little log cabin on top of twenty foot tall poles. The food cache had surely been used by the former occupant of the cabin to store frozen meat in the winter and keep it out of reach of animals. Paul had checked it out on one of the first days and found it empty. Because they had no meat to store in it, Paul thought about chopping it down, but decided against it. Chopping it down might make the owner of the cabin very unhappy and because it was made of cedar, the firewood would not last long anyway. He decided to keep it in reserve as a last resort, just like the skin stretchers in the cabin. He needed to find a new source of dead maple or ash.

Paul snowshoed along the lake until he could see up ahead that the sparse birch forest gave way to a thick conifer forest. Then he turned inland to skirt the edge of the dense evergreens. He had only snowshoed a few hundred yards when he came to a great birch tree. He slowly walked around it looking at it in amazement. He had seen many birch trees in his life but never a giant like this one. It was close to four foot in diameter and the first branch was over twenty feet off the ground. So that is how the Indians made birch bark canoes he thought. That is a question that had always puzzled Paul, how native people had made canoes out of the small birch trees he was familiar with. The answer was they did not, they used large ones like this giant. A large canoe could be made from this tree and with only one large piece of bark.

After resting for a few minutes leaning against the giant birch Paul continued his journey inland. A few hundred yards later the birch gave way to a poplar forest. Thinking that he was unlikely to find any maples in this direction he was about to turn around when he came across porcupine tracks. Finding these tracks was great news and maybe with a little luck he would have a birthday present for Sally after all. With only two days of rice left they were more in danger of starving than freezing so the goal of this hike instantly turned from wood gathering to a hunting trip. Porcupines have a difficult time maneuvering in deep snow and only tend to travel a short ways looking for a new tree with tastier bark.

Tracking the porcupine to its new tree only took Paul a few minutes and he spotted it high in the branches of a large poplar tree. If he had a rifle the porcupine would have made an easy target but of course he had only an ax. Paul let out an audible sigh when he saw the size of the tree. There was no way in his weakened condition that he felt up to chopping down a tree that large. However, he needed the nourishment that was in that animal and so he began laboriously chopping down the tree. His plan was to chop down the tree and kill the porcupine with the ax. He needed the tree to fall in an open area and not get hung up in another tree.

About halfway into chopping down the tree Paul had to take a break. His meager diet and this exertion made him feel faint. As he leaned against the tree to rest he prayed "Lord please give me strength for this task." After the rest, with renewed strength Paul went back to chopping. Cutting down a large tree like this is extra dangerous while wearing snowshoes. If the tree goes the wrong way snowshoes make getting out of the way more difficult and backing up with snowshoes is almost impossible. Fortunately, the wind was lightly blowing in just the right direction and Paul did not have any trouble making the tree fall where he wanted it to.

When the tree hit the ground the porcupine fell from the branches. Paul waded into the branches to dispatch the porcupine but the web on one of his snowshoes caught on a branch and he fell. Regaining ones footing after falling in deep snow with snowshoes on is difficult and by the time Paul was able to get back up the porcupine had abandoned the branches of the downed tree and was heading towards the base of another tree. Paul got to the other tree just as the porcupine climbed out of the reach of his ax.

The only good thing about the situation was that the second tree was much smaller in diameter than the first. After a long rest sitting on the trunk of the first tree and another prayer asking for a better outcome, Paul proceeded to chop down the second tree. This time there was no escape for the porcupine and Paul's ax swiftly ended its life with a blow to its head. Paul was overcome with thankfulness and gave thanks. He was also spent and needed to rest. He could not afford to expend any effort that was not absolutely necessary. So to lessen the weight he needed to carry back to camp he gutted and skinned the animal on the spot.

Skinning a porcupine can be dangerous, as the quills are very sharp and have small barbs on the end, but Paul had done the job once before. He never dreamed that the skills he learned as a Boy Scout on one of the survival weekend camps so many years before would ever come in so handy. After gutting the animal Paul placed the liver and heart in a plastic bag and put the plastic bag back into the pocket of his hunting coat. Paul hated liver with a passion but he could not afford to waste any protein and the iron in the liver would also go a long ways to restoring some proper nutrition in their diets.

It was an extremely large porcupine and the carcass weighed almost thirty pounds. That was too much for Paul to carry back in the shape he was in. He found an appropriate sized dead branch from the big poplar and chopped it off. He tied the carcass to the branch with his deer dragging rope from the pocket of his hunting coat. Then he used the branch as a traverse to drag the porcupine back to camp. The dead poplar branch would not make the best firewood but it would burn and dragging it was a lot easier than carrying the carcass. This adventure had used up most of the day and Paul was flat out exhausted and needed to rest. He would be lucky to make it back to the cabin by dark.

It had been another long boring day for Sally, just like many long boring days before it. She knew Paul had to keep going out to gather firewood if they were going to keep from freezing to death but she hated being there all alone. After her encounter with the wolf, being all by herself bothered her even more. At least when Paul was there talking with him made the time seem to go faster. Some of their talks about Christianity made her a little uncomfortable. Was there something to Christianity after all or was it as she had been taught at University just a bunch of fairy tales?

She knew that there were only two days of rice left. How long would they live when it was gone? She could also see they were using more firewood than Paul was able to supply but knew it would last a few days longer than the food. So would they starve to death or freeze to death? Maybe she should be preparing for her own death. She could write a final note to her parents with the paper and pencils in the trunk, but what would she say? Should she be asking Paul about how to get to heaven? No, she could not bring herself to do that. Her pride was standing in the way and besides, she just did not believe.

They were trying to conserve firewood so Paul was only filling the stove in the morning and evening. In the afternoon like it was now the temperature in the cabin would drop into the 50's and she was cold. Then she remembered how hot it had been in the loft so she carried a blanket up the ladder and wrapped up with it and laid down on the loft. The floor was hard and uncomfortable but it was warmer up there and she fell asleep. When she woke up, she had a stiff neck because she had not brought a pillow with her. While she worked the kink out of her neck, she once again noticed the cross hanging from a nail on the back side of the last log rafter. This time she decided to retrieve it, and tease Paul by pretending she thought he had given it to her for her birthday. She crawled to the back of the loft and when she reached out to the cross and slipped the chain from the nail she realized there was also something else on the chain, there was also a key.

CHAPTER 5

The Key to Survival

Sally slipped the gold chain of the necklace over her head. She would need both hands free to climb down the ladder. She had not even thought about the diary she had found in a few days because she had decided not to break the lock on it. Now, however, she had the key, and they could read it and return it to its resting place without the owner ever needing to know. She was very excited about finding the key but already knew she would need to wait until tomorrow, Christmas, to read the diary because it would soon be too dark to read it. Then she had a panicked thought. Where is Paul? He had been gone all day! Lately he had been coming back in to warm up at least a couple times during the day. She had not realized how late it was because she had been asleep most of the afternoon.

She was really worried. It was getting dark fast and Paul had never been this late before. What really worried her the most was what Paul had told her after her wolf encounter. Wolves hunt mainly at night. It was really cold in the cabin. Paul was usually the one who filled the stove but he had shown her how to do it. It was more complicated than just throwing in wood Willie Nilly. She decided that she would fill the stove herself and then go out into the night looking for Paul. As she filled the stove she thought about how scared she was of wolfs, but Paul may need her. Then she thought if she did run into wolves it really did not matter. They only had two days of rice left, and if she met her end at the tooth and fang of wolves at least it would be quick.

Sally quickly put on some heavier clothing and her coat, checked the latch of the door and left through the window because the door could not be latched from the outside. It was a still, cold and clear night. It was much colder than it had been and she could feel the lining in her nose freeze as she breathed in and thaw out as she breathed out. It was dark now but would be getting lighter soon as the full moon was just rising. She had brought her crutch with her and she walked down the path towards the outhouse until she came to the snowshoe path she saw Paul use that morning. The first few hundred meters down the snowshoe path were not too bad because it had been packed down by Paul traveling back and forth on it a number of times but then she reached the point where Paul had left his beaten path and she floundered in the deep snow.

This was hard and slow going and without snowshoes she would not be able to make much headway. She thought this is crazy, I do not even know if this is the right direction. Then she realized in her panic she had not been thinking clearly. She should have called out. She was afraid when she called out PAUL there would not be an answer, and was greatly relieved when she heard Paul answer from a short ways up the trail.

Sally turned and could see Paul wearily trudging toward her. Just as he reached her, there was a chorus of wolf howls from a couple of miles up the lake. Paul said, "It sounds like they just made a kill."

"Oh, Paul I was so worried! You have never been out this late." Sally said.

"Well, this morning you told me not to forget your birthday present, and shopping for both a birthday and Christmas present took longer than I planned. I have brought you both a birthday dinner and a Christmas dinner. " Paul replied. It was only then that Sally saw the branch he was dragging and the porcupine hanging from it.

Paul was really beat, and was happy to have Sally's help to finish dragging the branch and porcupine the rest of the way back to the cabin. During their frequent rest breaks on their way back he told her about chopping down the two trees. On their last break Sally surprised Paul by stating, "I have a Christmas present for you also."

When they reached the cabin, it was nice and warm because Sally had filled the stove. Paul laid the porcupine carcass on the table and opened the stove door so they could see what they were doing. Sally got the cast iron frying pan and the cooking oil down from the cupboard and Paul cut up the liver and heart into the pan and put it on the stove to cook. "I love beef liver. What does porcupine liver taste like?" Sally asked.

"I do not really care for liver and while I have eaten porcupine, I have never tried the liver. I have eaten both beef and venison liver and they both taste the same except venison liver has a more grainy texture, so I expect it will taste the same." Paul answered.

While they waited for the liver and heart to fry on the stove, Paul was dismantling the carcass into the large pan. "Too bad we do not have some potatoes, carrots, and onions, but this will make a fine Christmas dinner," Paul was saying.

Sally asked in anticipation "What does porcupine taste like?"

"Kind of like pork and if we stew it all night and half tomorrow it should be tender." Paul answered. "I have been thinking," Paul continued, "We have been real good with our rice ration but we have only two days left. What would you say if I asked if we should splurge and cook it all for Christmas in with the porcupine?"

Sally replied, "I think that would be a good idea. We might as well start our long fast with a full stomach." By this time the liver and heart were finished cooking and they ate it with relish. Even the liver-hating Paul was surprised at how much he enjoyed the meal.

When they finished eating, they were both full for the first time in many days but not stuffed. They both could and would have eaten more if there had been more food to eat. Sally said, "That was the best birthday dinner I ever had. Thank you."

"You know Sally, at my house we always opened Christmas presents on Christmas eve, so how about giving me my present tonight?" Paul asked.

"I cannot give it to you tonight but I could tell you what it is if you want." Sally answered.

"Well then, please do, or I will not be able to sleep tonight." Paul answered.

Sally had decided not to kid Paul by pretending that she thought he had given her the cross for her birthday. So she told him about getting cold, crawling up in the loft and falling to sleep only to wake up and find the birthday present the owner of the cabin had left for her. Then she told him about finding the key on the chain with the cross and that his Christmas present would be that she was going to read the diary to him.

"That is great!" Paul said, "Christmas dinner and entertainment."

The next morning, they both got up at the crack of dawn, and they both felt better than they had in a long time. It is amazing what a little nutrition and a full stomach can do. There was the wonderful smell of the porcupine cooking. Paul announced, "It is Christmas and we are going to celebrate. Today we will eat and be warm no matter how much wood we burn." He then filled the stove with wood and added more water and all the rest of the rice to the porcupine stew. He also seasoned it with salt and pepper. It was a bright, beautiful day and Sally asked, "Shall I start reading the diary while we wait for the stew to finish cooking?"

"Please do." Paul replied. So Sally retrieved the diary from the steamer trunk and unlocked its lock. The first page said this is the diary of Susan Le Forest Smith. The Le Forest was crossed out and Sally wondered if that meant that this woman was married.

The first few pages really weren't diary entries but more of a summation of what led this woman to start this diary. It went like this. My name is Susan Smith. My maiden name was Le Forest and I am the daughter of Pierre and Mary (Jones) Le Forest. Although no one is ever likely to read this, I feel the need to write down how the events of the last few months transpired to cause me to return to my childhood home. My father was from Quebec and was half French and half Algonquian Indian. He spoke Algonquian, French, and English. My Mother was English and met my father while she was working as a teacher. My father worked as a lumber jack, carpenter, handyman, hunting and fishing guide and a trapper.

During my childhood we moved around a lot and never stayed in the same place for two consecutive winters. I was born here and I can remember staying in this cabin five different winters so this place feels more like home than any other. One of the reasons is that when I was sixteen my mother died here so when I am here I feel close to her. I sewed her into her burial blanket and father and I buried her out back up the hill and marked her grave with a rock from the river. Father cut a cross into her head stone. We were always planning to get her a proper grave marker but never were able to afford it. Now I have brought Father's ashes back here and have sprinkled them on her grave so for once and for all, they are together again at last.

"Paul, did you know there was a grave out back?" Sally asked.

"No, the stone must be buried under the snow. Her Father could have told me what my name means." Paul said.

"I thought you told me that your name was Chippewa or Ottawa ." Sally stated. "I did, but the Chippewas, Ottawas, and Ojibwas were all part of the Algonquian Nation, and although they may identify themselves as Chippewas, Ottawas, Ojibwas or Algonquian they are all the same people group and speak the same language. The language is slightly different in the East than in the West but for the most part it is the same." Paul reported.

Sally continued reading the diary. As a child I spent most of my winters in the bush and only attended school for a few years when we lived close to a town. The rest of the time mother taught me. The Ministry of Education was not too happy about that but because my Mother was a teacher and I always passed my government test at a higher grade level than I should have, they never did much about it. After Mother died, Father got a job at a resort as a guide and handyman, so I could attend government school for my last two years of high school and I graduated with honors.

The last two years we lived at a cabin at the resort. Last winter I turned 18 and a guy by the name of James Smith moved into the cabin next to us. He worked on the ships on Lake Superior and was off for the winter. The owners of the resort were happy to rent him the cabin for the winter because they were only open from May to the end of September so they had plenty of empty cabins. We fell in love and were married in the spring before he went off to work on the ships for the summer.

Our plan was that we would get an apartment in the city for the winter and I was going to attend college. My father was going to move back to this cabin and run his trap line for the winter because the area had not been trapped in a couple of years. He and Mr. Johnsen flew in five hundred pounds of supplies to the cabin in preparation for him moving here for the winter. The plan was that he would guide during moose season and then after the lakes froze, I would haul him, his snowmobile, and sled to Sunrise in Jim's truck. There he would snowmobile from the end of the road to the cabin. He planned the trip into the cabin to take two or at the most three days, and I was a little worried about it, but he had done it many times before, sometimes with Mother and I.

In the spring he planned to canoe out with his pelts in his birch bark freight canoe that was at the cabin. He could have arranged for Mr. Johnsen fly to him out but a rich collector had offered him seven thousand dollars for his canoe sight unseen. When I asked him if he planned to buy an aluminum canoe to replace it he said no! His dad , uncle, and he had built that one and he still remembered how. He said that he knew where there was a suitable tree.

That passage really excited Paul. "That is the answer!" Paul exclaimed. "Yesterday, I found that tree. I could make a birch bark canoe and we could canoe out."

Sally stopped him, "Paul, sweetie, I am trying to be gentle, you are not talking sense. Have you ever made a birch bark canoe? Do you know what direction to canoe out? It is the middle of winter and it will be many months until the lakes thaw and we could leave, and all the food we have is on the stove right now."

The comments took the wind out of his sails and Paul realized how foolish what he had just blurted out was. Sheepishly, he changed the subject, "Our Christmas meal is ready, let's eat."

Paul asked a blessing over the meal, thanked God for providing the porcupine and thanked him for sending Jesus to save us from our sins. Then they both ate until they were truly stuffed. The porcupine meat was tender and falling off the bones and tasted heavenly. The rice had simmered in the broth from the porcupine and was better than any rice they had eaten so far in the cabin. The spruce tea even tasted good. The best part was that even after eating their fill there was enough food left for two or maybe three days if they stretched it.

After the meal and cleaning up the dishes Sally continued reading the diary. She was still reading the introduction and not the diary itself.

Unfortunately, none of our plans were to work out. Two tragedies occurred that left me numbed and unsure what to do. Father died during moose season in September, from a heart attack while packing out moose meat for one of his hunters. He was only 50. I knew that he wanted to be buried next to Mother but I had no way to arrange that so I had him cremated. Jim was off work at the time and had helped me think through what to do because I was not up to it. My plan was to ask Mr. Johnsen to fly me into the cabin next summer so I could sprinkle my father's ashes on my mother's grave and then fly back. That plan was doomed to fail also.

In mid November I was listening to the radio in the cabin at the resort when the news that blind sided me was announced. Jim's ship was missing and presumed sunk. I held out hope against hope that this was a big mistake or a bad dream, until the next day when an officer from the shipping company showed up at the cabin door with some papers to sign. He told me that he was very sorry for my loss and unless they found Jim's body, which he thought unlikely, I would not be able to collect Jim's life insurance until a year after the sinking.

Then there was more bad news. I went to the bank to withdraw some money and found that the bank had frozen our account because we had not filed the proper paper work when we got married. They said it would remain frozen until I could provide a death certificate and I knew that I would not be able to do that for a year. Then they told me I still needed to make the payments on Jim's truck and that there was a payment due in two weeks. I might have stated some of that wrong because I know I was not thinking clearly at the time and was still in shock.

I went back to the resort cabin to reassess my problems and pray. I had only fifty dollars, and the restaurant I sometimes worked at was closed for the winter. I am sure that the owners of the restaurant or the resort would have loaned me some money to tide me over until I could find a job but they had all gone South for the winter and I did not have their addresses. Jobs are hard to find here in the winter. I know I have some relatives in Quebec but I do not know them and they do not know me. They would also speak French or Algonquian and I only speak English. There I was, alone in the world after losing both my father and husband within a few months of each other and totally destitute. I prayed to God asking what should I do and cried myself to sleep.

The next morning, God had answered my prayer, because when I woke up I had the answer to my problem. I knew what to do. Father had taught me how to trap. I could run his trap line. His cabin was full of supplies. In the spring I would pack my pelts in Father's freight birch bark canoe and canoe out. Then I could sell it to the collector he told me about. I also planned to bring out Father's traps and will likely sell those also. I can still hear my father in my mind say keep right the first three lakes and left the next two and in three long days you will be out. I also wanted to retrieve my family Bible which was resting in a trunk in the cabin. I did not tell anyone of my plans because I knew they would try to talk me out of it and besides no one I trusted was around.

I packed all my winter clothes in garbage bags in my Father's duffel bag and strapped it in his sled. Father taught me to do this because dry clothes can be the difference between life and death. He would always say you never know when there will be a storm, the canoe will tip over, the snowmobile will break through the ice, or the roof will leak. Then I packed everything I thought I might need in my duffel and strapped that to the back of Father's snowmobile. I left a lot of my possessions in the resort cabin but I planned to be back by the time the resort opened at the end of May, so I knew they would be alright. Next, I backed Jim's truck up to a bank along the driveway of the resort. Then I opened the tailgate and drove Father's snowmobile into the bed and loaded his sled. Father had a scabbard mounted on the front of his snowmobile and I loaded his Model 99 Savage moose rifle in it.

Next, I wrote a letter to the bank explaining that I could not make the payments on the truck and they could repossess it. I told them that it would be parked at the end of the road in Sunrise. On my way I mailed the letter, stopped and bought the food I would need for my trip, and filled the snowmobile's gas tank and one extra gas can. Oh, and I also bought this diary. When I was finished I had three dollars left. The other extra gas cans I filled by siphoning gas from the truck. I was mad at the bank and did not feel like leaving them a full tank of gas. When I got to Sunrise and the end of the road I backed the truck up to a bank and unloaded my cargo. I had not been on this trail in three years and then my mother had been driving the snowmobile I was on and she was just following Father. I did not know for sure if I would remember the way but I felt God had led me to do this so I was not worried. I had to camp one night in the bush but I got to the cabin the next day.

"Paul, have you ever heard of a town called Sunrise? Sally asked.

"No, but now we know how to find our way out, three lakes to the right and two lakes to the left." Paul replied.

"Not for sure! We do not know for sure if she was talking about this river and we do not know if she was talking about going down stream or up stream." Sally said.

"You're right, we do not even know how many rivers come into or leave this lake." Paul agreed. "A three day canoe trip could be seventy five miles or three hundred miles and her two day snowmobile trip could have been up to 200 miles, so we really do not know much more now than before." Paul stated.

Sally asked, "Don't snowmobiles go faster than that? How many kilometers in a mile? I am used to kilometers and do not really have an idea how far 200 miles is." Paul replied that there were about 1.6 kilometers in a mile and that if the snowmobile she took into here was the one in the storage building it was so old he did not think it could go too fast if she was breaking trail with it.

Sally started reading again. "It looks like the diary starts here, because it says Dec.2"

"Does it say what year?" Paul asked.

"No, just Dec. 2." Sally replied. Then she resumed reading. I arrived at the cabin at 3:00 and had a lot of things I needed to do before dark but I went straight to my mother's grave. I spread Father's ashes on her grave before checking out the cabin because it was snowing. I wanted to complete this task while I could still find Mother's head stone. After performing this family duty and praying at what is now my parent's grave. I dropped the sled off at the porch and put the snowmobile in the shed. It looks like Father and Mr. Johnsen cut, split and stacked about twenty face cords of firewood. I should have plenty left by spring. That is a big relief because I was expecting that I would need to cut some to make it through the winter. I thought Father's chainsaw would be in the shed and it is not. All I have is the ax in the cabin.

The diary continued. The cabin is in good shape. The supplies that Father and Mr. Johnsen flew in here are all put away as I knew they would be. I found that the mice had gotten to my mattress in the loft, so it looks like I will be using my parents' bed. I never liked sleeping in the loft anyway because it was always too hot when I went to bed, then it would be cold by morning. By the time I unpacked, it was getting dark and the stove had the cabin nice and warm, so I went to bed.

Dec. 3 I woke up and filled the stove. It is a bright sunny day and I feel at peace for the first time since Father and Jim died. I feel that I am at long last home. I know a lot of people would be bothered by being alone but at least for now I relish it. I may be stir crazy by spring from cabin fever but for now I am happy and content to be alone. I am planning on reading through the Bible this winter and doing a lot of praying. I have read a lot of the Bible before but have never read it completely through.

Now I am going to take one of Father's fishing poles down to the river and see if I can catch breakfast. There are usually some big brook trout in the hole this time of year. I will have to keep this book locked and hid from the Mounties because the season is not open. Now that is funny. Father always followed all the trapping seasons and rules but never worried about the season when it came to fishing or shooting a moose for the larder. So I guess I am just like him. What would mother say?

Well, I caught breakfast and after I ate I went to work cleaning up the cabin and it is now ship shape. When I look around this cabin, I recall happier times. I can almost hear Mother and Father talking or Mother reading me a story or working with me on my lessons. I look over at the pump and remember Father saying that he never had a pump at any trapper's cabin but Mother would not move here if he did not put one in. He was mad about it at the time but later realized she had been right. The pump was a lot easier than hauling water from the river. My first full day here was great but just before bed a cold draft hit me in the face. I walked to the door and sure enough there was an east wind. I can only remember this happening a few times as a child. I hung a tarp over the door to cut down the draft. My mother had a rag rug she had made that we used over the door when there was an East wind, but it was old and worn out and Father laid it in Mother's grave before we put her body in.

I have my old mouse chewed mattress and all of Father's clothes that were stored here. So I plan to cut them up and make another rag rug. That project will keep me occupied when I am not running my trap line.

Sally asked if it was OK if she stopped reading, because it was getting dark. Then she asked Paul if he had ever read the Bible completely through. "Wouldn't not take more than a winter to read through it?" Paul answered that he had read it through a number of times and that it only takes about eighty hours. Sally said "I thought it would take a lot longer than that."

Paul, then said. "Well now we at least know that we are in Canada."

"How?" inquired Sally.

"Susan mentioned Mounties in her diary." Paul answered.

"Good thinking, I did not catch that." Sally replied.

Then Paul announced, "You entertained us all afternoon reading the diary. So now that it is too dark read I will tell you an amazing true story for your Christmas entertainment as my present to you, if you want." Sally eagerly agreed.

CHAPTER 6

Blessings Blowing in The Wind

P aul told the following story. A young man felt the calling of God to become a missionary to India. He raised support and a missions organization sent him. After twenty years of work he only had one convert to Christianity. His convert was his secretary and jobs were scarce in the area and so he was not even sure that she was a true convert. He felt like a failure and like he had wasted the money of his supporters. His secretary asked him to bring the Gospel to her remote mountain village. She could not go with him because she had been banned by her village years ago for some transgression. Lacking any other ideas, he decided to fulfill her request before he gave up.

He traveled through the jungle and up a treacherous mountain road in a Land Rover to his secretary's former village. The people were not used to outsiders visiting them and the leader called the whole village to a meeting to introduce the stranger. The missionary presented the Gospel and to his surprise the whole village accepted Christ as their Lord and Savior. The reason he later found was there had been an old woman in the village who had had a vision when she was a young girl that some day someone would come to their village and tell them about the one true God and how they should live their lives. Throughout her whole life that woman kept telling everyone that someday this missionary would come.

He spent a week with the people of the village, preaching and giving out literature and Bibles. When he ran out, he decided to go back to the city and get more. The whole village turned out to see him off, and because he could only drive slowly on the mountain road they were walking beside his Land Rover. When he went around the curve in the road they found that a six foot diameter tree had fallen and was blocking the road. There was no way around and the missionary said out loud, "What am I going to do now?" The leader of the village heard him and said, "Pray to God and see how he moves the tree." This distressed the missionary very much and he thought that if he prayed and nothing happened all these people would fall away, but what else could he do? He folded his hands and bowed his head and gave a long prayer beseeching God to move the tree. When he finished the prayer and opened his eyes the tree was still blocking the road and his heart sank. However, just then a young man came running down the road. When he got to the Land Rover he said, "I am from a village further up the mountain and I was here the day you arrived. I accepted Christ but when I returned to my village and told them about Christianity they refused to believe unless you would come and tell them."

So the missionary went with the young man to his village by a mountain foot path. He stayed in the second village for a week and all those people also accepted Christ. At the end of the week the missionary and all the people of the second village walked down the mountain path to the first village. The leader of the first village said, "Let's all go and see how God has moved the tree." So all the people of both villages walked down the mountain road to see how God had moved the tree, but when they rounded the bend the tree was still there. The missionary thought oh no, now all these people will fall away. However, just then an elephant came out of the jungle and stood by the tree. A short time later a man came out of the jungle. When he saw the tree blocking the road and all the people standing there, he hooked the elephant to the tree and had it pull the tree off the road to the cheers of the people. Then they asked him how he came to be there.

The man said he owned five elephants but this one was his favorite. A week ago it pulled up its stake and headed off through the jungle. It had never done anything like that before. He could not afford to lose his favorite elephant so he packed up some food and started following its tracks through the jungle. He had gotten close to the elephant a number of times but each time it ran off again. This was the first time it let him catch up to it and when he saw the tree blocking the road he thought he might as well move it.

The missionary was thankful to God but he was also ashamed that the new converts had more faith that God would answer his prayer than he did. The missionary also noted that the elephant had pulled up its stake and started coming this way a week ago, right when he asked God to move the tree.

Sally angrily said, "Paul I have a real problem with that story. When we were on the plane there were people praying that the plane would land safely, and they are all dead. I am sure you were praying for your wife's life and she is dead. We have two days worth of food left and then we will either starve or freeze to death and your prayers are not going to change that. I will bet that someone just made up that story for the gullible. Can't you see, your pretend God does not answer prayers? Oh, Paul I am sorry I blurted that out, I did not mean to offend you."

Paul did not say anything for a few minutes. They just sat quietly in the now dark cabin. Then Paul said, in a quavering voice "Sally, I have been praying almost all my life, and all of my prayers have been answered. It is just that sometimes they were not the answers I wanted and sometimes they were answers I did not understand. Some of the answers I did not understand at the time have become clear to me now."

There was another long pause, then he said, "I used to have a mongrel dog when I was a kid. He knew and understood twenty four different commands, and sometimes he even obeyed them. He was tied up outside because my mother would seldom let him in the house. When I would go outside he would vigorously wag his tail. When I would get on my bike and ride away, he would put his tail between his legs and looked dejected. As dogs go, he was a very smart one. I even saw him figure out things that I thought were beyond a dog's intellect. However, there was no way he could ever understand that I had to go run my paper route so I could afford to buy him dog food and dog toys."

" My dog was smart, but he could not hope to understand the reasons I did things. I may not be the sharpest knife in the drawer but most people would say that I was a lot smarter than my dog. Now if it were possible to draw a line graph to plot the intelligence of my dog, myself, and the One who created the universe you would see the dot that represented my dog and the dot that represented me would be almost touching each other and the one that represented God would be a billion trillion light years away. I have far less hope to understand the ways of God than my dog did to understand me. My dog did not understand me, but he trusted me. I do not always understand God but I trust him".

"The book of Romans says that "...All things work together for good for those who love God, to those who are the called according to his purpose." I do not understand why those people on the plane had to die,

I do not understand why I had to lose my wife, I do not understand why there are wars, fires, floods, hurricanes and tornadoes, but I do not need to because God is working things out for my good. I do not know why God has allowed us to be in this situation, but I believe it just may be for your sake."

Then Paul did something that startled Sally. He reached across the table and took her by both hands. Bowing his head, he prayed, "Our great and loving heavenly Father, Our Lord Jesus, the creator of the heavens and the earth, my designer and maker. I am your servant and will gladly accept anything you have planned for me, however I ask you to show your bountiful mercy to Sally and provide for her a way out of this situation. I ask that you show a blessing to her and that you provide some means for her to survive. I also ask that you allow her to find her way into a saving faith in you and into your kingdom. In Jesus name, Amen."

Sally felt terrible. She was sure she had not only offended Paul but had hurt him also. Why couldn't she have just kept her mouth closed. They were having such a nice day and she had to go and spoil it. She knew they had only a short time left before they starved or froze to death. Oh, why did she have to wreck their likely last chance for a little joy. They sat in silence for a time, then a cold draft hit Sally in the back of the head. Paul got up and opened the door. A strong cold wind was coming out of the East just as in Susan's diary.

Paul opened the door to the stove for light and grabbed the ax. "What are you going to do?" Sally asked.

"I am going to use the ax head to pry up the roofing nails that are holding down the rag rug so I can hang it over the door, like Susan's diary talked about. I don't know why someone nailed it down in the first place." Paul answered. Then Paul pried the rug up and hung it over the door to stop the draft.

After that Paul filled the stove for the night and Sally asked, "Should we go to bed now?"

"No, it is Christmas and it is still early. Would it be OK with you if we sang a few Christmas carols before we go to bed?" Paul asked.

"I would like that." Sally replied. She was thinking of it as a peace offering.

"Well, then I must warn you, I couldn't carry a tune in a bucket. There is one more thing I need to say before we sing. I now know why the rug was nailed down. It was covering up a trap door. The door is nailed down and we will have to wait until tomorrow to open it and see what is down there because my pen light is dead."

Now they were both filled with anticipation for what they might find under the floor. Then they sang Jingle Bells, Silent Night, and Oh Little Town of Bethlehem. When they went to bed, Sally felt much better and had some renewed hope, even if Paul did sing badly.

CHAPTER 7

The Discovery

Neither of them slept well that night, but Paul hardly slept at all. He kept praying to God that there would be food below that trap door. The diary did say that Susan had found that the 500 pounds of supplies had been put away as she knew they would be. Surely, that many supplies would not fit in the cupboards. Why had he not thought about that when Sally read that part? Of course, even if the owner of the cabin stored food in the cellar, that did not mean there would be any there now, but why was the trap door nailed shut?

They were both up at first light but they needed to wait until it was lighter so Paul built up the fire and they ate more porcupine. As it got lighter, Paul was trying to figure out how to open the trap door. They did not have a hammer or pry bar. He could, of course, chop it to pieces with the ax but then how could he fix the floor?

Sally said, "I have an idea." She went and got a wood chisel and a steel rod from the silverware drawer. What they were doing in the silverware drawer she did not know. "Could you drive the nails all the way through the floor board with the ax and this steel rod, and then maybe split the floor boards with the chisel if you have to?" Sally asked.

"That is a good idea." Paul said as he gave Sally a look that she interpreted to mean "How did you think of that, when I didn't?" Paul made short work of the job and soon had the trap door off and laying on the floor. They both peered into the hole in the floor, but could see nothing because of the darkness.

Paul lowered himself through the hole in the floor and found himself standing on the same rock formation the hearth was made of. The surface of the rock was about five feet below the floor of the cabin but there were steps chipped into the rock that led to a lower level. Paul had to bend over to avoid bumping his head as he descended the steps. It took a while for his eyes to adjust to the light. Sally yelled down the hole, "Paul, don't keep me in suspense! What do you see?" Paul came back up the steps and his head popped back up through the hole in the floor. One look at him dashed all of Sally's hopes. Tears were freely flowing down his cheeks and he was crying uncontrollably.

He could hardly speak, his voice was breaking up when he said, "Sally, I am sorry." His voice cracked and he had to start over. "I am sorry you hate rice because we have an awful lot of it to eat."

Paul ducked his head again and went back down the steps. Sally could not wait any longer and lowered herself into the hole. Soon she was standing beside Paul who was on his knees and silently praying. She hugged him. Tears were freely flowing from her eyes also. There were shelves on three sides of this cellar and they contained so many mason jars full of rice that Paul had made no effort to count them. Not only that but some of the jars were labeled pancake mix and others were flour. There were also jars that contained honey, sugar, salt, pepper, coffee, tea bags, and bags of yeast. There was even some bar soap, a container of lamp oil and also a couple of oil lamps. A stack of bushel baskets sat in the corner. At one time they likely contained potatoes, onions, and carrots. They were empty now, but Paul and Sally did not notice and would not have cared. They were not going to starve!

Still crying tears of happiness and relief, Sally left Paul's side and stepped across the small cellar to the shelves. When she did, a floor board creaked. This was a surprise because the floor of the cellar was dirt. "What is this?" Sally exclaimed as she bent over to examine what had made the noise.

Paul moved to her side and said, "It looks like another trap door.

They opened it and found that it covered an insulated wood compartment below the floor of the cellar. In the compartment, they found tins of maple syrup. They were both still overcome by emotion and between sobs, Sally asked what was the purpose of the compartment.

Paul said, "Its to keep the maple syrup from freezing."

When they regained their composure, Paul asked Sally if she knew how to make pancakes.

"I sure do!" she exclaimed.

"Well, then would you please make me about a dozen?" Paul asked as he handed her a jar of mix along with an empty box with the directions on the back.

"Sure, as long as this mix doesn't call for milk and eggs," Sally said taking the mix and the box. She found that there were some foot holds chipped out of the rock when she climbed back out to begin preparing the pancakes. Paul then started carrying jars of each of the items to the edge of the hole. He planned to replace the empty jars in the cupboards with these full jars. However, as he was transferring jars to the edge of the hole, he noticed a canvas bag hanging from the log floor joists. When he took it down and opened it, he found a Model 1906 Winchester pump .22 caliber rifle and a couple boxes of ammunition. This put an even bigger smile on Paul's face.

Just then Sally called down, "Are you sure you can eat a dozen pancakes? You know you already ate breakfast."

Paul called back, "If you make them I will eat them." Then he yelled, "Santa came a day late, but he brought me a .22 rifle."

Sally finished the pancakes and called Paul to a second breakfast and Paul did indeed eat twelve pancakes, covered in maple syrup. Sally had a bunch also. When Paul finished eating, he let out a groan and said, "I think I ate too much. He then said, "I need to get outside and chop more wood, but I am going to need to wait until these pancakes digest a little. Would you read some more of the diary?"

Sally replied, "Sure, but first I want to say that when you go out to chop wood, I want to go with you. My ankle is much better and I think I could be of help."

Paul said, "That sounds great to me."

Sally started reading the diary again. Dec. 4: I woke up sick this morning and threw up. I have been feeling a little off for the last few days but I thought it was just from my great sorrow. Now I think I may have a touch of the flu. Because I am not feeling well, I am not going to start my trap line today. I started cutting up my old mattress and some of Father's old clothes for the rag rug. I found that it was much harder cutting up Father's clothes than I thought it would be. I am cutting the material into long strips and braiding them in a long three way braid. When I am done braiding it, I will sew it into a spiral to make a rug, just as Mother showed me.

Dec. 5: I woke up sick again this morning and again threw up. Today I realized something I had not thought of before. Now I think that I do not have a touch of flu. I think I may be pregnant! Jim was home a week before his ship went down, so that would make me about three weeks pregnant. I feel stupid for not thinking about this possibility sooner, but I did have a lot of problems and grief the last couple of weeks.

If I am pregnant, I will be happy to still have a part of Jim to love and I am not worried about providing for our child. God will provide! However, if I am pregnant, I will need to make other plans about canoeing out. I should deliver in the middle of August. That would make me way too pregnant to canoe out in May. When I celebrate Christmas with the Johnsens, I will ask Mr. Johnsen to fly me out in May. I guess that there will be no pregnancy test for this girl, but I expect I will know for sure after a while.

Oh, I should add, I worked on the rag rug today and it was a sunshiny day and nice weather. I saw a moose today about a mile down the lake out on the ice. It would be way too much work to sneak up and shoot it, then haul it this far back. Besides, the wolves might get at it before I could get all the meat back, even with the snowmobile. Father's .300 savage is loaded and leaning against the wall by the door, so hopefully I will see one closer before the season closes. The wind swung back around to the Northwest.

A noise made Sally look up. It was Paul snoring. He was sitting in a kitchen chair across from her with one arm on the table and his head leaning against the wall. Evidently, the relief he felt from finding a cellar full of food combined with a full stomach had put him to sleep. Sally put the diary away and started exchanging empty jars from the cupboard with the full jars that Paul had set on the floor by the trap door. There was no question in her mind that Paul would assign the bounty of food they had found in the cellar to God's great providence. She knew it was just a coincidence, wasn't it? Wouldn't it have been ironic if they had starved to death with so much food under their feet? Then she thought about what she had read in the diary. She thought about a possibly pregnant teenager who keeps talking about God in the diary. It was like she was surrounded by Christians on all sides of her. Still, were all these things that had happened recently just the luck of the draw or was there some higher power at work? It would be hard for her to reject all she learned at University.

Paul woke up and stretched. Sally said, "I did not know I was reading you a bedtime story."

"Sorry I fell asleep, I did not sleep too well last night." Paul answered.

When he saw what she was doing he asked, "Would you like me to put those empty jars in the cellar?"

"No, I can handle it." she replied. Then she climbed back through the hole in the floor. When she had put all the jars away in the cellar and climbed back out, Paul was sitting at the table looking at the .22 rifle. When Paul noticed her, he asked her to come over and sit down. "Have you ever shot a rifle?" he asked.

"No, I don't like guns and I am afraid of them."

"Well, I want to show you how it works and how to handle it safely."

"I don't want to." Sally protested.

"Sally, in her diary, Susan said her Father died at 50, and I am 50. I am not planning on dying any time soon, but you never know. If I were to die, you may need to know how to shoot this gun to survive." Sally relented, and Paul showed her how to operate the rifle, how to put the hammer on half cock, which acts like a safety, and how to align the sights with a target. Then he said he wanted her to shoot it after he tested it to see if it was sighted in.

Paul opened the door and said, "I would never use a building as a target because it is normally unsafe but in this case I think it will be alright." Then he called out, "Is there anyone in the outhouse? If there is you better answer because I am about to use the outhouse as a target." There was, of course, no answer so he aligned sights with a knot in the board on the upper right hand corner. He used the door frame as a rest to steady the rifle, and he fired. "Darn," he said, "I can't see the hole. I must have missed." Then he went out the door, shutting it behind him and walked down to the outhouse. When he came back, there was a big grin on his face, "The bullet hole is right in the middle of the knot." he said. Paul then gave Sally some more instructions about holding her breath and squeezing the trigger and she took several shots. They were not as accurate as Paul's, but to her surprise, they were all centered around the knot. Also to her surprise, she found shooting the rifle was fun.

After their target practice session, they went out to gather more firewood. Paul had still not found a new source for small dead maples, but with Sally helping he decided to go back to the old area and cut some larger ones. With her help, they could haul a larger tree than he could by himself. Paul had already decided to change the way he chopped wood, even before Sally offered to help. He decided he would now chop the wood in five or six foot lengths.

They would be too long for the stove but they could load them in the stove and keep pushing them through the door as they burned. Of course it would only be safe to do that if they were there and attending the fire, but it meant lowering the number of times he needed to chop through a log by about a third. The other reason to go back to the old area was that he had already packed down a path from all his snowshoeing back and forth. The path would make it much easier for Sally. It had been below freezing for days and the snow was still deep but not as deep as it had been. After a time snow naturally settles and packs down, it also evaporates.

When they took a break from their hike in, Sally asked, "Paul, why do you think we have not been rescued? Isn't anyone looking for us?"

Paul answered, "Whenever I have been out in clear weather, I have been watching the sky and have yet to see a single plane. So it doesn't appear they are looking in this area and I think I may have figured out why. Do you remember our pilot saying there had been a lot of cancellations for our flight? I think there may have been a world wide flu pandemic."

"Oh!" Sally said with shock, she had not considered this possibility. Of course there had not been a pandemic, the flu outbreak had been minor and localized, but this is what was going through Paul's mind.

After they returned from gathering firewood, Paul was filling the stove when Sally said, "I am afraid that if you want me to make you some of this coffee, you will have to show me how. I don't like coffee and never learned how to make it."

"Really!" Paul said with surprise. "I have never drank a cup of coffee in my life, so I guess we can just put the jars back in the cellar." Then he stated, "Let's fill the lamps with oil, and explore the cellar more thoroughly and we will put the coffee jars back." Paul filled the lamps with lamp oil and lit them with an ember from the stove. They replaced the jars of coffee and only discovered a few new things: A mouse-chewed leather case with binoculars in it, two 500 round bricks of .22 long rifle cartridges, a tin of bag balm and about half a box of .300 savage ammunition. Paul was happy with their finds but was disappointed there was not any fishing tackle. They left the .300 Savage ammo where it was but carried up the other items.

"What is in that Bag Balm tin?" Sally asked.

Paul opened it and said, "Looks like bag balm to me."

"OK." Sally replied, "Let's try again. What is bag balm?"

"Farmers use it to put on the utters of cows." Paul answered.

"OK. I have not seen any cows or even a barn, so why is it here?" Sally asked.

Paul stuck his finger into the bag balm and pulled out a glob of the greasy stuff and started rubbing it into his hands. "I am sure that Susan or her Father used it on their hands when they were chapped from trapping." Then Paul handed the can to her, and she tried some.

CHAPTER 8

Silent Treatment

For the next several days, whenever they ate, Paul would bow his head and fold his hands, and offer a silent prayer of thanks. This bothered Sally far worse than his verbal prayers had. Likely, it was because of the guilt she felt over her indiscretion and strong words about Paul's praying. She gave some small hints that it was OK to resume praying out loud at meals. However, Paul persisted in his silent prayers. Sally could feel a wall between them that had not been there before. She could not figure out why his prayers had bothered her so much. After all, what harm could they do? Why couldn't she have just kept her big mouth shut about it? Sally was sure that she owed her survival to Paul, and she would not have lasted even for the first 24 hours if not for him. Over and over she kept beating herself up over her cross words to him.

The tension between them however was all in Sally's head, Paul was at peace with her. He had no idea what torment and anguish his silent prayers were causing her. She had objected to his prayers, so he had started praying silently. Paul only persisted in praying silently after her hints because he felt led by the Lord to do so. Through his whole life, Paul had mainly prayed silently because the Bible says that when you pray in secret, the Father will reward you openly. So, he was totally at peace with praying silently. Normally, Paul had only ever prayed out loud at meals with his family.

After a couple of days, the rest of the porcupine and all of its broth was gone. They had plenty of food now, but their diet lacked meat. So in the mornings, after he filled the stove and while he was waiting for the cabin to heat up, Paul would hunt. He would sit in a kitchen chair with the .22

and the door slightly ajar. He was hoping for a shot at a red squirrel but unfortunately he was not having any luck. Red squirrels make small targets and as they travel from place to place, they only pause occasionally long enough for a shot. While he was waiting for them, Paul had only seen two squirrels and neither of them offered him a shot.

For their first weeks at the cabin Paul had done most all the cooking, but starting with the dozen pancakes, Sally slowly took over that role. One day Sally stated, "I don't understand, why all the jars of flour and yeast? What would Susan have used them for?"

"I would guess for baking bread." Paul replied.

"But how could she bake bread without an oven?" Sally asked.

"There is an oven in the cupboard." Paul replied and he walked to the cupboard and took a cast iron Dutch oven down from the top shelf." The Dutch oven was a large cast iron pan with six inch high sides and the cast iron cover had a two inch rim turned up around the outside. They can be used for baking things on an open camp fire and the rim on the lid is for holding red hot coals so whatever is being made, bakes evenly. They require a lot closer attention when baking anything than a modern oven.

After Paul explained it's use, Sally tried her hand at baking some bread with the Dutch oven on top of the stove. She did not have a recipe and the only ingredients she had were flour, water, yeast, salt and the occasional weevil that was in the flour, but she and Paul were quite pleased with her results. So their diet became variations of rice, pancakes, bread and spruce tea. This was a great improvement over their all rice diet but was still lacking.

They were spending most of their daylight hours gathering firewood, only coming in to warm up and for a mid day meal. The urgency of building their stock pile of firewood back up prevented Sally from reading any of the diary for a few days. She could have read some at night with the oil lamp but they felt they should conserve the lamp oil and only use the lamps when really necessary. Besides, gathering firewood all day long wore her out and by the time night rolled around, she did not have the energy for anything but sleeping. They needed to bring in as much wood as possible. Who knew when the next long storm would hit and would prevent them from working.

Luckily, several things were working together to allow them to catch up on the firewood chopping and to build up a reserve. The first was Sally's help. The two of them together were able to haul larger trees than Paul could alone. While Paul was chopping, Sally was gathering limbs and hauling them back to camp. The limbs would make a fast, hot fire, but would not last long. Because of this, before Sally started helping, Paul could not afford to waste his time on the branches. They were also lucky to have a few days of nice weather with only a small accumulation of snow. The trail they were using had been well packed by Paul's snowshoes. However, the major advantage they had was that more food meant that they had more strength and stamina.

One day Sally even asked Paul to show her how to use the ax. At first he refused. He told her how one of the guys that was working for him chopped himself in the leg while clearing out a lot for a new home. The man would have bled to death had not Paul applied a tourniquet and, even then, would have died if not for the doctors at the hospital. Paul's employee had been using an ax his whole life and still had an accident, so Paul felt it was just too dangerous for Sally to try.

"Well, Mr. Sinhuna that is my point. What happens to me if you chop yourself in the leg and die or just drop dead of a heart attack?" Sally animatedly stated. That did the trick. Then Paul showed her how to stand and how to swing the ax, safely.

Then one morning, another storm rolled in. Paul went outside to check out the storm and when he came back in, he announced, "It is just too wicked out there to cut firewood today." Looking out the window, Sally agreed, and took the chance to read more of the diary out loud. Dec. 6: Well, I am really writing this on the 9th, I have had a lot to do and have not been keeping up writing in this diary. I started my trap line on this day. I got nine traps set in the East marsh. Four are set for beaver and five are set for muskrats. I plan on putting out a lot more, but nine traps are heavy, and I have all winter so it makes no sense killing myself doing all the work at once.

I was not sick at all today so I am thinking maybe I am not pregnant. If I am not, I will be disappointed, but it would make getting Father's birch bark canoe out easier. If I fly out in May with Mr. Johnsen, I would need to hire someone with a larger plane to fly out Father's canoe so I could sell it to the collector. I am thinking that would cost at least a thousand dollars and would sure cut into my money supply, plus what would I do if the collector would not buy it?

Dec. 7: I am writing this on the 9th also. I was not sick at all this day again. It is looking more and more like I did just have a touch of flu. However, I picked out a couple of names anyway. If I am pregnant and I have a girl, I will name her Lilly. I was thinking of naming a boy after my father, but then realized I should name him after his father. So if it is a boy, he will be named James.

I put out nine more traps. The traps I set on the 6th caught one beaver and three muskrats. I have the beaver cooking on the stove and the muskrat carcasses are freezing in the meat cache. Hopefully, I will shoot a moose and then I will use the muskrats for fisher and marten bait. I really do not like eating muskrats, but depending on how things work out I may need to. I skinned, stretched and fleshed all the hides and they are hanging from the cross ties.

Dec. 8: I was not sick this day also and set out six more traps, so now I have twenty four set. Only caught two muskrats today. Forgot to add that I am writing this on the 9th also. I cooked the beaver all day on the 7th and had some of it for dinner. It was really good, just like Mother used to cook it. There is enough left over for a few more days.

Dec. 9: Guess what; I am writing this on the 9th. I have been reading Genesis and have been reading about Abraham but will have to skip my Bible reading today because of a problem I ran into on my trap line. It was a good problem, though. I caught six beavers and nine muskrats. I had to spend the rest of the day hauling them back, and skinning, stretching, and fleshing. I think I am a lot slower at it than I used to be. I know I will never be as fast as Father was. With all these beavers I hopefully will not need to eat any muskrats even if I do not get a moose. Maybe I will cook a couple muskrats this winter just for variety.

Dec. 10: I did not check my trap line today because it looks like the worst storm I can remember. I went over all my hides today and fleshed them out better. The wind is really howling out there. I am glad to be in the cabin, staying nice and warm. When I bought the supplies I brought in here, I bought twelve cans of fruit. I had planned to ration them out, but despite my best efforts, they all froze and the cans bulged on the way in, so I have been thawing one each day and eating them.

Sally stopped reading, "I still can't understand how a woman could be so cruel to trap those animals."

Paul explained that when trapping both beaver and muskrat, the trap must be set in such a way that the animal dies right away or the animal would get away, so their deaths are not cruel. He also pointed out that she was eating them and saving the pelts, and that it really was not any different than domestic animals who are slaughtered for their meat and leather. Sally changed the subject by announcing that lunch was ready.

After eating, Paul said he was going to brave the storm to look for a new area to cut wood. "I am going to take the .22, so hopefully I will come across another porcupine."

Sally asked, "Where are you going to look, so I know where to come looking for you when you stay out after dark?"

"I was thinking I would try on the other side of the river because I have looked everywhere on this side within a reasonable distance from the cabin." Paul answered.

"How are you going to cross the river?" Sally asked with alarm.

"Don't worry, I will get to the other side of the river via the lake, and I will give the open water at the start of the river a wide berth. I may need a bath badly but I have no desire to go swimming today." Paul replied.

Then Sally stated, "Speaking about baths, I plan to take one while you are gone."

Paul made a wide arc around the open water near the start of the river. Besides not wanting to go swimming, he knew that swimming with snowshoes on is impossible. The ice on the lake was already close to four feet thick, so there was no reason for concern. When he he made his way half way around the open water, he stopped and looked to the west along the length of the lake. He could not see much because of the blowing snow, but he thought he should bring the binoculars out here on a clear day. Shortly after the lake froze, he had been out here near the same spot looking down the lake for any signs of human habitation and could see none. Now, after finding the binoculars, there was a possibility he would be able to see something on a clear day. He considered it a remote possibility because much of the North side of the lake had a high rock escarpment that came down to the edge of the water, and he had seen most of the South side from the plane.

When he reached the other side of the river, Paul pushed through the brush that lined the bank. When he broke out of the alder brush, he found himself in a thick young forest of small diameter and tall maple and ash trees. The best part was, that many, if not most, of these were standing dead trees. Paul wondered what had killed them and surmised that they had they may have died because they had been flooded out in the spring. Whatever the reason, he did not care and was grateful to find them and offered up one of his silent prayers of thanks. This was great news, because there were enough small dead trees here to easily see them through the rest of the winter. Also, they were actually closer to the cabin than the trees he had been cutting, and it was fairly flat most of the way and only up hill for the last forty yards from the shore of the lake to the cabin. All they needed to do was chop them down and drag them back. Paul knew he would need to clear a path through the alder brush to the lake.

He was just thinking that perhaps he should have brought the ax instead of the rifle for he knew he would not find any porcupines among the dead trees, when he noticed movement up ahead along the edge of the brush. The movement was coming from several spruce grouse that were eating the buds on the alder. Spruce grouse are also often called fools' hens because they are some of the least wary of all birds. However, from the distance Paul thought they were ruffled grouse which are much harder to sneak up on.

Paul spent the next half hour sneaking up on the birds, and used the crotch of a tree for a rest when he shot. With the crack of his rifle, one of the birds dropped from the brush to the snow. Paul was surprised when the other birds just turned and looked at their fallen comrade, but was not surprised enough to prevent him from lining up his sights with a second bird and firing. With the second shot, a second bird dropped to the snow, then the remaining birds took off. Paul was elated. These birds would make mighty fine eating.

Once he picked up his birds, Paul headed straight back to the cabin. He wanted to clean them as soon as possible before they froze. On his way back, he thought about how he would clean them. Normally, he would have skinned them. That is an easy job. He would have stood on the wings and pulled up on the legs, and in two minutes both birds would have been skinned. However, because of the situation they were in he thought he should pluck them. That way they would eat the skin and all the fat, and thereby get every bit of protein possible from these gifts from heaven.

When Paul reached the porch of the cabin he noticed the rag rug hanging over the window in the door. Something hanging over the window of the door was a signal that Sally had been using for a long time. It meant that she was still taking her bath, so Paul would not walk in on her. When he saw the rug in the window Paul wondered why she was not finished. Maybe she had not started her bath right away, he thought. Paul took off the snowshoes, and sat down on the porch and began plucking his birds. When he was finished, the rug was still in the window. Paul needed one of the pans on the stove so he could finish cleaning the birds. Now he was worried, it had been two hours since he had left. Sally should have been finished with her bath, especially considering that the water in the wash tub would only stay warm for a short time.

Paul got up and knocked on the door, but there was no answer. Now he was really worried. Paul called out, " Sally are you alright?"

"Yes." came the answer but not from inside the cabin. Just then, Sally came from around the corner of the cabin. When she saw the rug will still hanging in the door, she apologized for forgetting to take it down because she had left through the window. "I found the Le Forest grave, come and see it." Sally excitedly said.

"Can I first put these on to cook and warm up a little bit." Paul said, pointing to the birds laying on the porch.

"Oh, what have you got?" Sally asked.

Paul answered, "A couple of grouse, I need to finish cleaning them. Could you please bring me a pan off the stove?" Sally happily complied with Paul's request. Paul removed the innards but saved the hearts, livers and cleaned the gizzards and put them in the pan. Then he went in and washed them off with water from the pump and put them on the stove to cook.

"How did you find the grave?" Paul asked while he was warming up.

"I walked up the hill and looked for a spot that had a pretty view of the lake. Then I started probing through the snow with a stick. Actually, I found the stone in just a few minutes and when I dug down through the snow I found the cross cut in the stone." Sally answered. After he warmed up Sally led him up the hill to the grave.

"I can see why they picked this spot." Paul said, "It is pretty." Then Sally shocked Paul by asking him to bury her there, if she should die before they were rescued. Paul said he would, but then added if the ground was not frozen and he could find something to dig with.

Sally then asked if he wanted her to bury him there if he should die, and he replied that would be fine with him if it was not too much trouble. If it was too much trouble, it would also be fine with him if she left him for the wolves to clean up.

CHAPTER 9

God's Great Bounty

The grouse made a wonderful dinner, much better than the best chicken dinner either of them ever had. Paul told Sally the good news about finding a new source of firewood. There was some daylight left, and the weather outside had only gotten worse. So Sally started reading the diary again.

Dec. 11: Woke up this morning to the howling of the wind. The storm does not look like it has gotten any better. I am going to wait until this afternoon to check the trap line. Hopefully, the weather will improve by then.

I have not felt sick for a few days now, but last night I had a dream that I was holding my newborn Lilly in my arms. Was this a premonition from God, or just a silly dream? I do not know, but after that dream, I will be twice as disappointed if I am not pregnant. This has made me think about what others would say about me being pregnant. I am sure that many people would say, because my husband is dead, that I should abort my baby. I can just hear them saying, "You are young, and will find another husband. You don't want to saddle yourself with a baby." The way some people think almost brings tears to my eyes. A baby is a blessing from God not a burden! I will never understand how a mother could have her unborn baby killed. How could a woman be so cruel?

I did get out and checked my trap line, even if the weather did not improve very much. It was pretty much a waste of time. I did not catch anything. The only good thing I did discover, was that I needed to reset a couple of traps.

Just then the snow coming down outside the window got much heavier. That cut the light coming through the window to the point it was difficult to see to read. Sally put down the diary. Then Paul asked how she felt about abortion.

Sally stated that she supported a woman's right to have an abortion. Then she added that the diary sounded like Susan was not sophisticated enough to realize that a fetus is not a baby. Sally stated that a fetus is only a potential baby. "My friend at University became pregnant, and having the baby would have wrecked her life. She would have had to drop out, and she would have never gotten her degree."

Paul asked, "Did having an abortion improve her life?"

The thought of what had happened to her friend quickly flashed through Sally's mind. Her friend had two failed marriages and had ended up committing suicide. So Sally changed the subject by asking Paul what he thought about abortion.

"Well, you must understand that I am not sophisticated enough to realize that a fetus is not a baby. I believe that abortion is nothing less than the taking of an innocent life, but it might surprise you to learn that I am against abortion not for the sake of the unborn baby, but for the sake of the mother.

The Bible may not tell us about this, but I have read between the lines and believe that, because we have a loving and grace filled God, all of those aborted babies are with our God in heaven.

The words that Paul just used made Sally a little hot and she interrupted him and said, "You mean your God , not our God."

"No." Paul said gently. "I mean our God. You denying His existence changes nothing." Then Paul continued, "A woman cannot have her unborn baby killed without causing herself untold suffering. I knew of a woman who had two abortions. They left her unable to conceive, and she tried to kill herself twice before she asked Christ into her heart and could feel his forgiveness." "What happened to her then?" Sally coldly asked. "She married and adopted three kids. God can redeem the years the locusts have eaten." Paul could tell that Sally was angry, so he excused himself to carry in firewood.

As Sally sat alone in the darkening cabin, she felt surrounded and outnumbered. Reading the diary had been entertaining at first, but now she almost wished she had never found it. She was mad at Paul, and mad at herself for being mad at him. Then she thought to herself that perhaps she was just mad at God. She found the thought of being mad at someone she knew did not exist a little silly. By the time Paul had finished bringing in several arm loads of wood it was dark. He loaded up the stove for the night but because he had chopped the wood extra long they would need to sit up until the ends of the logs had burned enough that the whole log could be pushed all the way in and the stove's door would close.

Sally was wishing that they could have just gone to bed and avoided any more conversation until she had cooled off. She felt that she could just not excuse herself and go to bed. The irony was that Paul would not have thought anything of it if she had. So they just sat silently in the darkness, until Sally cooled down and made another statement. "Paul, you say that God is a God of love and that Christianity is all about love. One of the people I work with is a homosexual and a very good friend of mine. He is a very nice and kind man. Why do Christians and God hate him?"

Paul replied, "Sally, your premise is wrong. God and Christians do not hate homosexuals. Homosexuals hate God and Christians. Homosexuality is a sin, but so is adultery, stealing, murder, lying, taking God's name in vain, not honoring your father and your mother, plus a few others." The Bible tells us "The wages of sin is death." The Bible also says that "All have sinned and fallen short of the glories of God." "Because God is a just God, we must pay for our sins, however, we have nothing to pay for them with. The only way we can pay for our sins is to accept the payment that Jesus Christ made on our behalf by dying on the cross. The Bible also says "For by grace you have been saved, through faith, and that not of yourselves, it is the gift of God, and not of works, lest anyone should boast." Christ shed his blood to save me, you, and your friend from our sins.

For some reason, Paul's words were comforting to her, however she was not sure that she really understood them. She thought about asking more questions but she did not. She had too much pride to say she did not understand. So they just sat there in the dark until the ends of the logs had burned enough that Paul was able to push them all the way in. Then they went to bed.

The next morning, Sally heard Paul get out of bed and fix the fire, but she just turned over and went back to sleep, She normally did not get up until the cabin had warmed up. After a while, she opened her eyes momentarily and noticed that Paul was sitting by the door with the .22 rifle in hand waiting for a red squirrel. She was back, deep in sleep when a rifle shot rang out followed by two more. She was about to ask if he had hit the red squirrel when Paul ran out the door and yelled, for her to bring the ax. A few more shots rang out as she hurriedly pulled on her boots and put on her coat.

Sally ran out the door and to Paul's side, where he was standing on the bank above a thrashing cow moose. Out of breath, she said "Here is the ax." She held out the ax and he handed her the rifle. One mighty blow of the ax ended the cow's thrashing. Only a couple of months before, such a scene would have revolted Sally and made her sick to her stomach. Now, however, she was excited and glad. This meant that they would now have plenty of meat and it might assure their survival.

A cow calf was standing next to the river watching what was going on with its big brown eyes. Paul ran at it yelling and waving the ax. That caused the calf moose to turn and run off along the edge of the river. When Paul returned, he said, "I did not want it watching me butcher its mother. Don't worry about it. The calf is old enough to survive by itself." He then asked, "Can you help me with this, or don't you have the stomach for it?"

Sally answered, "I can't promise anything, but I think I can help."

"Good." Paul replied, "I can't ask for anything more than for you to try." Please take the rifle back to the cabin, and bring back the tarp and a couple of the biggest pans. Sally complied with his request and by the time she came back, Paul already had one of the front leg quarters skinned, off the moose, and laying in the snow up on the bank.

"Did you use the ax to cut through the leg bone?" Sally asked.

"No, the front leg bones are not attached to the rest of the skeleton." Paul answered.

Then Sally asked, "What do you want me to do?"

"First would you take my coat back to the cabin for me?" Even though it was cold, Paul knew he would not be needing his coat while working on the warm moose. He took the drag rope from the pocket then took off his hunting coat and handed the coat to her. When Sally returned from bringing Paul's coat to the cabin he had the first front quarter tied to his drag rope. "Now young lady, if you please, could you drag this up to the meat cache? If it is too heavy for you, don't strain yourself, I will help."

Sally laughed, and said, "I think I can handle that by myself." On the way dragging the front quarter to the meat cache, she realized it was a harder job than she thought. When she reached the cache she removed the drag rope and went back.

Paul was now working on removing the first back quarter. The back leg bone is attached to the rest of the skeleton, and Paul asked Sally to climb down the bank and help him.

"Aren't you going to gut it?" Sally asked.

"This moose is too big for us to even roll over without removing a couple of legs first." Paul replied. Then he asked her to hold the hunk of meat out of his way while he encircled the hip joint with his knife so he could remove the rear leg. Sally was surprised how hot the meat felt. Paul had not skinned out the rear quarter, but instead, had just cut through the hide. After removing the rear leg,. Paul tied the drag rope to the gamble and said, "You will need help with this one." Then he and Sally dragged the back leg up to the cache.

When they returned to the moose carcass Paul and Sally strained to turn the moose over and Paul butchered the second side exactly the same way as he did the first side. Paul then said, "I am getting kind of hungry. You know we missed breakfast. Would you like to cook moose liver, moose heart, moose steak, or moose roast for lunch?"

Sally replied, "I know you hate liver but that is what I would like."

"OK, then we will have moose liver for lunch and I will make you moose steak for dinner. Go ahead and go back up to the cabin, build up the fire, and get some oil in the frying pan hot and I will bring up some liver." Paul stated. Sally did as Paul had requested.

Paul had sent Sally up to the cabin, not only for her to get things ready, but to keep her from becoming queasy from the sight and smells from gutting the moose. Paul had gutted and butchered many deer but never a moose. Having never gutted a moose before, he was surprised by just how big the liver was. It was huge! He had asked Sally to bring down the two largest pans thinking that he would use them for the liver, but he estimated he could fill both pans several times with the liver. Paul filled one with liver and put the heart in the other, then brought the pans up to the cabin and dropped them off with Sally. "Call me when lunch is ready, I need to get back to work." Paul stated.

Back at the moose, Paul skinned out the back and removed the back straps and laid them on the tarp. Next, he removed the prized tenderloins from the underside of the back bone. These are the most tender and the best cuts of meat on the moose. He also laid the tenderloins on the tarp. He thought about removing meat from the ribs and the neck but he already knew if they ate moose three times a day for the rest of the winter they would not be able to use up all the meat he had already retrieved. The meat on the ribs and neck were interlaced with tallow and so these cuts were not as desirable as the cuts he had already retrieved. Paul added the rest of the liver to the tarp and then dragged the tarp to the porch, just as Sally called him for lunch.

After they ate and warmed up they went back out to the meat cache. Paul did not know what to do next. "I would like to skin out the hindquarters while they still have body heat in them. It will be impossible to skin them after they freeze. However, if I do and we put all this meat in the cache, it will freeze into one solid lump. We don't have a saw to cut pieces off and I do not know how we will ever get these heavy quarters up to the cache." Paul stated.

Sally said, "Maybe there is some way that we could hang them up separately in the cache to keep them from freezing together. Let me climb up there and check it out.

"OK, but please be careful." Paul replied.

Sally climbed one of the poles that was holding up the cache by using the spikes that had been driven into the pole for that purpose, by the owner. When she got to the top she removed a spike that was keeping the hasp closed, opened the door and crawled in. She called out, "Paul I have found the answer on how we are going to lift the meat up here. There is a block and tackle behind a corner of the cache. Also, there are some meat hooks hanging from the rafters, so we can hang the quarters separately."

"Great!" Paul called out and he started to skin out the hind quarters, while Sally rigged the block and tackle. The ridge log of the cache stuck out beyond the overhang and Sally recognized that its purpose was to hold the block and tackle. She rigged it up and lowered down the rope.

Paul tied a front quarter to the rope and hoisted it up to Sally. Then Sally swung it into the cache and Paul let up on the rope. "That was easy." She called out. She untied the rope and threw the end back down and then struggled to lift the quarter to a meat hook. The front quarters weighed over seventy pounds each and it took all her strength to manage them. Sally was able to just turn them up on end. The hind quarters were much heavier and Paul had to climb up to help with them. Between the two of them they could barely hang up the hind quarters. After all the quarters were hanging, Paul sliced into them with the knife, hoping that that would make chopping them up after they froze easier. Next, they hoisted up the tarp with the rest of the meat and liver. Paul cut the meat and liver into serving sizes with the knife and they arranged the pieces on the floor of the cache so they would not freeze together. Paul finished up by hanging the pieces of moose hide over the cross supports of the food cache, high above the ground.

By the time Paul was done frying the tenderloin for dinner they were both exhausted. Butchering and putting away the moose had taken all day. They sat down at the table and Paul bowed his head and folded his hands to say a silent prayer when Sally reached out and took his hands. "Paul, will you please pray out loud?" she asked.

So Paul prayed, "Thank you, heavenly Father, for sending this moose to us and making my aim true. I know there was no reason to believe a .22 Long Rifle would be able to drop a moose, if not for Your help. Thank You for providing this great bounty. Just days ago, we were starving and now we have an abundance of food. Thank you for providing for us, years ago, when the owner of this cabin built it, and stocked it with firewood and food. Also, thank you for Susan's diary which has provided guidance to us. I ask a special blessing on Susan Smith because of the blessings she has given us through You. In Jesus name amen." Then they ate the best steak Sally ever had.

CHAPTER 10

A Changed Life

Sally kept mulling some of the things that Paul said over and over again in her head. Why am I doing this, she thought, I have never done anything like this before. She had never let anything anyone said in her corporation bother her, and certainly never replayed anything over and over in her head. Still she could not help herself from rerunning things Paul had said over in her mind. The words that bothered her most were, "I believe this may have happened for your sake." What had Paul meant by that? Finally she could stand it no more. That night while they waited for the ends of the logs to burn so they could be pushed all the way into the stove, Sally asked, "Paul do you think all of this is my fault?"

"All of what?" Paul asked.

"This! You said that you thought that this may have happened for my sake." Sally said.

Paul answered, "Gosh no, it is certainly not your fault, but I do believe that God may be using the circumstances that we find ourselves in to reach out to you." Paul continued. "The Bible tells us that God does not want anyone to perish and sometimes he will use extra ordinary things to cause a person to turn towards Him."

"What do you mean by extra ordinary?" Sally asked.

Paul replied, "Maybe I should use the word miracle. I have a perfect example of God working miracles in a man's life in order to reach him. I know this story is true, beyond all shadow of a doubt. Unlike the story I told you about the missionary in India, that I only read.

Paul pushed a log further into the fire and began to speak, "The last two years of my wife's life, she was in a wheelchair. The cancer and chemo therapy had sapped all her strength. She needed a power wheelchair so she could get around by herself and not have to depend on other people to push her. By that time, I had widened all the doors in the house so she could get around with her manual wheelchair. However the power wheelchair she wanted was larger than her manual one and we did not know if she would be able to turn around in the bathroom. So the wheelchair store we were dealing with offered to send someone out with a similar power wheelchair to see if it would work in our house."

"A man arrived at our house with the power wheelchair and introduced himself as Pete Holbrook. As soon as I met him I knew he was a Christian. He proceeded to demonstrate the wheelchair to us and showed us that it would work out fine in our house. Then he wanted my wife to try it out. She transferred from her manual wheelchair to the power one and Pete wanted to make an adjustment to it so it would fit her better. He reached into his pocket to pull out a tool and a coin fell on the floor. He picked up the coin and said, "I have a story to tell about this coin if you folks have a few minutes." We told him we had time and this is what he told us."

"Before I got a job as a wheelchair mechanic I had three part time jobs and two hobbies. My hobbies were drug addiction and alcoholism, and my part time jobs were drug pusher, break in artist, and bank robber. One day while working my part time job as a bank robber, I got in a shoot out with the police and lost. I ended up in a California Penitentiary sentenced to life in prison without the possibility of parole. After I had been in prison for awhile, my wife told me she was going to divorce me because she could see no future for our marriage. I did not like that, but I knew she was right. I was in prison for the rest of my life. My wife and kids deserved some kind of future."

"I was far from a model prisoner, and it took me a while to realize that no matter how much trouble I could cause for the guards, they could cause more for me. One day when I was causing trouble, a couple of guards beat me up and threw me back into my cell. I found myself laying face down on the urine stained concrete floor. I pounded my fist on the floor and said, I can't make it, I can't make it, I just can't make it." Just then another guard came along and threw my mail into me through the bars. When an envelope hit the floor, the seam opened up and this coin rolled out across the floor and hit me in the hand. I thought what the #@% and picked it up and looked at it. The face of the coin said YOU CAN MAKE IT. What is this I thought, and I turned it over. The reverse side said GOD LOVES YOU AND HAS A WONDERFUL PLAN FOR YOUR LIFE."

"I had thought about God before. I thought about him just like I thought about Santa Claus and the Easter Bunny. There could not really be a God that knew I existed, and despite all my faults loved me, could there? Yet here was this coin in my hand that showed up at precisely the lowest point of my life to give me a glimmer of hope. Maybe there really was a God after all. I began reading the Bible and attending services at the prison chapel. After a couple of weeks I committed my life to Christ."

Still, I was in prison for the rest of my life with no hope for parole. How could I serve Christ in a place like that? One thing I decided I needed to do was clean up my language. I could not put a sentence together without swearing or using a foul word. I prayed to God and asked him to help me clean up my language. Overnight, He worked a miracle and took all my swearing and foul words away.

"Shortly after becoming a Christian, I received a letter from the Parole Board saying I was being paroled because of a technical problem with my trial. This was my chance. I went back to my wife and begged her to take me back. When she asked me why she should, I told her I was a new man and had accepted Christ as my Lord and Savior. She did not know what that meant because she was not a Christian and she did not know if she could believe me, but she took me back anyway".

"However we had a problem. Back when I was following my part time job as drug pusher I had bought some drugs on credit and failed to repay my supplier. There were people in California that wanted me dead. My wife had relatives in Northern Michigan that offered to take us in while I looked for a job. I asked for permission to be paroled in Michigan because of the danger to my family and it was granted".

"We moved to Northern Michigan and I started looking for a job. I applied everywhere I could think of. It seemed no one was willing to give an ex con a second chance. Then I went into the wheelchair store and asked to talk to the owner. He said, " I am the owner. What can I do for you?" I asked if, by any chance, he had a job opening, and he said if I had come in yesterday he would have said no. However, that morning one of his employees had given him two weeks notice.

Then he asked if I had any experience as a wheelchair mechanic. I told him no. He then inquired, "Well, what kind of experience do you have?" I told him about my part time jobs as a drug pusher, break in artist, and bank robber. "Then he busted out laughing, and asked seriously, "What kind of experience do you have?" I told him seriously, I had not had an honest job in my life and that I had been in prison. Then he asked me, "Why should I hire you?" I told him that I had accepted Christ as my Lord and if he hired, me I believed that God would bless him and his business."

"He told me that he was not a Christian and that he would have to think about hiring me and he would get back to me. When I left the store, I figured I would never hear from him again, but he called the next day. He told me to come in and talk to his employees and if they said it was OK, he would hire me. They did and he did. That was three years ago. Now, I am Business Manager of the store."

Then Paul said, "My wife bought the power wheelchair from the store and a month later we had it back for some adjustments. When we saw Pete, he told us he had just given two weeks notice at the wheelchair store and was going to work as Business Manager of his church. The last time I saw him, he had become one of the Pastors of his church. So you see Sally, God still uses miracles to change peoples lives."

Paul was now able to push the logs all the way into the stove. He waited for Sally to get in bed, then he shut the stove door. Paul was really beat, and was fast asleep soon after his head hit the pillow. Sally, however, laid awake for a long time thinking about the things that Paul had said. Was God tugging at her heart? Or was she feeling the way she was from eating too much moose meat for dinner? Just a few days ago she was expecting to starve or freeze to death soon, and now she fully expected to survive until they were rescued. Had God arranged this? She knew she was not quite ready to believe yet. However, there was one thing she knew for sure. If God was really trying to reach her He certainly needed to use something as severe as a plane crash to get her attention and now He finally had it.

Chapter 11

Neighbors?

The next morning, Paul was a little slow to get going. He was out of bed at the crack of dawn and built up the fire in the stove as usual, but his added aches and pains from butchering the moose were slowing him down. His back was bothering him and it caused him to sit around the kitchen table longer than normal. He asked Sally if she would read some more of the diary. Sally was really not all that eager to read more but she complied with his request.

Dec. 11: When I checked my trap line, I found that I caught another beaver and three muskrats. I came across some moose tracks near the edge of the marsh, so I know for sure that there are some moose in the area. Father always waited until he could shoot a moose from the cabin because he said it was too much work retrieving them otherwise. Father shot one every year that we stayed here except one. That year Mother shot one from the front porch while he was running the trap line. When the snow is deep the moose often travel along the river and feed in the cedar. The last day of moose season is the 15th so I am hoping to get one in the next few days so I don't have to break the law.

At this point, Sally stopped reading for a moment and gave Paul a stern look and said, "Paul you are a moose poacher! The season is closed." Then she continued on reading.

Dec. 12 : Well, I have one less .300 Savage cartridge than I did this morning. I shot a calf moose in the neck and she dropped in her tracks just to the side of the outhouse. I shot rifles a lot, but this is my first moose. I shot it at first light, but it took me a couple of hours to get the mother to run off. I thought I might have to shoot the mother too, as they can be very dangerous. I could have shot the mother instead of the calf, but Father always said not to be wasteful and I know I will not even be able to eat the whole calf by spring. It took me into the night to get it butchered and put away in the cache. I am happy I had Father's gas lantern. Tomorrow, I am going to make some jerky, but I am too tired to do anything but go to bed now.

"Mr. Sinhuna, it sounds like Susan is a better shot than you. She only used one shot," Sally teased.

In defense of his marksmanship Paul said, "There is a big difference between shooting a moose with a .300 Savage and a .22 long rifle. My first shot was aiming for the brain and a .22 bullet could easily glance off the skull. I needed to hit it just right to put it down. I believe I got it only through Divine Providence." Sally continued on reading.

Dec. 13: I slept in today. When I woke up, I thought of something that makes me feel a little foolish for not thinking about it before. I am praying that it is a true sign. I have missed my period. It may not mean anything because, just like my mother, I have always had irregular periods and I think I have missed at least one a year since I first started getting them. Well, if I still have not had one by next month, I guess I will be able to say for sure that I am pregnant.

Only caught two muskrats, and the traps have been set for two days. If my catch or the weather don't improve, I may pull all my traps and wait until after Christmas to try again. I have started making moose jerky out of a whole front quarter. I am using Mother's secret recipe. I know that the Johnsens always loved Mother's jerky, so I am planning to take them a bunch for Christmas. Mrs. Johnsen always wanted Mother's recipe but mother would never tell her.

Dec. 14: Only one muskrat today, and bad weather. My jerky is turning out good. I have another batch hanging above the stove drying. I have been thinking about if I should take the snowmobile to the Johnsen's cabin or snowshoe. I think the snowmobile decided for me. I tried to start it today and could not. I checked the gas tank and it was empty. It appears that there is a leak in the gas line. I could smell the faint smell of gas. Maybe Mr. Johnsen can fix it for me after Christmas. I guess I will be snowshoeing.

The last passage made Paul really excited. "Maybe rescue is within a days hike of here." He exclaimed.

"Yes, but what direction?" Sally asked, bringing Paul back to reality.

"Skip ahead in the diary to around Christmas to see if Susan says anything about where the Johnsen cabin is." Paul requested. Sally found a part where Susan was about to leave the cabin and head down the lake pulling a sled loaded with presents. Paul said, "That settles it, on the first nice day, I will hike down the lake with the snowshoes and see if I can find neighbors. Perhaps, we will be rescued within the next couple of days." Paul's statement and decision made Sally uneasy but she did not say anything about it because she did not think she could change his mind.

Paul announced that they needed to get out and cut some firewood because even if he could find the Johnsen's cabin, and even if they were home they may not have any way to get a message out until spring. They both quickly put on their warm clothes and left the cabin. When they reached the point on the frozen lake near the open water of the river, they stopped and both took turns looking down the length of the lake with the binoculars, but neither could see any sign of a cabin.

They proceeded to the other side of the river and Paul started chopping a path through the alder brush. Sally carried the brush back to the beginning of the path and put it in a pile. When he finished clearing a path through to the timber, Paul asked Sally to go back to the start of the path and sort through the pile of brush and haul the twenty or thirty largest pieces back to the cabin.

Sally stated, "I thought you said we should not burn green wood, and this alder is green."

"You're right." Paul answered, "I don't want to burn them. I want to use them to make jerky."

"Oh." Sally said. She did not understand but also did not ask any more questions.

By the time Sally returned to the timber from bringing the alder to the cabin, Paul had chopped down a couple of small dead trees. They worked together to haul the trees back to the cabin. There Paul surveyed their firewood stock pile. "It looks like we have about two weeks worth." He announced. By that time, they were both cold, so after they retrieved a front moose quarter from the cache, they both quit for the day.

Sally and Paul hung the frozen quarter from a cross tie and put the wash tub under it to catch anything dripping from it as it thawed out. Paul then got out the sheath knife and started peeling the bark off an alder branch.

"OK, what are we doing now?" Sally asked.

"I plan to hang these between the cross ties and hang strips of moose meat from them to dry it out and make jerky." Paul answered.

"Don't you cook the meat first?" Sally asked with alarm."

"No." Paul answered, "We will just rub the strips with pepper and salt and string them on these branches and let them dry out. People have been persevering meat like this for thousands of years."

"Well, I am not sure I will be eating any. It seems like the meat will spoil." Sally said.

Paul asked if she ever ate jerky and if she liked it. She replied that she had and she did like it. "Well then, the jerky you ate was made by the same process." Paul stated. Sally, went and got a sharp knife from the silverware drawer, and started to help peel the bark from the alder branches.

The front moose quarter was frozen solid when they hung it from the cross tie, but after a few hours of hanging in the warm cabin, it had thawed just enough for Paul to be able to cut some strips of meat from the outside. Paul and Sally rubbed the strips with salt and pepper, drilled holes in them with the points of their knives and strung them on the peeled alder branches. When they had strung several on a branch, Paul would hang the branch between the cross ties. Soon Paul had cut all the semi frozen meat off the front quarter. The rest of the meat was still frozen rock hard, and would need to wait until the next day. Another storm blew in and Paul announced that he could already tell from the sound of the wind that he would not be going out looking for neighbors tomorrow.

After they had hung up all the jerky makings they could that night, they just sat silently watching the fire through the open stove door. They were resting up and waiting until they could push the logs all the way into the stove so they could go to bed. Sally asked a question. " I know a man who is Jewish and is the most religious person I know except perhaps you. He keeps all the Jewish holidays and feasts, eats only kosher foods and attends Synagogue every week. Will he go to heaven when he dies?"

Paul answered, "The Bible calls the Jews God's chosen people, and the roots of Christianity is Jewish. Christ was a Jew, and there are lots of completed Jews who know Christ as their Lord. However, the Bible makes it clear that the only way to the Father is through Jesus Christ. A lot of Christians would say that a Jewish person has no hope of heaven unless they accept Christ in this life. However, it is not my place to put limits on Christ's grace, so I would have to answer, I just don't know for sure, but would say that the only sure way would be for him to accept Christ in this life."

"On a related subject, most Christians have wondered about what happens to people who have never even heard of Jesus. It doesn't seem fair that they should be condemned to Hell when they never had an opportunity to accept Christ.

The Bible is silent on these matters, and some believe that Christ will judge these people based on the amount of light they received. That is, of course, just speculation, and the only sure way into heaven is to accept Christ now.

The next morning, Paul's prediction about the weather being too bad for him to start out looking for the Johnsen cabin proved accurate. So they just sat around the kitchen table and worked on making more jerky. Paul also cut a couple of steaks off the moose front quarter. He explained to Sally that they would be far less tender than the tenderloin they had been having. Then he took a meat tenderizer out of the silverware drawer and pounded the steaks. When Sally cooked them up for their breakfast she found that Paul was right. They were not nearly as tender. Paul took down the driest piece of jerky they had hung up the previous night to sample it. He cut a piece off and gave it to Sally. Against her better judgment she tried it and found that it was good. It had a slight smoky taste from the occasional whiff of smoke that escaped the open stove door.

The jerky tasted good, but it was tough chewing. Paul explained that in order to preserve the meat for a long period of time it had to be completely dry. However, if they took it down while there was still some moisture left in it, the jerky would make a lot better eating. So his plan was to make some of both. Some he would let hang until it was dry as shoe leather and about as tender. That jerky would then be placed in mason jars with the lids screwed on, and be held in reserve, in case they ever really needed it.

After breakfast, they went out and chopped more firewood and had another uneventful day. Except, that after they hauled the last load for the day, Paul told Sally that he wanted to show her something. Sally followed him off the beaten path and had trouble wading through the snow. At last they came to the great birch tree that Paul had found earlier. Sally was impressed by the tree's huge size. Paul announced that he was sure that this was the very tree that Susan's father had told her about and Susan wrote about in her diary. "If I can't find the Johnsen cabin or it proves to be abandoned, I plan on using this tree to make a birch bark canoe. We now have the moose hide that I can cut into raw hide lashings, and we can get pine sap from the white pines down the river. We can also use some small live ash trees uphill from where we have been cutting for the frame."

"I don't know." Sally said. "We still do not really know which way to paddle out, and that sounds like it would be a really big job to build a canoe."

Paul said, "You are right on both counts. We may be forced to explore to find our way out if Susan does not tell us more about it in her diary, but we may not have any other choice, if we are not rescued. I have read in a book about how a skilled birch bark canoe builder could make one in a day, but I think that was just the author's imagination. I would guess that it would take a skilled builder at least a week or two and it would likely take me a lot longer. In any case, I need to wait until spring and the sap starts flowing to remove the bark from the tree. I just wanted you to see this great tree because it is the largest one you are ever likely to see and I thought it would be something to tell your grandkids about." Paul did not mean anything by the expression about grandkids. If he had been thinking he would not have used it. The expression was just one he had heard used before and had used on occasion himself. However, Sally picked up on it and wondered what he had meant by it. She knew she was likely never to have children, let alone grandchildren.

That night they were both awakened from a sound sleep by a chorus of wolves howling just outside the cabin. Paul flew out of bed towards the door. When he reached the door, he grabbed the .22 rifle off its hooks. There were several wolves consuming the remains of the moose below the bank. When they heard Paul open the door they all stopped and looked up. Paul leveled the rifle at them but it was too dark to see the sights. So he just pointed the rifle at the nearest wolf and fired. The wolf let out a yelp and took off down the lake followed by the rest of the pack. Paul took several more shots as they departed.

"Paul, aren't wolves considered endangered animals?" Sally asked.

"Well, they will be endangered if they ever make the mistake of giving me a clear shot at them. I don't want them hanging out around here and I don't want them to associate this cabin with food."

Sally said, "It sounds like you hate wolves."

"I don't hate them, but I don't trust them either." Paul replied.

The next morning proved to be a bright, sunny, still and clear day. Paul prepared for his expedition to look for the Johnsen cabin by borrowing an extra pair of Susan's blue jeans from Sally. His intentions were to use them as a back pack. First he laid his sweat shirt out on the bed, then he added his quilted shirt, Sally's scooped neck sweater, some jerky and a mason jar with a box of kitchen matches in it. Sally insisted that he put every thing in garbage bags just in case. Then he pulled everything up into a ball and tied it off. Sally helped him stuff this ball into the waist of the jeans. At this point he drew up the waist by running a piece of cord though the belt lopes of the jeans and pulling it tight. Next he tied off the pant legs to the cord with some leather thongs that had been in the cabin. This effectively turned the pant legs into shoulder straps.

Sally said, "Paul I wish you wouldn't go. I am worried about you"

"You need not worry, everything will turn out as God wills. I might be back tonight but more likely I will not be back until tomorrow night. Whatever you do, don't try to follow me. Without snowshoes it would be a waste of effort." Paul replied. Then he gave Sally a big hug and was out the door. Sally read more into the hug than Paul had intended. Paul meant it as just a little reassurance, but Sally thought of it as something more.

When Paul left the cabin he startled a flock of about a dozen jays which had been feeding on scraps of tallow clinging to the moose hide he had left hanging from the food cache. It surprised him because, up until now, he had not even noticed a single jay around there. Paul started his trek with .22 rifle in hand, but first he examined the remains of his moose. The wolves had cleaned up most of it. There were just some tuffs of hair and the head and a short length of back bone left. It appeared that they had crunched through the bones with ease. Paul thought about the bodies the wolves had eaten after the crash. The bones in a human body offered no real resistance to their powerful jaws.

When Paul reached the wolf tracks from the night before he followed them out on to the lake. Every once in a while he noticed a spot of blood as he followed the tracks down the edge of the lake. He did not know if these drops of blood meant that one of his bullets had found its mark, or if the blood had been transferred from the remains of the moose. After he followed the tracks about a mile he noticed something about the tracks had changed. He just was not sure what it was. Then he noticed there was more blood, and he took that as a sign that he had hit a wolf, most likely the first one he shot at. After a little over a mile, he came to a large bloody area in the snow. There were patches of wolf fur all around along with a couple of wolf paws. Paul knew that this meant that he had killed the wolf he shot at and the rest of the pack had eaten it.

Paul continued in a Westerly direction along the length of the lake, but he ventured out toward the center of the lake. The snow was not as deep there, so it was easier snowshoeing. Also he was a little leery of being ambushed by wolves. Being out in the middle of the lake would give him added time to spot any wolves before they could attack. Every so often, he would turn and check his back trail. After a couple of hours hiking he noticed a couple of black dots on his back trail about a mile behind him. He did not know for sure, but he figured they were wolves. What else could they be?

Now, every few minutes he would turn and watch his back trail and each time the dots would be larger. After a little while he knew for sure they were wolves, and he was uncomfortable about the situation. Although he had used the little rifle in his hands to kill both a wolf and a moose he knew that the fact that he had been able to drop a moose with it had more to do with Divine Providence than the stopping power of a .22 Long Rifle. The 1906 Winchester Pump was loaded with eighteen cartridges and he had a box of fifty in his pocket. However, those facts did not make him feel warm and fuzzy inside, so he sent out a short prayer.

Paul kept looking to the front of him and the two sides. The last thing he wanted was to be surrounded or flanked. Fortunately, the two that were following were the only ones he saw. He had read about wolves following people out of curiosity and maybe that was the reason they were on his back trail, but he was not counting on it. Whenever he would stop and look at them, it appeared that they would stop also. When the wolves had closed the distance to three hundred yards, Paul decided that was close enough and he took action. Paul turned around and aimed the little rifle two or three feet above the wolves heads, and rapidly pumped the rifle's action firing several shots. He wasn't aiming over their heads to miss. A .22 bullet drops quite a bit at three hundred yards and Paul knew he would have to aim high to have any chance at all to hit them. He also knew that at that distance, if he did get lucky and hit one, it would likely just sting it. There is not much ump left in a .22 fired from a short barreled rifle at that range.

The shots accomplished Paul's objective. The two wolves turned around and high tailed it back to where they came from. Paul stood and watched as the wolves made their retreat. In just a short time, they were out of sight. He said a short prayer of thanks as he reloaded the rifle. Then he took out the binoculars and glassed the area up ahead. He could still see nothing but nature.

After Paul snowshoed another hour he noticed a bay of the lake that headed off to the North. Now what should I do, he thought. He had already come what he estimated to be six to eight miles and it was past noon. If he turned around right now, it was doubtful he could be back before night. Susan's diary had only said that she headed West along the lake towards the Johnsen cabin. Paul was only assuming the cabin was on this lake. Now he had two choices. The right choice might mean a warm cabin and rescue. The wrong choice would mean that he would have to spend the night outside.

He took out the binoculars and again scanned the area up ahead. He was thinking that the cabin would not be on the south side of the lake because he had seen most of that side from the plane. Of course, he could have missed it. He was looking North towards the bay when he saw it. There was something glimmering. Could that be a pane of glass in a window? He was still too far off to tell, so he headed off in that direction.

Paul picked up his pace. As he got closer he stopped again and looked through the binoculars. YES! It was a cabin and it looked like there were lights on the inside. Now Paul had to keep telling himself to slow down and pace himself. It is never a good idea to work up a sweat in freezing temperatures. The cabin was on the West side of the North bay and the sun was going down. Because of the angle of the sun and the glare from the snow it was hard to see.

When Paul was three hundred yards from the cabin he stopped to catch his breath and looked through the binoculars again. This time he noticed that something was not right. He could see no tracks in the snow out front and no smoke coming from the chimney, but it still looked like there was light coming from inside the cabin. When Paul reached the shore of the lake he was close enough to see a sign above the door that said The Johnsen's. This was the place. It was not until he reached the porch that he could see why it looked like light was coming from the inside. The roof was caved in. To say he was disappointed would not be telling it all. He had no other choice than to spend an uncomfortable night in this ruin. To make matters worse it was starting to snow and the wind was picking up.

The door was unlocked, but the snow on the inside prevented Paul from opening it, however, he was able to gain entry through a front window. By most standards it was a small cabin, about 24'x36' with a half loft, plus two bedrooms. However, after spending over a month in a one room 12'x16' cabin, it seemed spacious to Paul. His first question was how long had the roof been caved in. It did not look like it happened this year and he guessed two or three years ago. There were lots of things left from the previous occupants, but it looked like some things were missing. Still, he did not have time now to play detective. It would be dark in less than an hour and he needed to get things ready to spend the night.

The part of the cabin with the wood stove still had a roof over it. Paul opened the stove's door and was happy to find dry wood all arranged to make starting a fire easy. It looked to him that the person who had prepared this stove for the fire was the same one who had prepared the stove in the other cabin. There was some birch bark in the stove and it looked like someone had folded it to carry in their pocket. Paul already knew that there were no birch trees around outside the cabin. He made a note of this to himself and decided that when he returned to the other cabin he would always carry some birch bark in his pockets for emergency fire starting, until they were rescued. Paul realized that he would have been up a creek getting a fire going if someone had not already prepared this stove for a fire.

Paul cleared the floor in front of the door of snow by digging the snow out with one of his snowshoes. He had noticed several cords of dry wood under the front porch and he wanted to be able to access it easily through the front door. It was ironic he thought, that the snow on the inside was deeper than it was on the outside porch. Paul found a leather Lazy Boy recliner in the corner away from the wood stove. He brushed the snow off it and dragged it over close to the stove. It would have to serve as his bed tonight. Paul took off his pack and laid it on the recliner. Opening it , he removed the mason jar with the matches and soon he had a cheery fire going. It took him four matches because of the wind. That made a total of five that he used since the plane crash. The fire in the other stove was started with one match and had never been allowed to go out.

There was a tarp covering the firewood on the porch. Paul pulled it off and took it into the cabin. There were already short ropes tied to the grommets of the tarp, and Paul used them to tie the tarp off in a vertical position to help block the wind coming in from the caved in roof. He used an eight foot toboggan that was leaning against the corner to help hold the tarp vertical, and he noticed that the name Pierre Le Forest was painted on it. Paul planned to take the toboggan back with him. It would greatly aid their firewood hauling. Besides, because of the name, the toboggan seemed like it belonged at the other cabin anyway. Also, he noticed a couple of canoe paddles hanging on the gable of the cabin, crossed as a decoration. He planned to take them with him also, if he could figure out a way to get up to them.

Paul was hungry but even more thirsty. He had not eaten or drank anything since morning. The caved in roof was blocking some of the kitchen cabinets but there were a couple he could get at. In the base cabinet, he found three pans, and he packed them with snow and put them on the stove. Melted snow does not taste the best, but if he melted enough, it would at least quench his thirst. He would be having moose jerky for dinner, but he wondered if, by chance, there was any type of food in the cupboard. He did not find much of use in the upper cabinet, but he did find a prize. There was a glass jar with a plastic screw on lid that had been unopened and was full of Tang, an orange flavored breakfast drink. He would be having hot Tang with his jerky dinner, and was sure Sally would be pleased with this treat when he brought the jar back with him.

He needed a spoon to mix the Tang with, and went and pulled out what he thought might be the silverware drawer. In the fading light, at first, he thought that the drawer was empty but quickly realized that it was packed full of wind driven snow. Paul pulled out the drawer from the cabinet and brought it over and dumped its contents on the recliner. He found the spoon he was looking for and another sheath knife and sheath. Paul put the knife in his pocket and planned to give it to Sally. The thought of this city girl wearing a sheath knife on her belt gave Paul a little giggle. Paul could see that there had been big changes in Sally's life and wondered if these changes would be permanent after she got back to the big city. The thought about how she had been holding his hands while he asked the blessing over their meals spurred him to add another little prayer to the others he had already prayed for her salvation.

Paul enjoyed his meal of moose jerky and hot Tang. The hot Tang was so good that he melted more snow and made more. When his meal was finished, he took off his coat and T-shirt because it was wet from perspiration. Then he put on Sally's sweater, his quilted shirt and added his sweatshirt and his hunting coat. Paul mentally kicked himself for not thinking of looking through the ruins of the cabin for some blankets or a sleeping bag when there was still enough light to see. He took his glove off and felt the leather of the recliner. Because it was so close to the stove, it actually felt hot. Paul thought that the night might not be as uncomfortable as he thought it would be. He was, however, wrong about that. The surface of the leather of the chair was hot, but the stuffing inside was still frozen, and once he reclined and laid down, the cold would seep back to the surface.

Sally had an uneventful day. Paul had asked her to promise that she would not go out and chop wood by herself, before he had left. She had kept her promise but she had carried in several arm loads of wood that

Paul had already chopped. She had also kept herself occupied by taking a bath and washing down the entire cabin with a wet rag. There had been fine dust, mostly from wood ash, all over the cabin and a few new mouse droppings. Now the cabin was spic and span. She had been worried about Paul all day, but now, that the sun was going down and it was becoming apparent that Paul would not return that night, she was even more worried. She kept trying to talk herself out of her uneasiness by telling herself that if anyone could take care of themselves in the wilderness, it was Paul. Her talks with herself were not working. She was becoming more worried by the minute.

When she crawled into bed, she was very worried, but what could she do about it? Then a novel idea came to her. She could pray! Sally kind of laughed at the thought. If there really was a God, why should he listen to her? After all, she did not even believe in him. When was the last time she prayed? Way back when she was a very little girl and still believed in Santa Claus! Still, what could praying hurt? So she prayed, "Dear God, if you do exist, you know I do not believe in you, but I am making this request of you anyway. Please watch over Paul and bring him safely back to me. In Jesus name, Amen.

Strangely, after the prayer, she felt more at ease, and surprisingly she fell to sleep quickly.

Paul slept with the .22 rifle in his lap and had a fitful night, just dosing off and waking up every few minutes. He alternated from being too hot to too cold. Every time he woke up he would get up and add more wood to the stove. This would give the surface of the chair a chance to warm back up. There was no reason to conserve firewood, there was plenty on the porch and he doubted that the owner of the cabin would ever repair the damage to the cabin, so the wood would just go to waste. He left the stove door open. The fire would burn faster with the door open and would put out more heat. Because of the unfamiliar surroundings, the light from the open door came in handy when he would get up to add wood.

Close to morning, Paul finally fell into a deep sleep and had a terrible nightmare. He dreamed that he was in the branches of a tree and watching helplessly as a pack of wolves grotesquely tore apart and consumed the bodies of the people that had been on the plane. The wolves had eaten almost all the remains when another pack howled off in the distance. The pack that was eating the bodies let loose with a chorus of howls and suddenly Paul was wide awake and the howls were not only in his dreams.

It was sunrise and the howls were coming from the other side of the bay, off the top of the rock escarpment.

Paul got up. Sleeping on the frozen recliner had made his back stiff. He painfully moved to look out the cabin's picture window. He looked across the four hundred yard wide bay to see if he could spot the source of the howls. After a few minutes he could see movement along the edge of the escarpment. He looked through the binoculars and could see a pack of wolves chasing something, but what? It looked to be a small bear, but that did not make sense to Paul because a bear would be denned up this time of year. When they reached a cleft in the rock, that worked as a pass from the top of the escarpment to the shore of the lake, the animal being chased took the exit. It ran down the pass and out onto the lake . The pack followed suit. Paul could now identify the animal as a wolverine. The wolverine ran out onto the lake and headed for some rocks that jetted through the ice. It ran into a dead end pocket in the rocks and turned to face its attackers.

It would seem that the wolverine had trapped its self, but it knew what it was doing. The wolverine was more than a match for one or two wolves at a time but not the whole pack. Nestled into the dead end pocket, it was protected from the rear and the sides. The wolves could not attack by more than one or two at once. So they had reached a standoff. The wolves could not get at the wolverine and the wolverine could not leave.

For close to half an hour, Paul watched as the drama unfolded. The wolves danced around taunting the wolverine, daring him to come out and fight. The wolverine, however, was having none of it, and refused to budge from it's position. Finally one wolf ventured too close and instantly turned from hunter to hunted. It paid for its transgression with its life. It looked to Paul like a quick and powerful swipe of the wolverine's paw had instantly snapped the wolf's neck.

For awhile, the rest of the pack just stood and watched their fallen comrade. Then as quickly as they had come, they left and returned up the pass to the escarpment. This left the wolverine alone and gave it a chance to enjoy the meal it made of its attacker. When it was finished, it crossed the bay to the North of the cabin. Paul had enjoyed watching this event but was now even more concerned about the wolves. If they were desperate enough to try to attack a wolverine, he would need to be extra alert. The fact that there had seldom been a wolf attack of a human in North America was now far from his mind.

Paul's thoughts turned back to the task at hand, salvaging whatever he could find useful in this cabin and returning to the Le Forest cabin. He started laying out things he would take back with him using the reclined recliner as a table. First, he put the toboggan on the recliner. There were rope hand holds on both sides of the toboggan and he would use those to tie down cargo. He took down the tarp and laid it and the jar of Tang on the toboggan. Paul then got out his jerky and proceeded to eat it as he looked for other things to salvage. This was an effort to save time because he wanted to start back as soon as possible. He also melted more snow so he could make more hot Tang.

Without his snowshoes on, he climbed over the deep snow that was on the collapsed roofing. He reached the rear of the cabin, which still had a roof, and explored the bedrooms. They each contained a bed with blankets, but even in their frozen state, they smelled of mildew and so Paul had no use for the blankets. He checked out a couple of closets which were mostly empty and contained nothing useful. The last closet, however, contained a treasure trove for him. There were some shirts and pants and other clothing that would fit him. They were dry and smelled alright. He also found a new sleeping bag still in the plastic bag it came in from the factory.

These finds pleased him very much but he may have been even a little more pleased with the tackle box and two fishing poles that he found. Paul opened the tackle box and found that it was full of all kinds of artificial baits, hooks, sinkers, and even a fillet knife. He thought about taking the sleeping bag but he really did not need it so he left it in the closet. Paul took all the rest of his treasures and laid them on the toboggan.

Paul had noticed that there was a black board with chalk in one of the bedrooms. Why it was there puzzled him, but he returned to leave a note on it. He could not have known, but Mrs. Johnsen had used it for teaching her son school lessons. Paul wrote, HELP! TWO PLANE CRASH SURVIVORS IN CABIN ON EAST END OF LAKE. PAUL SINHUNA AND SALLY... What is Sally's last name he thought. Oh yes, it is McPHEARSON. Paul went back to the toboggan and began tying his treasures down.

He happened to look across the room to where the toboggan had been leaning against the wall and noticed something sticking out of the snow. He walked over to it and was delighted when he pulled a bow saw out of the snow. The blade was rusty but he was still very happy with his find. He could use it to cut frozen moose meat and firewood. He laid out all his treasures on the toboggan and lashed them down. He even added a few

112

pieces of fire wood and covered everything with the tarp and tied it down. Paul tied on his snowshoes and had pulled the toboggan down to the lake when he remembered the canoe paddles on the gable of the cabin. Leaving the toboggan at the edge of the lake Paul returned up the hill to the cabin. Paul had noticed a long piece of pipe that was being used as a curtain rod in the largest bedroom. Maybe I could use that to reach up and knock down the canoe paddles, he thought. He was involved with taking down this curtain rod when he heard something drop down from the wall to the collapsed roof in the former living room.

He moved to the doorway of the bedroom to see what had made the noise and found himself eye ball to eye ball with a large wolverine. Paul's grip tightened on the .22 rifle. Paul had been caught flat footed. He knew that the wolverine had much faster reflexes than he did and it could be on him before he could raise the rifle and fire. They stood there and stared at each other for what Paul perceived as a long time but was really just a fraction of a second. Then the wolverine let out a huffing sound, turned and scrambled up the collapsed roof, cleared the wall of the cabin, and was gone. After Paul's heartbeat returned to normal, he offered up a quick prayer of thanks. After the prayer he thought I should be thankful it had a full stomach from eating that wolf. Paul went back outside and with rifle at the ready, he looked around the corner of the cabin to make sure that the wolverine was truly gone. It was, and he could see where it had made long leaps in the snow as it made its retreat.

After Paul went around the corner of the cabin and could see that the wolverine was truly gone, he took time to say a more complete prayer, thanking God for causing the wolverine to leave and for sending it to him in the first place. That prayer of thanks was important to Paul, because he knew if God had not sent the wolverine, he would not have looked around the corner of the cabin and would not have seen the bow of an aluminum canoe sticking out of the snow bank. The canoe was about four feet off the ground on a cedar log rack, but both the rack and the canoe were almost completely covered with snow.

Paul dug out the canoe using one of his snowshoes as a shovel, until he could determine that the canoe was in good shape. It was frozen in, and dragging it back to the other cabin would not have been practical anyway. He would have to come back for it and he figured he might as well also leave the canoe paddles where they were. "I guess that means I will not be making a birch bark canoe." he said to himself. Paul had kind of been looking forward to building a canoe, but he was happy that now he would not have to. Taking the bark from the giant birch would have killed it, and though it might sound silly, Paul really did not want to be responsible for its demise.

CHAPTER 12

Homecoming

O nce Paul had checked out the canoe and decided to leave the canoe paddles where they were, he started out for home, pulling the toboggan behind him. There was already an improvised harness attached to the toboggan's tow rope, so this left Paul's hands free. He carried the .22 rifle in one hand, always ready for use, if need be. When one hand would get cold, he would switch the rifle over to the other. All the way back, he was keeping a sharp look out for wolves and happily he would not see any. With all the trouble he had experienced with wolves in the last two days, he wanted to make sure that he was home before dark. There was a cold West wind pushing him along. He was making good time but about halfway back he could feel his back muscles were starting to stiffen up. The further he snowshoed, the tighter his back muscles became.

Under other circumstances, Paul would have stopped to rest his back. He knew that if he could apply heat to it, his muscles would loosen right up. However, he had no way of applying heat to them. He feared that if he kept on going that the muscles in his back would tie themselves in knots and he would be incapacitated for a few days, but he did not have a choice. He had to keep moving. The cold West wind kept pushing him along and making his back stiffen more. After a while, it began to snow, lightly at first but then it increased in intensity. Soon the visibility decreased until Paul could no longer see the sides of the lake.

Paul was now following the tracks he had made the day before, backwards. Soon the new snow added to the snow from the previous night obliterated his tracks from yesterday. After awhile he found himself blindly walking down the ice in a whiteout condition. A whiteout occurs when the snow is coming down so hard that a person can only see white in any direction. Now he was using the wind at his back as his only source of direction. There were now two things bothering him besides his back. One was the open water at the end of the lake where the lake met the river. He knew that he was still a long way off and he was praying that the snow would let up before he got there. The other thing he was worried about was wolves. It was not necessary for wolves to see him for them to find him. They have an excellent sense of smell and Paul was walking blindly down wind. If there were wolves down wind, all they needed to do was wait until their lunch came to them. Paul prayed about these fears and neither of these fears proved to be of any consequence.

When Sally woke up that morning, she went outside, climbed the food cache and picked out a hunk of moose meat that she figured would make a nice pot roast. She wanted to have a nice meal ready when Paul returned. After she thawed the meat somewhat by pouring hot water over it, she put it on to cook. She seasoned it with some salt and pepper and knew it could slowly cook for the rest of the day. With that task finished she had the rest of the day to just sit there and think.

She was the CEO of a major Canadian corporation. The key word in that sentence is was. She had been missing for almost two months, and was most likely presumed dead. Her hand picked board of directors had surely picked someone to replace her as CEO by now. Who did they pick? Sally's father still held a lot of sway over the board. Who would have been his choice? He would probably have picked her cousin Beth, the Christian. He would want to keep as much family control over the corporation as possible. Sally's cousin, Beth, was already managing the newspaper in Edmonton. Sally had looked at the numbers and knew the newspaper that Beth was managing was doing better than the others that the corporation owned. Beth would be a good choice, Sally thought.

That thought really surprised Sally, because two months before Beth would have been her last choice. Sally had never really liked Beth. Sally had never gotten along too well with Beth, but now she realized that was probably her fault and not Beth's. Perhaps now things would be different because she now had a better understanding of Christians. Two months before, the thought of being replaced as CEO would have horrified Sally; her job was her life. Now, if she could not get her job back, she knew she would be just fine. After she thought about it, she was amazed at her change in attitude.

Sally thoughts turned to her life in her past. How had her life ended up so different than how she had envisioned it? When she was young, she had wanted to grow up and be a wife and a mother. The thought of a career was not her number one priority. Instead, her career had turned into her whole life. How had that happened?

For a brief moment, she thought about Vince, the guy she had dated at University. That had ended so badly, that even after all these years, thinking about what had happened still hurt. Sally forced herself to think about something else to avoid the pain. In the last sixteen years, she had only dated a few different men. Most of those had been only one or two dates until she had dropped them. She had told herself that she was just too busy to have a personal relationship, but she knew that the real reason was the pain she felt over what had happened to her back at University. There I go again. Hadn't I just promised myself that I was not going to think about what Vince did to me? She then thought about the other guys she had dated since her University days. She had not trusted any of them. Were they all really just after her money or after what she could do for them because she was a CEO? Sally laughed out loud. Yes, she thought to herself, I believe they all were!

Since day one in the cabin they had been plagued with mice and they left their dirty little droppings everywhere. The worst time was on a still night when they could hear the little varmints crawling all over the cabin. What Sally hated the most was when a mouse would wake her up by running on the blankets of the bed or worst yet, across her face. Paul had killed a couple of them by throwing a piece of firewood across the room at them. Sally was thankful for that, but even more thankful that Paul had killed the mice after they found the food in the cellar, because she was sure if he had killed them before, he would have made soup out of them. While she was waiting for Paul to return, she saw a very unusual mouse dart back and forth several times during the day. It moved much faster than the other mice and in jerky motions. The really strange thing about it was that it was all white. Sally thought I must remember to tell Paul about it.

Sally hated being left alone for several reasons. One reason was the boredom. When she was bored, she would reflect on things and sometimes that was painful. She knew for sure that Paul was a true believer and was at peace with himself. She knew also that she was not a believer and that she was not at peace. What is lacking in me, that I cannot believe? She was beginning to think that everything would be so much easer if she could only believe. Another reason she hated being alone was that she would begin to worry. The later it became, the more she worried. She decided that she would fill the stove with wood so the cabin would be nice and warm when Paul got back. Then she would dress in her warm clothes and go out on the ice and see if she could see Paul coming. First she checked her roast and found it was tender. Then she added some rice, filled the stove, and left through the window.

There was about an hour of light left, and as Sally walked down the path to the lake she was afraid that when she got out on the lake she would see nothing. It had been snowing hard earlier but now it was almost clear. She decided to try another prayer. Dear God, its me again; the woman who does not believe in You. I am asking that You send Paul safely back to me tonight. If You are really real, please help me to believe in You. In Jesus name, Amen. When Sally got out on the ice, she could see a lone figure off to the West. The snow in the center of the lake was not as deep as the snow around the edges and it was also harder packed. Sally was able to walk on it, and was only sinking in about 14 to 18 centimeters with each step so she started walking towards the figure. Fifteen minutes later she met up with Paul.

When she reached him she noticed the toboggan and said, "I take it that you found the Johnsen cabin and that no one was home?"

"You got that right. The roof was caved in and it looked like it has been that way for a long time." Paul answered.

It was then that Sally noticed that Paul's face was grimaced with pain, and she asked with alarm, "Paul are you alright?"

"No, I am not. My back has stiffened up and I am afraid that as soon as I stop moving it will stiffen up so bad I will not be able to move." Paul stated.

"Paul, let me pull the toboggan the rest of the way," Sally said, as she removed the harness from Paul and put it on herself. Paul did not protest. When they reached the outhouse, Paul asked Sally to bring the toboggan up and into the cabin and then come back and help him up to the cabin. By the time she came back, Paul was finished using the outhouse and was standing and leaning on the door. Sally, helped him up to the cabin and carried the snowshoes, as he could barely move.

Paul said, "If I could get some heat on my lower back, I think the muscles would loosen back up."

Sally said, "I have an idea." She helped him into the cabin and sat him down facing the table in a chair that was sitting sideways to the table. Then she helped him strip down to the waist. He especially needed help removing Sally's scooped neck sweater because he was not able to lift his arms over his head. Sally instructed Paul to lean over the table. Then she poured hot water from a pot on the stove over the towel in the sink. When it was cool enough, she took the towel and wrung it out and laid it on his back.

Sally kept monitoring the towel. Whenever it cooled down, she would take it back to the sink and pour more hot water on it. In between applying the hot towel to Paul's back, Sally unloaded the toboggan.

Paul asked her if she would make some hot Tang to go with dinner.

She said, "OK, but first I want to work the kinks out of your back." Sally pulled over the other kitchen chair, sat down and began massaging Paul's back.

While she was rubbing his back, a surprising thought occurred to her. It had been in the back of her mind for a long time already but now it had been moved to the front. The thought was so shocking that at first she tried to avoid it. The harder she tried to avoid it, the more clear the thought became. It was hopeless. She might as well admit it to herself, because it was unavoidable. Sally now knew she was in love with Paul. After this realization had sunk in, Sally wondered if she should tell him how she felt, but wisely she thought, no. If I tell him now, and he does not feel the same way about me, it would be awkward at best. After all, we are still stuck here all alone in this cabin. She decided to wait to tell him until they were rescued. Instead of confessing her love for him, Sally told Paul of how worried she had been and made him promise that he would never leave her like that again.

It was a good thing that Sally did not tell Paul of her love for him at that point in time. From the time that Paul had met his future wife in high school, he had never thought of another woman in a romantic way. At that time he thought of Sally like he had thought of his little sister before she was murdered. Sally was someone that needed his help and protection. He had never thought about it, but if he had, he would have realized that he loved Sally in the way that someone loves a close friend. If, at that time he would have had a romantic thought about her, he would have put it out of his mind. After all, it would never have occurred to him that a beautiful young woman like Sally could ever have feelings for him.

After the hot towel treatment and Sally's massaging, Paul's back felt much better, but he was still in pain. Paul thanked her. Sally made the hot Tang and Paul asked a short blessing, thanking the Heavenly Father for finding the canoe, the safe journey home, and the food. Then they ate the pot roast and rice that Sally had prepared. While they ate, Paul complimented Sally on the meal and told her about the wolves and the wolverine. He told her how God had sent the wolverine to pay him a visit so that he would look around the corner of the cabin and find the canoe sticking out of the snow bank. Then he announced that when spring came, he would need to go back for the canoe.

Sally corrected him, "You mean that when spring comes, WE will need to go back for the canoe. Remember, you just promised that you would never leave me."

Paul replied, "I stand corrected."

Sally thought about what Paul said. About how God had sent a wolverine to lead him to the canoe. Could that really be? Or was it just a lucky coincidence? She could see a beauty in Paul's simple child like faith. Paul saw God's hand in everything that happened and he was so sure of it. Sally wished she could have a simple faith like that, but she knew that still, deep down in her heart, she simply did not believe. However, things were slowly changing. She was now praying and God was becoming more real to her.

The next morning, Paul's back muscles were too tight to work chopping wood. Not that it mattered; the storm, that had blown in overnight was too bad to work in anyway. Sally gave Paul's back another treatment of hot towel and massage. Then she said Dr. McPhearson prescribes rest for your back the whole day today." Sally then made them pancakes for breakfast. After breakfast, Paul asked if Sally would read more of Susan's diary. Sally just skimmed through the part from where she had left off reading to where Susan was leaving for the Johnsen's cabin. That part was not all that interesting anyway. Susan had just talked about how she had been reading her family Bible and how she had pulled her traps because she was not catching much and the weather had been bad. Sally started reading again with the Dec. 23 rd entry.

I am leaving to spend Christmas with the Johnsens tomorrow morning. It is sort of a Christmas tradition. We spent Christmas with the Johnsens every year we stayed at this cabin. I will be snowshoeing because there is something wrong with the snowmobile. Some extra clothes are packed in my duffel bag and I have already tied it down to Father's sled and have made a harness so I can easily pull it. The jerky I made for the Johnsens is already packed as is a present that Father had made for Mr. & Mrs. Johnsen. It is a moose antler on which Father carved a scene of two people fishing from a canoe.

Paul interrupted, "I wonder if the sled she is talking about is the toboggan that I brought back. There is a harness on it and the name painted on it is Susan's Father.

Sally just said, "Could be." and continued reading.

I will bring Father's .300 Savage in case I see a wolf. A .30 caliber hole in the hide will really knock down the price the fur buyers will pay me for it, but at least I will have the hide to sell. I was not having much luck lately with the trap line. Hopefully the weather will improve and when I put the traps back out, I will have more luck.

Dec. 24 I am leaving, pulling the sled, first thing this morning. God has given me a clear and calm day for my hike. I am looking forward to seeing the Johnsens as this is likely to be the only time I will talk to anyone for the rest of the winter. I can't wait to see how much Matt Johnsen has grown. I think he is about fourteen now. I will likely stay a few days so I will be skipping writing in this diary.

I have noticed that my pants are getting tighter and pray that is another sign that I am pregnant. I have already checked out some of Mother's clothes that were stored in this cabin and will be wearing them for maternity clothes because she was bigger around than I am but the same height that I am now. Mrs. Johnsen is also the same height as I am, and she is even bigger around. When she hears my good news, I am sure she will loan me some of her clothes.

Dec. 25 Well I am back home again. I got to the Johnsen's cabin early in the afternoon yesterday just as I planned. Only trouble was I found no one was home. It doesn't look like anyone has been there in at least a couple of years. The thought of the possibility that they would not be there had never entered my mind, but now I realize that Mr. Johnsen likely has several trapping cabins, just like Father used to. I guess that means that I will be canoeing out with Father's birch bark freight canoe after all, no matter how pregnant I am. I should be alright. I just don't look forward to taking the canoe down the first rapids from the lake to the calm part of the river. The brush along the bank is too thick to line the canoe along those rapids. Father only ran those rapids a few times. He preferred to portage around them, but the canoe weighs too much for me to portage myself, so I guess I have no other choice.

I stayed at the Johnsen cabin overnight and slept in the recliner next to the wood stove. There was not even a fire laid up in the stove when I got there. There is now! In the morning I shoveled out the ashes and arranged the wood in the stove for the next fire. I even left some of the birch bark I had folded up in my pocket so that whoever builds the next fire will have an easy time starting it. Father always said to make sure that there was always wood in the stove to make starting a fire easy. Who knows when that could make a difference between life and death.

Just then Sally looked up at Paul, and saw that a tear was running down his cheek. "What's wrong?" she asked.

Paul was embarrassed that Sally had seen his tears, "There is nothing wrong, my tears are tears of joy. I am just amazed how God looked into the future and used Susan to provide for me. When I got to the Johnsen cabin, I needed to build a fire in the stove. I had matches and there was plenty of wood, but I did not have anything to get a fire started. There are no birch trees around there for a source of bark. If God had not used Susan to prepare the wood for a fire, I would have been out of luck. The wood stacked outside on the porch was covered with a tarp, but still had snow in it. The wood Susan had in the stove was dry and the birch bark made starting the fire easy even if it did take me four matches because of the wind." Then Paul asked Sally to remind him to load up his pockets with birch bark. She said she would and would put some in her pockets as well.

Sally started reading the diary again. While I was there, I looked though Mrs. Johnsen's closet and borrowed some of her largest clothes. I left her a note saying that I borrowed them. I felt a little funny about it, but I am sure she would not mind. It is kind of the code of the North, that you should lend something to anyone who needs it. Doesn't the Good Book say, "From those who would borrow of thee turn not thou away." I packed Mrs. Johnsen's clothes in my duffel and used it as a back pack. I left Father's sled there so they would know they had company if they ever showed up. Besides pulling it there had been a lot harder than I expected it to be. Finding that the Johnsens were not home was a big disappointment to me, but I had a merry Christmas in spite of it. I sang Christmas carols almost all the way home. Any wolves that may have been watching me, must have thought I was crazy.

Sally stopped reading at this point and gave Paul's back another treatment of hot towel and massage. Then she served some leftover moose roast and rice from the day before for lunch. After lunch Sally said, "When we crashed, my heart and mind was closed to God and the Bible. However now, because of what you have said and the things that have happened, my heart and mind are open. I want to, err, really want to believe but there are things I need to work through in my mind before I can. I am not a Bible expert by any means. In fact, I cannot remember ever reading it. There are some Bible stories I remember from Sunday School that I have questions about. You say that you believe the whole Bible is true, so can you explain how the story of Jonah and the whale could possibly be true?"

Paul was smiling, because he could see that what Sally had said about being open to God and the Bible was an answer to his prayers. He said, "I would be happy to. First I would like to point out that the the Book of Jonah in the Bible doesn't say anything about Jonah and a whale. It talks about Jonah and a great fish. In the book of Matthew, the (OLD) King James version of the Bible does call it a whale but a newer translation, such as the New International Version calls it a huge fish. However, I have read that in the original Greek the word means something like sea monster, so no one can say for sure what type of creature it was."

"Now, some Christians believe that the story of Jonah is just a story or morality tale. As you know, I believe it really happened and so did a much better authority than I. Jesus mentioned the stories of both Noah and Jonah. Jesus knew it to be true so I believe it also. Before I get into an explanation, I would like to review the whole story for you. It has been a long time since you were in Sunday School and you may not remember all the details." Sally said that would be fine with her.

"OK then, this is the Paul Sinhuna paraphrased edition of the book of Jonah. God told Jonah to arise and go to the city of Nineveh and to speak out against its wickedness. Jonah considered the people of Nineveh his enemies, and he did not want to go because the people might repent of their evil ways and then God would not destroy the city and its people. So Jonah arose and went to Joppa and got on a ship that was going to Tarshish. Jonah knew that Tarshish is about as far from Nineveh as he could get, but God caused the ship he was on to be caught in a terrible storm. Jonah had gone down to the lowest part of the ship and was fast asleep. The captain of the ship came to Jonah and woke him up. The captain said call on your God; perhaps your God will consider us, so that we may not perish. Jonah told the mariners that the storm was his fault because he had disobeyed his God. Then Jonah told them to pick him up and throw him into the sea and the sea would become calm. At first the mariners refused to throw him overboard because they feared God would punish them if they did.

Instead, they rowed hard to bring the ship to land, but when they found they could not, they did throw Jonah overboard and the sea ceased from its raging. Now, the Lord had prepared a great fish to swallow Jonah. And Jonah was in the belly of the fish for three days and three nights."

Paul continued the story. "Then Jonah prayed to the Lord from the fish's belly and repented. So the Lord spoke to the fish and it vomited Jonah onto dry land. Then the Lord told Jonah to arise and go to Nineveh and preach the message that I tell you. Nineveh was a great city with more than one hundred twenty thousand people. Jonah walked throughout the city and cried out that in forty days Nineveh would be overthrown. So the people of Nineveh believed God and proclaimed a fast, and put on sackcloth from the greatest to the least of them. The King of the city said, "Who can tell if God will turn and relent, and turn away from His fierce anger, so that we may not perish?" When God saw their works and that they turned from their evil ways; God relented and had compassion on them. So He did not allow the disaster that he said he would bring upon them."

Paul stopped and finished the glass of Tang Sally had made for lunch, then he continued. "The Bible tells us that God had prepared a great fish to swallow Jonah. So some Christians think that the great fish may have been a special one-of-a-kind fish, and it very well may have been. However, something I read about a long time ago makes me think that the fish that swallowed Jonah may have been an ordinary fish and that the Bible may have just meant that God had prepared the great fish by arranging for it to be in the right place at the right time."

"I read about an incident that, if I remember correctly, happened around the year 1900 off the coast of England in the English channel. There were a number of small boats a short ways off the coast that were harpooning basking sharks. The basking shark grows to about 40 feet long but the ones they were harpooning were only around 20 feet long. They would harpoon a shark and let it tow their boat around for a while, until it would tire. Then they would slit its gills to bleed it out and row to shore towing the shark behind them. Once in shallow water, close to the shore, they would butcher the shark to sell its meat and sell the skin for sand paper."

"One of the boats made the mistake of harpooning a much larger whale shark. Whale sharks can grow to be 46 feet long and weigh over 13 ½ tons. The whale shark was large enough to pull the boat they were in underwater. Fishermen in another boat saw what happened and rushed to save the fishermen of the stricken boat. They were able to rescue all but one. The next day, the boats were out again when one of them spotted the whale shark from the day before. These fishermen also harpooned it and were able to bring it to shore because it had lost most of its strength from the actions of the previous day. When they began butchering it, they noticed something thrashing around in its stomach. When they opened the stomach, they found the missing fisherman from the day before, still alive. His skin was bleached white and his entire body was devoid of hair. He did not regain his ability to speak for about 30 days. They put him in a London Museum as a living exhibit and charged a shilling admittance fee. The exhibit was advertised as "The Jonah of the Twentieth Century"

Now, let me add that the original story I read was represented as fact. Years later I tried to find some additional information on the Internet and was only able to find a similar story. That one claimed the fisherman was in the shark for 48 hours and was rescued by a larger ship that winched the shark on board. There were parts of that story that did not sound as plausible as the first story I read so it is quite possible that they were both fiction. However, here are some interesting things I found out that lends some feasibility to the first story. Both basking sharks and whale sharks are filter feeders that feed on plankton and so do not have rows of razor sharp teeth. Unlike the basking shark, the whale shark has a large enough throat to swallow a person whole. The stomach of a large whale shark is large enough to hold several people and it uses its stomach to hold air to help it swim at certain depths because it lacks an air bladder that fish like a lake trout have."

In the story of Jonah, the Bible tells us that the whole city of more than one hundred and twenty thousand people repented and turned from their evil ways. The question I see is why? Jonah was speaking the words of the Lord but a lot of people have done that and the words fell on deaf ears. In the story I read about a fisherman being swallowed by a whale shark, the skin of the man had been bleached white by the acid in the fish's stomach. Now the Bible doesn't say anything about Jonah's skin being bleached white, but it stands to reason that it would have been. Perhaps the reason that all the people repented was that Jonah's skin had been bleached white and that made them believe the words of the Lord."

"Remember a number of days ago, when I said the things that modern science believes as fact are constantly changing? Were you taught in school that all fish are cold blooded?" Paul asked.

"Yes, I was." Sally replied.

Then Paul said, "So was I, but we were both taught wrong." We now know that the Great White Shark, Salmon Shark, and Whale Shark are not cold blooded. There is still research going on and by now, they may have discovered more non-cold-blooded fish, but those are the three I know about. They are not cold blooded, but they are not exactly warm blooded either. Their body temperature remains about ten degrees warmer than the surrounding water. So here we have one of the few semi-warm blooded fish. Did God design them like that to keep Jonah from going into hypothermic shock?"

While I was looking for information about the whale shark swallowing a man, I found a lot of information about people being swallowed by sperm whales. I could see holes in most of those stories and they all supposedly happened long ago but who knows, some of those stories could be true. However, it is hard to understand how someone in the stomach of a whale could breathe, as they do not, to my knowledge, carry air in their stomachs. I guess my whole point is we do not know for sure if it was a great fish, a whale, or some other type of sea creature that swallowed Jonah, but we do know that God prepared it for its task.

By now it was time for dinner and Sally served more moose meat, but this time she prepared cold Tang. While they were eating, she asked, "How and when are we going to retrieve the canoe from the Johnsen cabin?"

Paul said, "I have been thinking about that. If we both went back there, I think that working together, we could drag it back across the ice. The snow is too deep to get there without snowshoes. Because of the aluminum canoe, I no longer need to build a birch bark one, so I have been thinking that I should make a pair of snowshoes for myself and you can wear the ones I have been using."

"Paul do you know how to make snowshoes?" Sally questioned.

"No," Paul admitted, "But then I did not know how I was going to build a birch bark canoe either, and I think the snowshoes will be a lot easier. Plus we have a set to look at for guidance. Except, I will make a couple of changes."

"Like what?" Sally asked.

"Well, first I will make them larger. The ones we have are sized for a person about your size and not for me. The other thing I will change is the style. The ones we have are called Algonquian or Michigan style. I like that style the best, but it requires the wood to be steamed so it can be bent around the toe, and given our limited resources, we have no way to do that. So I am planning to make the Ojibway Style, the outside frame is made from two pieces of wood instead of just one. So, I think that they will be much easier to make. There are some small diameter and tall, live ash trees uphill from where we have been cutting wood. I am planning on using some of those for the frame.

CHAPTER 13

Jacques and the Eggs

The next day, Paul's back was much better but it was still bothering him. Dr. McPhearson gave him another hot towel and massage treatment, then she prescribed another full day of rest. Paul said, "Dr., please just make it a half day if the weather improves."

"Well, we will see. Maybe I can knock a half a day off for good behavior." Sally replied. She made some pancakes and after breakfast she asked if Paul wanted to hear more from the diary. Paul said he did, so she started reading. At first Sally just skimmed the next few entries, none were very long and they did not hold much interest for her. Just a few things, about what Susan was reading in her Bible, and how the weather had turned bad and she was not going to start her trap line up until it improved. The first entry of the new year looked interesting so Sally started reading there.

Jan 1: I woke up at sunrise on the first day of this new year and prayed to God asking that the new year would be a good one for me and my unborn baby. Just as I finished my prayer, I heard dogs barking. I went to the door and looked out and saw Father's friend, Jacques, tying up his dog team. Suddenly a thought struck me funny. Mother and Father always taught me to address everyone by Mr. & Mrs. and their last names. Everyone, except Father's friend Jacques. I don't even know what his last name is. Even when I was very little, I just called him Jacques. I hurried up and put on my coat and boots and went outside to greet him.

When he saw me come out the door, he called out, "Bonjour, Mademoiselle Le Forest, is your Pa Pa home?" I told him I was no longer a mademoiselle, I was now Mrs. Smith and that Father had died during moose season in September. He said, "Mon Cherie, Jacques's heart is very heavy for you. Are you and Monsieur Smith running your Pa Pa's trap line?" I told him that my husband had lost his life in a shipwreck in November and he said, "Mon Cherie, now Jacques' heart is breaking for you." Then his eyes got wide and he said, "Surely Madam Smith is not staying in this cabin all alone?" I told him no, I was not alone, I had my Heavenly Father with me and my baby and I patted my belly. The look on his face turned from great sorrow to great joy and that really made me happy.

Then I noticed how skinny his dogs looked and asked him about it. He told me they had not eaten in two days. I told him that I could fix that and asked him to get his ax from his sled and I retrieved mine from the cabin. Then we chopped up the remains of my moose; the ribs and neck, and fed it to his hungry dogs. When we were finished, Jacques said, "You feed my dogs, now I feed you." Then he untied one of his dogs and got a basket from his sled. We went up to the cabin. He let his dog in and set the basket on the table. When he unwrapped the blankets from around the basket, I saw that it contained another basket with about three dozen eggs. Surrounding the inner basket with the eggs were five small puppies and Jacques took them and gave them to their mother so they could nurse. He had packed them like that to keep the eggs from freezing. I immediately took six eggs and fried them up for our breakfast. I had not had eggs in over a month and this was a treat.

We sat down to eat breakfast and I gave him four eggs and I took two. He finished before I did, so I got up and gave him a loaf of bread I had baked and a jar of honey. When he finished that, I gave him the left over moose roast from the day before, along with some rice. When he had finished that, he was finally full. It appeared that Jacques had not eaten in two days also. I asked him how he came to be here and he said, "I thought I had a very sad story, until I heard yours. My trap line has been plagued by Monsieur Glutton. He got almost all the animals I trapped. Then two nights ago, Monsieur Glutton broke into my hen house and ate all my hens. Jacques shot no moose this year and with his hens gone, he has ran out of food." I told him I could spare a front and hind quarter off a calf moose, a dozen muskrat carcasses and a few jars of rice. He said, "Mon Cheri, you make Jacques very happy." Then he told me that he was moving to his other cabin 160 kilometers away, and asked if he could spend the night here. I told him he could have my bed and I would sleep in the loft. Then he said

"No, no Mon Cheri, Jacques sleep in loft." He went back out to his sled and got his sleeping roll and pad and spread them out in the loft. It was still morning but in a few minutes I heard heavy snoring coming from the loft. I don't think he even took his boots off.

I know that the cabin that he was using was west down the lake, up the river and on another lake, about 64 kilometers from here, even though I have never been there. Father pointed it out one time when we flew over it. The Monsieur Glutton he was talking about is a wolverine and I know they can be a nightmare to a trapper. Father had trouble with one at another cabin we were staying at. He was finally able to shoot it and it was a good thing that the wolverine's hide brought good money because it was about the only money he made that winter.

I went out and got some moose tenderloin from the cache so it would thaw and I could fry it for dinner. Then I played with his puppies all afternoon. All that time from morning to just before sundown I heard a steady stream of snoring coming from the loft. Then I fried the tenderloins and woke him up. He ate a pile of food and went back up in the loft and started snoring again. He snored all night long and I barely got any sleep.

Jan. 2: I woke up and made Jacques a big breakfast of pancakes and maple syrup. He ate a full dozen.

Sally stopped, sternly looked at Paul and said, "That sounds like someone else I know." Then she continued reading. After breakfast, we went outside and loaded his sled with the moose quarters, muskrats, and rice I gave him. Then he turned to me and asked if there was anything he could do for me before he left. I almost said no, but then I had an idea, and asked if he could portage Father's canoe for me past the rapids. He said "But of course." and we went down and shoveled the snow off father's canoe and took it down from its rack. Jacques tied a rope to each side of the front thwart and then to his dogs harness. He then instructed me to sit in the back of the canoe and steer with a paddle.(Yea, right!)

Then off we went. If I never do that again it will be too soon. At first, all went well. Jacques was snowshoeing along the front of the canoe, controlling the dogs with his voice, and I was in the back of the canoe "steering" with the paddle in the snow, kind of like I would in water. I was able to steer it around some corners in the trail. Then I don't know what happened, perhaps the dogs got wind of a snowshoe rabbit or a moose. The next thing I knew, I was careening down the trail out of control. Jacques was running at the front of the canoe when he tripped and the canoe ran over him. Happily I can report the only damage was to his pride. He was not hurt and there was no damage to the canoe. However, I was still flying out of control down the steep part of the trail and then the canoe paddle broke and I had no control at all.

Sally stopped and said, "Oh my gosh, do you think that is the broken paddle I was using for a crutch?

Paul just replied, "I would not be surprised."

Then Sally continued reading.

I don't know where I would have ended up, if the dog team had not jumped off the bank at the sharp turn at the beginning of the marsh and become entangled with a downed tree. The dogs were unhappy about being tangled up and a couple were nipping at each other. When Jacques finally caught up he was out of breath, and it took him half an hour to untangle his team. I thought he would be mad at me for running him over, but when he finished untangling the dogs, he turned to me with a big grin and said, "Mon ami, do you want to do that again?" I just answered, "NO."

When we got back to the cabin I made him a big lunch and he left me the rest of the eggs. Then he packed up his bed roll and wrapped the puppies back up with the blanket and put them back in the basket. I walked with him back to his sled and helped him attach his team to his sled. He said, "Adieu, Madam Smith, adieu. adieu." and he was off. Now I am not likely to see another single soul until I canoe out in May

Jan. 3: I was going to put out some traps today, but I decided to do a little scouting first. It was a good thing I did because now I do not think I will set any out for a couple of weeks. While I was out snowshoeing and scouting I crossed Jacques' sled tracks from yesterday, and there right on top were wolverine tracks that were made last night. I followed Jacques' sled tracks and the wolverine's tracks for about three kilometers. So it looks like Jacques' trouble with Monsieur Glutton may not be over. If the wolverine gives up following him and doubles back, I don't want him finding my trap line.

Sally stopped reading and said, "Eggs, I sure wish we had some of those eggs that Susan was talking about in her diary. I would dearly love some eggs. I really miss them." Paul was standing by the door and looking out the window. He had stood up because his back was hurting from sitting too long in a kitchen chair.

Paul said, "I have an idea on how we could get some eggs if we have not been rescued by spring. Have you noticed the nest on the top of the white pine across the lake?"

"Yes, I have noticed it." Sally replied.

Then Paul said, "Unless I miss my guess, that is a Bald Eagle nest, and come spring, after the eagles return, I could climb the tree and gather a few eggs. Of course, Paul was making a joke, perhaps one that he alone would find funny. He knew that an eagle would defend its nest and trying to steal its eggs would be a fool's mission. However, Sally did not realize that this was just Paul's poor attempt at humor.

Horrified, Sally said, "Paul you can't do that. Bald Eagles are an endangered species, you can't steal their eggs."

"Why not?" Paul asked.

"Because, you would go to prison for killing eagles." Sally answered. "Well, I would not kill any eagles, I would just take a few of their eggs. The eggs are not eagles, just potential eagles." he replied.

Paul had not meant for his little joke to turn into an analogy on abortion, but that is exactly what had happened. He remembered that their last discussion on abortion had made Sally angry. So Paul put on his coat and said, "I am going to try and see if I can chop some firewood. That will either help work the kinks out of my back or make my back worse. Then he went out the door.

Sally continued sitting at the table. She was angry; not as angry as the first time the topic came up, but angry, none the less. He had basically just used her own words against her. She had said that a fetus was not a baby, just a potential baby. Paul had just said that an eagle egg was not an eagle, just a potential eagle. Sally could now see just how weak of an argument she had made. An eagle egg is an eagle and a fetus is a baby. It was hard to admit that she had been wrong all those years, and it hurt. She found that there were tears in her eyes.

Then she thought, did Paul know? No, there was no way. She had never told anyone. She was angry with Paul, but then she thought she should not be; he could not have known. If there was anyone she should be angry with besides herself, it was Vince. Sally brushed the tears from her eyes, and thought, I better get out there and help Paul before he figures out there is something wrong. She put some moose meat and rice on the stove to cook. Then she quickly put on her coat and boots. Sally checked the door to make sure it was latched and then left through the window.

Sally followed Paul's tracks in the snow, down the path, across the lake, and through the brush to where they had been cutting wood. Paul already had a couple of eight foot logs loaded on the toboggan and there were a couple more trees cut down, but he was nowhere to be seen. When Paul had left, Sally noticed he had taken the rifle. Was he out hunting? She saw his tracks in the snow leading up the hill so she followed them. Soon she heard some chopping and as she walked up on Paul, she could see he was chopping some small live ash trees to use for making the snowshoes.

"Where is the rifle?" Sally asked.

"It is hanging on a broken branch, by the trigger guard on that tree over there. If you would, I would appreciate it if you would carry it for me." Sally went over and retrieved the rifle from the branch. Paul did not need her help right then, so she thought she would look around. A packed down game trail ran up a cleft in the rock escarpment. She walked a short way over to the base of the escarpment, where a multi-trunked tree had blown over in the wind. Sally was looking for a place to sit down while she waited for Paul to finish chopping down and removing the limbs from the trees he was working on. Most of the trunks of the tree were covered with a couple of feet of snow, but there was a small part on one of the trunks that was almost bare. So Sally sat down there and waited.

Paul was almost finished with his task, when a fool's hen came flying through the small trees and landed in some branches less than fifty feet from Sally. After having moose for most every meal for the last few days, Sally was ready for a change. She raised the rifle and aligned the sights and fired. Sally almost missed. She was aiming for the body but hit it in the head. The fool's hen fluttered to the snow below. Paul looked up when he heard the shot and saw the bird flopping around in the snow. He quickly snowshoed to the bird so the bird would not get away. When he picked it up, Paul noticed that the bullet had neatly removed the bird's head. He turned around and was about to congratulate Sally on a perfect shot when he noticed Sally was standing facing away from him. He snowshoed to her side and saw a look of concern on her face.

Paul asked, "What's the matter?"

"When I shot, a strange noise came from under the tree trunk I was sitting on and it scared me." Sally replied.

When he saw where she had been sitting, Paul immediately knew what had made the noise. He put his hand on her shoulder and quietly said, "Just just back away quietly" That is what they did, and when they reached the area where Paul had been chopping the trees to make into snowshoes, Sally asked, "What was going on?"

"You, my dear lady, were sitting on a bear den, and when you shot you woke it up." Paul answered. Then he said, "Bears are not true hibernators and can be awakened, but I do not think you disturbed it too much and it should go right back to sleep. We will come back tomorrow with an oil lamp and I will go into the den and shoot it. Then we will have bear roast instead of moose roast for awhile. We can render its fat into cooking oil, because we are running short." Paul's idea was not welcomed with enthusiasm. In fact, she was not happy about it at all.

CHAPTER 14

Snowshoes

They gathered up the material Paul had cut for making snowshoes and walked back to where Paul left the toboggan. Paul told Sally that she was a crack shot having shot the head off the fool's hen, and Sally told him that she had a bridge to sell him if he believed that she was aiming for the head. They secured the additional trees to the toboggan and began pulling it back to the cabin.

As they pulled the toboggan, Sally said, "Paul, I don't think it is wise for you to try to shoot the bear and I have a really bad feeling about it. If a .22 is too small of a gun to shoot a moose, wouldn't it also be too small to shoot a bear?"

"That is why I want to bring the oil lamp. I need to go inside the bear den and shoot it in the head. It should not be a problem, as long as I can see what I am doing." Paul replied.

"How are you going to hold the lamp and rifle at the same time?" Sally asked.

"I will just hold one in each hand, unless of course you want to hold the lamp for me." Paul said.

"NO THANKS, and I really wish you wouldn't try it. We can get along without the meat." Sally answered.

When they got back to the cabin, Paul skinned the bird. Skinning it was much faster than plucking it and there was no need to try and get every last calorie and ounce of protein out of it as there was before Paul shot the moose. Sally went in and got a pan off the stove for Paul and he prepared the fool's hen for cooking. Of course he saved the liver, heart, and gizzard.

He put the bird in the pan and Sally washed it off. She added water to the pan and put it on the stove to boil. While they were waiting for the bird to cook, Paul took out his sheath knife and began paring down one of the ash trees he was going to turn into a snowshoe frame.

Sally sat at the table and said, "I would like to help, but the paring knife I was using to peel the alder branches with is not up to the task."

"Oh, I almost forgot, I have a present for you." Paul said as he removed the sheath knife he had found at the Johnsen cabin from the pocket of his hunting coat.

Paul slid the sheath knife across the table to Sally. With a smile Sally said, "Other women get diamond rings and I get a sheath knife, but I would rather have the knife right now anyway, it is a lot more practical." Sally took the knife out of the sheath and put the sheath on her belt. Then she picked up another piece of ash tree trunk and began carving. Paul smiled, in approval. Then Sally said, "That reminds me about something that happened while you were off to the Johnsen cabin that I was going to tell you about but forgot about until now. While you were gone, I saw a really long white mouse darting around the cabin."

"Oh, that explains why I have not seen a mouse since I got back. Your "really long" white mouse sounds like an ermine to me." Paul replied.

"Ermine? I have heard of ermine, but I did not know there were any in Canada." Sally said.

"Well, most people would call it a weasel and we can be thankful that it eliminated our mouse problem for us."

When the fool's hen was finished cooking, Sally served half to Paul and took half for herself, then divided up the moose roast and rice. Paul asked a blessing over the meal and made a special point to thank God for the accuracy of Sally's shot. After the meal, it was getting dark and Paul loaded the stove with long logs. While they were waiting for the ends of the logs to burn, Sally stated, "I have another question for you that I would like you to answer before you go and get yourself killed by the bear." When I was at University, I was told that archaeological evidence does not support the Bible. What do you say about that?"

Paul replied, "In the early days of archeology, people were looking for how archaeological evidence supported the Bible. Then something changed and the leading archaeologists decided that the Bible was a bunch of myths and therefore, if the evidence they found supported the Bible, then they must be misinterpreting it.

At the time they said such things as the time line of ancient Egypt and the Bible did not line up, that there was no evidence in Egypt of Joseph, there was no archaeological evidence of the exodus in the Sinai Peninsula, and that they had not found archaeological evidence of King David and that showed the Bible was just a collection of myths.

Many archaeologists puzzled over the Egyptian time line because no matter how they put it together, it did not completely line up. Then a modern Biblical Archaeologist was looking at some Egyptian hieroglyphics when he noticed that someone long ago had interpreted one line wrong. When that one line was read correctly the Egyptian time line came together and fit perfectly. The intriguing thing to me is than once the Egyptian time line came together it matched that of the Bible. I learned about this from a television program and if I remember correctly, other non-Biblical Archaeologists did not completely accept his findings.

The next problem I listed is that they had not found any evidence of Joseph in Egypt. Remember that the Bible says that Joseph rose from a slave to Pharaoh's right hand man and Pharaoh put him in charge of all of Egypt. For a number of years Joseph was Egypt's true ruler because Pharaoh had turned all the responsibility to him. It would stand to reason that if the Bible account is true, there should be some archaeological evidence. Early archaeologists looked but could find none. However, there are some things that need to be remembered. Early Egyptians believed that if they could erase a person's name on every monument than that person would be erased from history and that meant person never really existed. Egypt is full of evidence where people attempted to erase a leader that they did not like by removing their cartouche on monuments.

I saw a television program where a modern archaeologist was showing a tomb in the Egyptian land of Goshen which is where the Bible says the Children of Israel settled. The tomb had been looted by grave robbers of everything except a large statue. The statue was of a man who had semitic features. The statue had no Egyptian features at all.. The coat on the statue shows traces of many colors of paint, just like Joseph's coat of many colors the Bible talks about. The tomb was empty and the Bible says that the Children of Israel took Joseph's bones with them when they left Egypt. Of course that does not prove anything because most of the tombs that have been found in Egypt were empty because of grave robbers in antiquity. The Biblical Archaeologist in the program believed that this was Joseph's tomb but there is no way to prove it.

Type in "proof of the exodus" into a search engine on the Internet and many pages will come up. Many of these pages will state that there has never been any archaeological evidence found that the Exodus of the Bible ever happened. Why is that? It is because the possibility that the Exodus happened just as the Bible says does not fit the world view of many Non-Biblical Archaeologists. The Exodus happened about 3500 years ago. Just how much evidence could reasonably be expected to still be around to be found? However, there is archaeological evidence that does support the Biblical account of the Exodus.

Chariot wheels have been found at the bottom of the Red Sea encrusted in coral. This find may support the story of the Exodus, but the only thing that it proves is chariots somehow found their way to the bottom of the Red Sea. There is no way to tell if the chariot wheels relate to Exodus or some other event.

I read about a cemetery that was discovered in Egypt where all graves are believed to be Hebrews not Egyptians. The graves contain many more bones from females than males. Does that support the Bible where it says that Pharaoh ordered all the newborn Hebrew males killed and the females were allowed to live? Of course it does, but after 3500 years, there is no way to prove it. There could be another explanation.

I also have read about a large Jewish cemetery that was found in a desolate area on the Sinai Peninsula. Supposedly, it was a great distance from this cemetery to any inhabited areas. The grave markers were engraved in an early form of Hebrew and many talked about things that happened in the book of Exodus. The wording did not match the scriptures. It appears that the people who engraved the head stones were using their own words and were witnesses to the events of the Exodus. If the people that were buried in that cemetery did not come from the Children of Israel when they were wandering in the wilderness, where did they come from? Were the bodies in this cemetery shipped great distances by camel caravan in the heat of the desert? That possibility does not seem likely. Think about the smell.

The best evidence that the Exodus actually did occur may be the Egyptian hieroglyphic graffiti found throughout the Sinai Peninsula. The Rosetta Stone Stele allowed linguists to begin the process of deciphering hieroglyphs. The Rosetta Stone had three translations of the same passage, Egyptian Demotic which is a script form of written Egyptian, Classical Greek and Egyptian hieroglyphics. Deciphering Egyptian hieroglyphics requires a thorough understanding of Classical Greek and Egyptian, so there are not that many people who can do it. The graffiti in the Sinai was not deciphered until recently. Many of the passages talked about things that happened during the Exodus in the first person. The Children of Israel were slaves in Egypt for over 400 years. It just stands to reason that a number of them would be able to read and write Egyptian hieroglyphics.

Lastly, many people pointed to the fact that there had never been any archaeological evidence found that supported the Bible stories about King David as proof that the Bible is just a collections of myths. However, in 1993 a Stele was deciphered that talked about King David. Since that time there has been more evidence of King David uncovered so their argument does not hold water anymore.

The ends of the logs had burned off, so Paul was able to push them all the way in. He left the stove door open so Sally had light to get into bed, then he shut the door and went to bed himself.

The next day proved to be windy and Paul announced that he did not want to go after the bear on that day because it might prove difficult to keep the oil lamp burning. He needed the lamp to see to shoot the bear in the head. The announcement that he was not going after the bear that day was much to the relief of Sally. At least until Paul said that there was no reason to rush things, as the bear was not going anywhere. In the morning they worked on cutting and hauling more firewood and in the afternoon they worked on carving the snowshoe frames. The next few days turned out to be too windy for the bear hunt, so they fell into a pattern of cutting wood in the morning and working on the snowshoe frames in the afternoon. A couple times Paul took some time off to try some fishing, in the open water at the beginning of the river but had no luck.

At the start of the snowshoe project, Paul had told Sally that he wanted to end up with four 1"x1"x60" pieces for the outside of the frames. The Ojibway snowshoe style uses two pieces for the outside frame. Both the toe and the heel of the snowshoe are fastened together and the center part is spread by inserting spreader boards which fit by mortise and tenoned into the frame. Carving the frames was proving to be more work than Paul had envisioned. After two days of work by both he and Sally, they did not even have the outside pieces of one frame finished for one snowshoe.

For the next two weeks, the wind kept up and prevented the bear hunt, but the snowshoes were beginning to take shape. When the two pieces for the outside of the first snowshoe frame were finished, Sally started working on the outside pieces of the next snowshoe, and Paul started working on assembling the first frame. First, he split the spreader boards out of a piece of ash log that he had cut to length with the saw. The ax made short work of that job. Next he cut the holes for the tenons in the frame. The small chisel they had found in the silverware drawer greatly aided in this task.

Paul wanted to use some 1/8 inch diameter bolts with nuts and washers he had found in a jar in the collapsed storage shed to attach the ends of the snowshoe together. However, he had a problem. He did not have any way to drill the holes he needed. Three minutes at home with his drill press would have completed the job, but without the proper tools, drilling the holes was proving to be a daunting task. Finally it was Sally who came up with a solution to his problem. "Why don't you burn the holes through?" she had asked. Why not indeed?" Still it took most of a day to burn the sixteen holes required for both snowshoes using a red hot nail, heated in the stove and held with a rusty pair of pliers he found in the shed.

The snowshoes needed an up turn at the toe. When Paul put together the frames he took advantage of a natural curve in the wood for the up turned toe, but that was not enough. So, as they were working on making the webbing Paul had used rocks from the river to give the snowshoes an extra bend at the toe by stacking the stones on the frames so that the extra bend would be set into the wood as the wood seasoned and dried.

To make the rawhide webbing, Paul retrieved the pieces of moose hide he had hanging from the cross supports on the food cache. The jays had done a good job of removing the tallow from the hide. The hide was frozen as stiff as a board and reminded Paul of a piece of plywood more than a moose hide. He laid the pieces of hide hair down on the porch and cut it into half inch wide strips with his knife. Paul had read that letting the hide soak in a mixture of wood ashes and water for a few days would loosen the hair. So he mixed some up and soaked the strips in the wash tub for a few days, much to the dismay of Sally. She missed her bath tub.

At first Paul thought the mixture was not working but then the hair started coming off, and Paul and Sally finished taking the hair off by working the strips back and forth with the hair side up against a tree, thereby rubbing the hair off the hide. Then each of them laced the wet raw hide webbing on one of the snowshoes, weaving it into a pattern by using Susan's snowshoes as a guide. It was necessary to keep tying the strips together as they worked.

When they were done, Paul had to admit that the snowshoe that Sally was working on looked better than the one he laced. The raw hide had to dry out for a few days before Paul could try them out. As rawhide dries, it shrinks and Paul was worried that they may have pulled the wet rawhide webbing too tight and that it would shrink to the point that it would damage the frame. But in the end it turned out that they had guessed correctly on how tight to pull the wet rawhide and the webbing turned out nice and tight. Over all they were both proud of the job they had done, but Paul was concerned about one more thing. He explained to Sally that snowshoes are normally varnished to keep the webbing from absorbing moisture and becoming loose.

They did not have any varnish, so that was not an option. Then Sally asked, "Would wax work?"

Paul replied, "I suppose so ,but we don't have any of that either."

"Yes. We do!" Sally said with excitement. "The other day, I was putting some empty jars back in the cellar and was moving jars on the shelf, when I discovered a block of paraffin." So Sally retrieved the block of paraffin from the cellar and added water to a larger pan and put the block of paraffin in a smaller pan. Then she put the small pan in the larger and put them on the stove so they would act as a double boiler. Once the wax was melted, Sally and Paul each applied the melted wax to one of the snowshoes' webbing with rags.

The next day the sun rose on the day Sally had been dreading. It was perfectly calm. When she served Paul pancakes for breakfast she was hoping that he had forgotten about the bear den, but when they were finished eating Paul asked if she was going with him to get the bear.

"Paul I really wish you would not try and shoot that bear. We can get along without the meat and I see it as an unnecessary risk." Sally pleaded.

"Don't worry, if I thought that it was risky I would not do it. If you are uncomfortable with it, Just pray for me." Paul replied.

Then Sally said, "If I can not talk you out of it. I will go with you. After all, we are partners in this survival thing."

On their trip to the bear den, they brought the tobaggon to retrieve the bear with, and the ax to chop the bear out of the den. When they neared the lake Sally said, "I was supposed to remind you to get some birch bark for fire starting." So they stopped and both filled their pockets with birch bark from a dead birch near the edge of the lake. As they crossed the lake Paul pointed out a high flying jet to Sally. It was just a little dot high in the sky and there was no hope that the jet would spot them, but it was nice to know that they weren't the only two people left on the earth, just the same. The high flying jet was the first plane they had seen since the crash.

When they reached the den, Sally asked, "What is the plan Chief, and how can I help?"

Paul was already removing his new snowshoes and as he took off his coat he said, "After we light the lamp, I will crawl into the den and will use the light to find the bear's head, then I will shoot it. When you hear the shot, I would appreciate it if you would grab me by the legs and pull for all you are worth." Sally promised that she would and then held the lamp for Paul to light. After he replaced the globe on the lamp, Paul said a short silent prayer and started head first into the bear den.

The opening into the den was smaller than Paul had envisioned, and he had to snake his way between the tree trunks. The den was also deeper than he thought it would be and by the time he was in deep enough to see the bear, only his feet were sticking out of the opening. Just as Paul was able to make out the head and was about to shoot he heard a soft crying sound. He turned his head and saw three small cubs, each about the size of his clenched fist. This bear was a sow with cubs. That possibility had somehow not occurred to Paul. Now he did not want to shoot the bear and he began wiggling trying to work his way back out of the den. This disturbed the mother bear enough that she partly woke up and let out a low growl. Sally had not heard a shot, but when she heard the growl she took it upon herself to grab Paul by the boots and pull.

When Paul cleared the den opening, he quietly thanked Sally for her assistance and explained that the bear was a sow and that he was not going to shoot it. This was much to Sally's relief. As Paul put his coat and snowshoes back on, a flock of a dozen or so spruce grouse flew high over their heads. It appeared that they had come from the alder brush that lined the river and Paul guessed that they would land in the spruce trees on top of the rock escarpment. Paul asked Sally if she thought that they should climb the passage in the cleft in the rock and go after them.

Sally replied, "Yes, I think I like eating those a lot better than I would bear meat anyway."

They left the toboggan, oil lamp and ax behind and began following the game trail up the cleft in the rock. When the reached they top of the escarpment they could see that there were several spruce trees well back from the edge of the rock face. Beyond these few sparse spruce trees was a dense spruce forest. Paul and Sally snowshoed to the nearest trees and stopped to scan the trees ahead for the grouse. After looking for quite some time, Paul spotted the birds in a tree about two hundred feet away. That was too far away to assure the success of the shot but there was no more cover to use to sneak closer. Paul figured that he could make the shot and used the trunk and branch of a tree as a rest to steady the rifle. At the shot, all the grouse just looked up. It was a clean miss. Paul pumped the rifle's action and realigned the sights with his target. When he shot, all the grouse took off and sailed out over the edge of the cliff. However, one of the birds broke off from the flock and was losing elevation as it flew over the edge of the cliff.

That was a sign to Paul that his bullet had hit its mark, and he quickly snowshoed to the edge of the cliff to see where his quarry went. Sally was about to yell out to stay back from the edge when, in a split second, Paul dropped out of sight. The man she loved was standing next to her one moment and mere seconds later, he was gone. Sally screamed, "PAUL!", but she already knew there would be no answer. The cliff was forty meters high and no one could survive the fall. Without even knowing what she was doing she prayed out loud, "Oh God, how can I go on without him?"

Sally just stood there in disbelief and shock for several minutes. What would she do now that Paul was dead. She thought about the promise she had made to bury him at the grave site of Susan's parents and how he had said that she could leave him for the wolves. The ground would be frozen, but the thought of leaving him for the wolves was just to terrible for her too think about. She knew that she owed him a lot and was determined to give him a Christian burial. Maybe, if she built a large bonfire near the Le Forest grave, it would thaw the ground enough to dig a grave. What could she use to dig with?

What had happened? She slowly edged towards the edge of the cliff. Soon she could see what had caused Paul's demise. The snow had drifted out over the edge of the cliff and made an overhang. From the top Paul thought that he was well back from the edge but when he stepped out on the snow overhang it had collapsed. Sally was now crying uncontrollably, and as she inched closer to the edge she was girting herself for the sight of Paul's broken body at the base of the cliff.

As Sally edged closer to the precipice a strange feeling came over her that she should call out again and she did. "PAUL!" This time however, she heard a moan. When she peered over the edge she could see Paul's mangled body laying on a ledge five meters below. When he fell, his left leg had scraped a pinnacle of rock. Blood had seeped through his pants, and the pure white snow, that surrounded him, was being stained crimson red. "Paul, why didn't you answer me?" Sally yelled in panic.

"I had the wind knocked out of me and I couldn't." Paul replied.

"How am I going to get you out of there?" Sally asked with alarm.

Paul replied calmly, "Go get the ax and chop down one of the larger spruce trees up on top. Cut off all except a foot of each branch and lower the bottom end down to me. Hopefully, I will be able to climb it."

"Will you be able to walk?" Sally inquired.

"I don't think so. I think my leg is broken." came Paul's reply.

As she flew down the pass to get the toboggan and the ax, she just kept repeating, Thank you God, Thank you God, Thank you God, over and over again in her head. She was going down the pass too fast and almost lost her footing. Slow down she told herself. It would be no help to Paul if, in her haste she fell also. When she reached the bottom of the pass, she lashed the ax to the toboggan and started back up the pass, leaving the oil lamp behind. When she reached the top, Sally quickly selected a suitable tree and chopped it down. Then she pruned back each limb, leaving about a foot, just as Paul had requested. Only a half to three quarters of an hour had passed when Sally lowered the butt end of the tree to Paul. The tree really weighed too much for her to manage, but somewhere she found the strength.

In the meantime Paul had removed his snowshoes and had tied them together with the drawstring from the hood of his sweatshirt. Then he had tied the other end of the string to his hood. There was, of course, no way for him to climb the tree with snowshoes on and he could not spare an arm to carry them. Paul had a difficult time climbing the tree. His bad leg was worst than useless. As he climbed, the spruce needles scratched his face. When he got to the top, Sally helped him over the edge. They were both exhausted, but there was no rest for Sally yet. She helped roll him on to the toboggan and then she tied him down. Lowering Paul and the toboggan down the pass was perilous, but somehow she made it. Dragging the toboggan back to the cabin from the bottom was not a problem until Sally reached the edge of the lake. It was all up hill from there.

By the time she reached the outhouse she needed a break and she asked Paul if he needed to use the outhouse. Paul replied that getting up would be extra painful and asked Sally to look the other way. She did, and Paul turned on his side and urinated from the toboggan. When Sally turned back around she could see in the snow that there had been blood in his urine. That meant that there was internal bleeding. Could someone survive that without medical attention? As Sally pulled him the remaining way to the cabin, she redoubled her prayers that the Lord would spare Paul's life.

When they reached the cabin, Sally used all her remaining strength to help Paul through the door. Paul asked Sally to bring in his snowshoes because he had gotten blood on them and did not want some animal ruining them. Normally he had left the snowshoes outside so they would stay cold. If the snowshoes were brought inside the cabin, they would warm up and the snow would stick to them the next time they were used.

When Sally brought Paul in she sat him in a kitchen chair. Then Sally started attending to his first aid. A few months before, Sally would not have been up to the task she was now being called on to perform, especially on someone she loved. Sally took out her sheath knife and cut Paul's pants leg from the hem to the hip. The skin was missing or badly abraded in a continuous patch, two to three inches wide by about two feet long. The whole leg appeared to be black and blue and was swollen to twice its normal size. Blood was still seeping from the wound. The sight of it made Sally sick to her stomach but she steeled herself for the work she needed to do.

Sally went to the steamer trunk and got out the sheets that were in it. She had not used them on the bed because of the sleeping bags. She would need to use these sheets for bandages. Sally cut the corner from one of the sheets to use it to clean the wound. She poured boiling water on this corner to sterilize it and after it cooled, she used it to mop up the blood that was still oozing from the wound. "Paul, I have cleaned this as best I can but I am afraid that it will become infected because we don't have any antibiotics."

Paul was still conscious despite his overwhelming pain. He said to get the jar of honey down from the cupboard and put that on his leg as that would work as an antibiotic.

"You mean that jar of crystallized stuff in the cupboard?" Sally asked. "Isn't that spoiled?"

Paul answered, "Honey never spoils, but you will need to heat it up in a double boiler like we melted the wax so it will turn back into a liquid." Sally did as Paul said and after it melted into a liquid she let it cool down and then applied it to Paul's wound with her fingers.

Sally said, "At least there are not any bones sticking through so you probably do not have a compound fracture."

"Sally, I need you to grab me by my foot and really pull hard on my leg just in case there is a fracture and it is out of alignment." Paul said.

Sally did as she was told. She could not tell if anything moved but when she had finished, Paul had passed out.

The fact that he had passed out worried her, but she thought that it was perhaps a blessing in disguise. Next Sally wrapped Paul's leg with the sheet. It was not sterile but it was clean and she thought that if Paul was right about the honey, acting as an antibiotic it would be OK. Then she thought if he was wrong about the honey he was sure to get an infection. Even if he did not get an infection, the internal bleeding might be more than he could overcome. I have to stop thinking like that, she thought. As Sally bandaged Paul's leg, tears were flowing down both of her cheeks and she was praying earnestly. When she finished wrapping his leg, Sally went outside and retrieved two extra pieces of green ash that was left over from the snowshoe project. She brought them inside and cut the ash to length with the bow saw. Then she tied them to Paul's leg to use as a splints with several strips of sheet that she had ripped from the larger sheet.

By the time she was finished, Paul had come to and she helped him get his coat off and get into bed. Sally just had Paul lay on top of his sleeping bag. She rolled her sleeping bag up and used it and Paul's coat to prop up his leg. Then she covered him up with the blankets. "Where are you going to sleep?" Paul asked.

"Don't worry about that," Sally ordered, " I am not going to bed, I have something important to do." Paul did not respond, and Sally did not know if he had passed out again or didn't know what to say. She sat up and kept putting wood in the stove to keep the cabin warm all night so Paul would not be cold. In between firing the stove, she was praying.

Sometime before morning, Sally fell asleep with her arms folded and her head laying on the kitchen table. The cabin had cooled down and she awoke with a cold shiver. Sally got up and put more wood in the stove. Paul, always an early riser, woke up and asked Sally for help because he needed to go to the outhouse. Sally helped him out of bed and through the door. Then Paul said, "It is just too painful I can't make it to the outhouse." Then he asked Sally to turn her head again. Paul leaned against the porch post and relieved himself in the snow. When Sally turned back she could see that Paul still had blood in his urine but not as much as yesterday. Maybe her prayers were being answered. Neither Paul nor Sally said anything about the blood in his urine. Sally helped him back into the cabin and back into bed.

After Paul was back in bed Sally said, "I don't understand. Why did God have to allow this to happen to you? We have been through so much already, why did this have to happen?"

Paul just said, "Sally, God is always good." Then he asked her a question that had her wondering if he was completely coherent. "Is the oil lamp still on the other side of the river?"

"Yes, it is." Sally answered.

"Well then, would you please go back there and bring it back? While you are there I want you to stand back and look at the rock escarpment, both to the west and to the east. Then when you come back, please tell me what you saw." Sally put on her coat and boots and went outside without saying anything.

As she sat on the porch tying on her snowshoes she was wondering if Paul was alright mentally. Why did he feel the need to send her back for the oil lamp? After all, they had another in the cellar and why had he asked her to look at the escarpment? A chilling thought passed through her head. Did Paul know he was dying and thought it would be easier on her if she was not there when he did? Sally was mentally and physically drained. She had hardly slept that night and now she was off on a mission she did not understand. She was thinking that maybe she should have questioned Paul more, why did he want her to do this?

When she got to the other side of the river, she went over and retrieved the oil lamp. Then she noticed the spruce grouse that had caused all this trouble laying dead in the snow. She snowshoed over and picked it up. It was frozen solid and hard. Sally thought she could bring it back, thaw it out and clean it. She had watched Paul clean the others and though she did not welcome the thought of cleaning it, she figured she could. Then she remembered Paul had asked her to stand back and look at the escarpment. She still did not understand but she did what Paul had asked her to do. From the area where they had been chopping trees for the snow shoe frames she stood and looked, first to the west and then to the east.

What did Paul want her to see? She could see about a kilometer in each direction but what was she looking for? Then Sally had a strange thought. Perhaps she should ask God for help to see what Paul wanted her to. She was all prayed out from praying all night but closed her eyes and said a brief prayer anyway, "God please open my eyes." When she opened her eyes again she immediately saw what she was looking for. She could see the tree she had chopped down and lowered to the ledge that Paul was on. What Paul wanted her to see was the ledge he was on. That ledge was the only ledge in sight! Had Paul been a few meters right or left he would have fell to his death. Paul was right. God was always good.

While on her way back to the cabin Sally realized that she was beginning to think the way Paul did. Had God prepared that ledge thousands of years ago, from the foundations of time, just to save Paul's life? If God had in fact done that, surely he wouldn't let Paul die a slow painful death from his wounds, would he? Why would God prepare a ledge to save him only to let him die? This thought bolstered her spirits and instead of the fear and panic she had been feeling she now felt relief and thankfulness. When she returned to the cabin, Paul asked her if she saw what he wanted her to.

Sally just said, "Yes, I did, and you are right. God is always good."

Sally told Paul that she had found his bird and showed it to him.

He just said, "Good, I hate to think I put you through all this for nothing." She then went back outside, sat on the porch and plucked the grouse. When she came back in she put the frozen bird in a pan to thaw. After it thawed, she cleaned it and cooked it. Paul did not eat much of its meat but Sally made sure he drank most of its broth. She sat by the bed and spoon fed him.

Sally asked Paul if it would be OK with him if she changed his bandage.

Paul replied that he wanted her to leave the bandage alone for now but asked if she would tighten the splint because it appeared the swelling in his leg had receded somewhat and had made the ties loose. Sally did what he asked and was happy that it appeared that the swelling was going down some.

For three days Paul refused to let Sally change the bandage but then finally he said it was OK. Sally found that the honey had prevented an infection also it had an added advantage of keeping the scab that was forming from sticking to the bandage and it had kept the scab soft. Paul's leg was far from looking good but it did look better. There was still swelling in the leg but it was not nearly as bad as it had been. The leg was still all black and blue. All the trips to the outhouse were hard for Paul and he needed Sally's help every time. Paul was in constant pain and spent most of the time semi-sleeping. The pain was so severe it prevented him from falling into a deep sleep, yet the lack of deep sleep kept him from being fully awake much of the time.

At one of Paul's more lucid moments, while Sally was feeding him, Sally was saying that if he had been in a hospital they would have had his leg in a hyper barometric chamber with oxygen under pressure. The oxygen would have kept it from being infected and the pressure would have made it heal much faster.

Paul said that fit in with many Creationists' thoughts on the meaning of the book of Genesis. The Bible says that God made the firmament and divided the waters which were under the firmament from the waters which were above the firmament. Some Christians believe that that means that there was a layer of water vapor or liquid water high above the earth and this layer would have kept the atmospheric pressure much higher than it is today. Perhaps this higher pressure and higher oxygen levels were why people lived much longer lives before the flood of Noah.

Paul kept apologizing to Sally for his accident. What bothered him the most was the thought that the canoe was still at the Johnsen cabin and they had not been able to retrieve it after all the effort they put into making his snowshoes. Sally told him to stop apologizing. She had actually had fun helping him make the snowshoes. Especially because the one she laced turned out better than his had. She enjoyed rubbing that in. The project had kept them occupied for quite some time and that was time that she was not bored. Besides, she had come to peace with the accident and decided that God had meant the accident somehow for their good. That statement had pleased Paul and he could see how much Sally had changed. However, neither Paul or Sally knew then just how true Sally's statement had been. The Lord had meant Paul's accident for their good and one day the details would be revealed to them.

As the days went by, Paul's leg slowly improved. After about a month Paul's leg only hurt when he moved it. Paul and Sally had lost track of the date it was on the calender. Paul's watch had stopped on January 5th and because he was not constantly checking it he didn't notice it for several days. So they did not really know what day of the month it was. After Paul's watch stopped, Sally started cutting notches in the log post that went to the ridge log in the center of the cabin, to keep track of time. Someone had done that on the post before. The only trouble was, occasionally she would forget to cut a notch and some days she would forget she had already cut one so she ended up cutting two. The best they could figure, it was about the middle of March. The days were getting longer and the weather a little warmer, but winter still had a firm grip on the north country.

While Paul convalesced, Sally finished reading Susan's diary to him. Sally had skipped a lot of entries because they just were not that interesting. Actually it looked like Susan had skipped a lot also. Lots of days the entry only said something about the weather or talked about reading a part in her Bible. There were a number of weeks where she made only one entry and there were a couple of weeks where she had no entries at all. One thing was for sure. She was pregnant and her morning sickness had returned. Sally kept thinking that poor girl, pregnant and here in this wilderness all alone.

Paul said perhaps the lack of entries meant that Susan was suffering from cabin fever, but would have expected more entries instead of less, if that was true. Susan had not started up her trap line again because of her morning sickness. Oh, and there was also an entry about how Susan had finished her rag rug. One of her last entries talked about how her mother's clothes were not fitting any more and that she was now wearing Mrs. Johnsen's.

The last entry was dated May 15 and talked about how sad she was about leaving this cabin, but today was the day she was leaving for civilization. She had packed everything she was taking in garbage bags and tied them into her Father's freight, birch bark canoe. She only had three paddles because she had broken one, but she figured that was two more than she needed. Then she repeated what her father had told her. Keep right on the first three lakes and left on the next two and in three long days you will be out.

Susan had been writing her diary for her own entertainment only. She had no idea that anyone would ever read it. Susan knew that getting back to civilization was not merely a long three day canoe ride, and her diary was not meant as a guide. If it had been, she would have told of two dangerous rapids that even her father would have not considered running. Susan knew that when she came to those rapids she would need to get out and walk along the rock bank, controlling the canoe with ropes; a process called lining a canoe. Susan also knew what her father meant by the words "In three long days you will be out. They would be very long days indeed and it did not mean she would be back to civilization; only that she would be out of the river system and a longer and far more perilous trip awaited her. Paul and Sally could not have known any of that at this time.

When she was not reading the diary to Paul, or cooking, Sally was going out alone and cutting firewood. The firewood cutting was not as urgent now as it had been because the weather was warmer and she had built up a reserve supply. Paul was venturing out to the outhouse alone, using only the crutch he had made for Sally out of the broken canoe paddle.

It was much too short for him but he was making do. In the months since the crash, Paul had lost over one hundred pounds, at first because they were short of food and then because he was in too much pain to eat much.

They still had plenty of food. The moose meat was still holding up well and they had a lot left. Paul planned to turn all the rest into jerky when the weather warmed to the point it would thaw. Sally had managed to supplement their food supply by catching a couple of walleyes in the open water at the beginning of the river, but the fishing was not very good. As March turned into April, Paul was beginning to bear weight on his bad leg. By the middle of April, he was walking short distances without the crutch. He was still in a lot of pain when he walked, but you could never realize it by watching him. He hid it well. Finally, near the end of April, the time had come and Paul and Sally made most of the rest of the moose meat into jerky.

CHAPTER 15

Call of the Loon

Near the end of April or the beginning of May, winter was finally losing its grip on the area around the cabin. There had been a few days that were actually above freezing. One night on his way back from the outhouse, Paul noticed how vivid the Aurora Borealis was and when he got back to the cabin, he called Sally to come out and see the Northern Lights. As they stood there together, side by side, admiring the great beauty of God's handiwork, they heard the lonesome call of a loon. Paul said, "That call must mean that there is open water somewhere on the lake. If we are going after that canoe, we will need to leave tomorrow morning, while we can still cross the lake to get to the other side of the river."

Sally asked, "Paul, do you think you can walk that far on your bad leg?"

"I think I can make it if we don't push too hard and take some breaks. We should be able to get there in two days. My plan is to cross the lake to the other side of the river and climb to the top of the escarpment. Then we will walk along the escarpment to the north bay where the Johnsen cabin is. When we get there, I do not know what we will do. Perhaps we can walk around the bay, or maybe we will build a raft and cross it. It is only about 400 yards across at the cabin and more narrow further north."

Sally said, "Surely you do not mean that we will walk along the edge of the escarpment."

Paul laughed, "No, don't worry, I have learned my lesson. I don't want to be anywhere near the edge. We will walk back by the tree line." So the plans were made. In the morning they would be leaving the cabin, at least temporarily. It had been their shelter for about five months. All because of the call of the loon, things were going to change. They would spend other nights in that cabin, but this was the last night this cabin would ever be home to them.

The next morning, Sally carefully packed Susan's diary back where she had found it in the steamer trunk. Then she climbed to the loft, and put the gold chain with the key and crucifix back on the nail. Paul was busy deciding what they should bring with them. They did not have back packs, so he planned to wrap everything they needed in his sleeping bag then the sleeping bag would hang from a long pole. That way they could both carry one end of the pole. Of course, everything would be wrapped in garbage bags to keep it dry. They needed a pan for cooking and boiling drinking water, some rice and some jerky. They would also take extra clothes, blankets, the ax, rifle, matches, fishing poles and some tackle.

Paul retrieved an eight foot ash pole from the porch. It had been left over from the snowshoe project. He sat on the porch because it was such a nice day and whittled the ends of the poles smooth with his knife. Sally was cooking them the last moose steaks she saved from being made into jerky. When the steaks were finished cooking she served them on the porch, along with some homemade bread and the last of the Tang. They both ate their breakfast on the porch without saying much. Like Susan mentioned in her diary, both of them were strangely somehow sad about leaving this cabin.

After breakfast, Paul brought the pole he had been working on into the cabin and laid it on the bed. Sally helped him pack everything up. They had not heard any wolves howling for a couple of months and Paul figured they had moved on to a better hunting territory. So Paul did not want to carry the rifle but he wanted it where he could get at it in a hurry, if need be. They rolled everything up in the sleeping bag but they had the butt stock of the rifle near the edge of the bag, so it would be easy to pull out without unpacking everything. The rifle was loaded in the magazine, but not in the chamber for safety and Paul pointed this out to Sally. The action would need to be pumped to put a round in the chamber before it could be fired.

All the extra clothing was placed in garbage bags. The sleeping bag was wrapped around the pole and tied off with cord. Around this, their two tarps were wrapped and tied off. Lastly a hole was poked in the bottom of two garbage bags and they were threaded over each end of the pole and over the sleeping bag. The bags were also tied off with cords. They carried the pole out to the porch, then Paul went back in and shoveled the ash and coals out of the stove and into the wash tub. He laid up firewood in the stove to make building a new fire easy. He had learned something from Susan. Paul dumped the ashes in the snow and put the wash tub back inside and then brought his snowshoes out and laid them on the porch. Sally closed and latched the door and left through the window.

Paul and Sally both sat on the edge of the porch and tied on their snowshoes. They each hoisted an end of the pole to their shoulder and they were off. They needed their snowshoes, because there were still areas of deep snow and because the snowshoes spread out their weight so it would be safer crossing the ice. This was the first time since his accident that Paul had put on his snowshoes and that fact would become very apparent to him before they had snowshoed very far, but at this point, his leg was feeling OK. They crossed the ice of the lake without incident and reached the bear den at the base of the escarpment, near the cleft in the rock passageway. They did not go close to the den, but Paul could tell that the mother bear and her cubs were still inside, because he could not see their tracks in the snow. Up the pass they went, but by the time they reached the top, Paul's leg was already hurting and he was ready to take a break.

At the tree line, Paul bent over a spruce tree for them to sit on and they both took a seat. From this vantage point they could see far to the west on the lake and they could see some open water in the distance. It was turning out to be a beautiful day, clear and warm. So warm, in fact, that they both removed their coats and tied them to the outside of their parcel, when they were finished with their break. They started off again but after a mile, Paul's leg needed another rest so they stopped. This time they removed their snowshoes because they had reached an area where there were only a few inches of snow. They tied the snowshoes to the parcel also. Up ahead about a half a mile on the path they were taking they could see bare rock. The snow there had already melted. While they rested, they both ate a couple of handfuls of snow to keep hydrated. They would need to boil any drinking water, but snow is generally safe to eat.

They started their sojourn again and soon reached the point in their path where there was no snow. After trudging through snow for months, walking on bare rock was like a new experience for them. Around noon, they stopped for another break and lunch. There were some appropriately sized rocks for them to sit on while they took their break. Having been in the sun all morning, the rocks were comfortably warm and sitting on them felt good. Sally had thought ahead to put some jerky in a plastic bag in the pocket of her coat, so they did not need to open their pack to get food. As they sat on the warm rocks eating their lunch, their spirits were high and other than Paul's leg, they were both feeling good.

They sat there looking down at the beautiful panoramic vista of the lake. Paul said. "Today, while we are sitting here I feel like you and I are queen and king of the world."

Sally answered, "I feel the same way." Moments later two bald eagles appeared on the South side of the lake, below them. Sally pointed them out. One of the eagles swooped low over a patch of open water on the lake and scooped up a fish. It flew up and landed in a tree, where its mate joined it for lunch.

Paul said, "My dear queen, it looks like a pair of our subjects are also enjoying their lunch."

Sally said, "They look happy now, but they do not know you are planning on stealing their eggs." With that, they both burst out laughing.

After their rest and lunch they started back on their long hike. The trek that Paul had made to the Johnsen cabin had been shorter and a more direct route. The rock escarpment wove in and out along the north shoreline. Overall, this made their route two or three miles longer than the one Paul took on the ice. It was such a nice, clear, and warm day neither Paul nor Sally had given the extra distance a thought. Early in the afternoon Paul called a halt to their advance. His leg was really hurting and he called a stop long before he otherwise would have.

Paul asked, "Sally, do you mind if we set up camp here for the night?"

"That is fine with me, Boss." was her reply.

There was a little brook that flowed close to their camp site in a low spot in the rock. It went over the edge of the escarpment and turned into a waterfall. The sound of the waterfall could be heard from their camp. Paul thought it might just be from seasonal melt water, but in any case it was located conveniently for getting water for cooking. There was a pile of rocks that would block the prevailing northwest wind if it were to come up but it was still perfectly calm. Because of the bedrock they were on, the camp site lacked anywhere to tie off the tarps that they had brought. It looked like the night would be clear and hopefully the tarps would not be needed.

They laid down their burden at the camp site, and they both went off in different directions to gather dead wood for the camp fire. Both of them brought back enough to last the night, so they had plenty. There was a depression in the rock that would make a good fire pit and Paul pointed out to Sally that they were not the first people to camp in that spot. The depression contained charcoal from some long ago fire.

"How long ago do you think this fire was?" Sally asked.

Paul said. "It is hard to tell. It could have been last year or even two hundred years ago."

Sally said, "I guess without carbon 14 dating there is no way to tell."

Paul replied, "Even with carbon 14 dating an exact date would be hard to tell. Carbon 14 dating could be used to tell when the wood that had turned to charcoal was last alive, but not when the fire was made. It can only date things that were once alive. The man who invented it thought it would be highly accurate to date things 500 years old and less because samples of things with known ages exist for comparison. He also thought that it would make a good guess at ages up to around 3000 years. He held out much less hope that it would even be remotely accurate for ages much beyond 5000 years. Yet carbon 14 dating is often used to date things at tens of thousands of years old."

Sally started to untie and unpack their bundle so she could get out the pan and the rice. Paul got the ax as she unpacked it and left to get some spruce boughs to use to make a bed. They would make something softer to sleep on than the hard rock and more importantly, the boughs would separate them from the rock. The surface of the rock was warm now, but as soon as the sun went down the great frozen mass of the rock would quickly overcome the warmth of the surface.

Paul laid out the spruce boughs to make a bed and covered them with the tarps and his sleeping bag. His plan was to use the sleeping bag as a sleeping mat and only cover up with the blankets. Hopefully, the night would stay warm, and between the blankets and the fire, they would be warm enough. Then Paul started a fire using some of the birch bark in his pocket for kindling. Sally got some water from the brook, and put it on to boil and when it did she added three cups of rice for their dinner. When it was done, they both ate their share of rice from the same pan. She had brought silverware for both of them, but to save weight they did not bring bowls.

Perhaps it was the location or maybe they were extra hungry because of the hike, but the rice tasted extra good. It could not have been the fact that they were sharing the same pan, could it? After eating, they just sat around the camp fire and talked. The talk turned to home. Home for Sally was any of three different penthouse apartments all in big Canadian cities, but she did not completely explain that or the fact that she owned the buildings they were in. She just said she lived in an apartment in a big city. Paul told her that he could never live in a city and that he lived in a log home that he had built for his family on a small Northern Michigan lake.

"That is ironic. We just spent the winter in a log cabin on a lake and you live in one." Sally said. Then she said "I thought I would always want to live in the big city, but after this winter I think I would like to try country living."

As the evening turned into darkness they were treated to another Aurora Borealis light show. It was almost like God had gone to the trouble to put on the light show just for them.

When they became sleepy, they laid out on the sleeping bag they were using for a mattress. They had their coats on and each wrapped up in a blanket. The rock pile to the northwest was reflecting some of the heat from the camp fire back at them, but Sally asked Paul to hold her because she was cold. They were not in separate sleeping bags, but Sally trusted him and knew he would not "try anything funny". Paul wrapped his blanket around her and held her to keep her warm. Sally had been a little cold, but mainly she, just wanted Paul to hold her and she faded off to sleep quickly. Just before he went to sleep himself, Paul finally realized that he loved this woman. Instead of making him happy, the thought made him sad. He was sure that Sally could never feel that way about him, so he must never tell her of his feelings for her. After all, what would be the point, it would just make her feel bad. The verse in the Bible about not being unequally yoked with a non-believer came to mind also. Perhaps he was misinterpreting his feelings for Sally or maybe he was just missing his late wife, Joan.

Paul got up several times that night to add more wood to the fire. Each time he went back to bed he would wrap his blanket back around Sally and hold her to keep her warm. Late into the night, Sally woke up. She was facing away from Paul but he had his arm around her and he was deep in sleep. Something had awakened her. When she opened her eyes, she saw the camp fire softly burning, but then she saw something else. A large creature was standing just on the other side of the fire and was silhouetted against the sky. Sally was too scared to speak. Instead, she grabbed Paul's arm and shook it to wake him up.

Paul had always been a light sleeper and as soon as he opened his eyes he could see the creature looming over them. Paul just sat up and yelled, "Get out of here." The creature immediately followed his order, turned and ran off. The sound of its hoofs on the rock could be heard, as it faded off in the distance.

"What was that?" Sally asked with alarm.

"It was just a moose." Paul replied as he got up and added more wood to the fire.

"What was it doing?" Sally asked, as her heartbeat started to return to normal.

"Oh, it probably was just curious about the fire." Paul surmised.

"I thought animals were scared of fire." Sally stated.

"In most cases that is just a myth. That moose had likely never even seen a fire before so it had no reason to be afraid of it." Paul answered.

When Paul returned to the makeshift bed he laid down facing away from Sally. His muscles ached from remaining in the same position most of the night, so he needed to sleep on his other side. Sally turned over wrapped her blanket around and held him. They woke up at first light and Paul got up to tend the fire. When Paul saw that Sally was awake he said, "Thank you for keeping me warm the second half of the night."

With a big smile, Sally said, "You're welcome, and thank you for keeping me warm the first half of the night and keeping the fire going." Sally got up, filled the pan with water from the brook, and put it on the fire to boil. Paul asked if it was OK with her if they started out their breakfast with some spruce tea, because he was really thirsty. Sally replied that she was very thirsty also.

Paul took the ax and left to retrieve a fresh spruce branch so Sally could use the needles for tea. When he returned, Sally took the branch and started stripping the needles from it into the pan. After it had brewed to the proper color, Sally strained the needles out with a fork. Once the pan had cooled, they took turns drinking from it as they ate their breakfast jerky. Paul commented that he could not believe how much better the spruce tea tasted than it did the first time he tried it. Sally smiled at the compliment on her spruce tea brewing ability and added that she was even beginning to like it.

After breakfast, they packed everything up just as they had originally done the day before. Then they hoisted the pole back to their shoulders and resumed their mission to reach the Johnsen cabin and the coveted canoe. It was another warm and clear day. As their eyes surveyed the lake below them, they could see a lot of open water. There was still a patch of ice here and there but for the most part it was open. Sally said, "It is a good thing we left yesterday morning, because I do not think that we would have been able to cross the lake if we had waited until today."

Paul replied, "I believe you are right."

Paul needed to take a few less breaks, because of the pain in his leg that day than he did the day before. They did not even stop for lunch, so they were making good time. It was mid afternoon when they reached the edge of the escarpment overlooking the north bay and the Johnsen cabin. As they surveyed the scene below from their high vantage point, both Paul and Sally were surprised to find that the north bay was still locked in ice. The ice looked rotten and they could not cross it. Looking north, Paul could see that the bay extended far out of sight. His original idea about walking around it was not going to be practical. There was a stony beach at the base of the rock escarpment but beyond that the shoreline was thick brush that went right to the water. He also realized that his thought about building a raft was not going to work either. To build a raft, dry dead logs would be needed, preferably cedar. It appeared that all the trees on this side of the bay were alive and were other species.

Paul had a knot in his stomach. How was he going to tell Sally that he had led her on this trek for nothing. Worse yet, they were now on the side of the lake opposite the Le Forest cabin. How were they going to get back? The ice bridge they had crossed would surely be melted by the time they could get back if it was not already. They had only taken enough food with them for a few days. Paul swallowed hard and explained the situation to Sally as he saw it.

"Paul, I am surprised at you." Sally stated. "The Lord would not have brought us this far, only to put a permanent road block in our way. We just need to pray and ask for his guidance. He has to have an answer to our problem."

This response caught Paul off guard, but it surprised and delighted him. They stopped and held hands, bowed their heads and each silently asked for the Lord's help.

After the prayer, Sally said, "Now we just need to wait and see how the Lord answers our prayer like the missionary did in the story you told." This really surprised Paul and a couple of questions ran through his mind. Was Sally mocking him? No, he did not believe that, as she seemed sincere. Had Sally asked Jesus to be her Lord and Savior? If she had, she had not told him about it. Paul decided he would wait until he felt the time was right and ask her, and he said a silent prayer to God asking for guidance on the matter of when to talk to Sally about her salvation.

The answer to their problem on how to cross the north bay, did not reveal itself immediately. Paul and Sally gathered some firewood and brought it with them when they traveled down the same cleft in the escarpment that Paul had watched the wolverine come down months before. When they got to the shore of the lake, they set up camp. They used one of their tarps as a ground cloth and the other was tied up as a shed type tent to block the northwest wind. They made a fire pit between their lean-to and the rock face of the escarpment. Then they walked up and down the shoreline gathering driftwood to bring back to camp for a firewood reserve.

Paul chopped a hole in the rotten ice and Sally filled the pan with water and put it on to boil on their newly kindled fire. When the water was boiling Sally took it upon herself to only add one cup of rice. It looked like they may be here for awhile and she was putting them back on the ration they decided on, at the beginning of their adventure. While the rice was cooking, Sally asked Paul when he thought the bay would be clear of ice. "My guess would be tomorrow afternoon, why do you ask?" Paul replied.

"I was thinking that after the ice is out, on a warm day we could swim across the bay where it necks down to two hundred meters wide."

Paul nervously laughed, " I don't know. I have always been chicken of swimming in really cold water, and I am afraid that we would both have hypothermia by the time we got to the other side, but you may have come up with our only answer. We will just have to wait and see."

Just then, the sun went behind the clouds and the wind picked up. They could feel the temperature was dropping. That night the temperature dropped even more and despite their campfire, the fact that they shared Paul's sleeping bag, both blankets, and wore all their coats to bed, they still spent the second most uncomfortable night of this whole ordeal.

The next morning, Paul got up at first light and added more wood to the fire. Then he realized that the answer to their problem, about crossing the bay was at hand. He rousted Sally from bed by saying, "We need to pack up in a hurry. There is a skim of new ice and we need to cross the bay before the sun comes up and it melts." Sally got up right away and began packing. "Leave the tarps; we can come back for them with the canoe after the ice melts." Paul ordered. Soon they had their things wrapped up in the sleeping bag and tied to the pole as they had packed before. Only this time, they did not have the garbage bags on the outside of the sleeping bag because the bags had become shredded while going through thick brush on the way there.

Quickly they walked down the beach to where the bay was only two hundred meters across. They were carrying their pole and their snowshoes. When they reached the narrow spot of the bay they squatted down and started putting on their snowshoes. The snowshoes would spread their weight on the thin ice. Paul said, "Sally make sure that you have your sheath knife. You cannot swim with snowshoes, so if you go through the ice, take your knife and cut the bindings. If I go through the ice, just keep going until you get to shore. If I go through the ice, you will be more help to me by getting to shore and getting a fire going, than by trying to help me and getting wet yourself."

On their way there, Paul had always been in the lead, but now Paul asked Sally to go first. Paul realized that his chances of going through the ice were a lot greater than Sally's. If he went through, he wanted to make sure that she made it safely across. Off they went with Sally in the lead, and all went fine until they were only a few yards from the other side. Then, with a crack, the ice broke and Paul fell through. Fortunately, the water, where he broke through, was only three feet deep. Paul yelled for Sally to keep going and she continued on, dragging the pole with the now semi-soggy sleeping bag behind her. Paul took his knife and cut his snowshoe bindings, but in doing so he had to bend over and get his coat soaked and submerge his arm in the icy water.

After he had cut loose the bindings, Paul stepped off his snowshoes and retrieved them as they floated to the surface. Paul laid the snowshoes on the unbroken ice in front of him and kind of laid down and rolled out of the lake on top of them. In so doing he got even wetter. By the time Paul reached the shore he was pretty soaked. He was shaking and his teeth were chattering. He had never done anything like that before, and was surprised how difficult it had been. Fortunately for Paul, Sally had followed his orders perfectly, and she already had a fire going. She was adding fuel to the fire to make it even larger. Sally unpacked their soggy sleeping bag and was happy that the garbage bags inside had kept Paul's extra clothes dry. She helped Paul remove his wet clothes down to his underwear and turned and looked away while Paul changed into dry underwear. After that, Sally went into the woods to get more wood for the fire.

When she returned with the wood, Paul said, through chattering teeth "Thank you. That is the second time you saved my life."

Sally replied, "You are more than welcome, but I think this time you would have made it on your own. In any case, if you had not saved my life on our first night, I would not have been able to save yours."

Soon, the sun rose, and with it, the temperature climbed. It was turning out to be the warmest day they had so far. With his dry clothing and the blazing fire, Paul's teeth soon quit chattering. While Sally was waiting for Paul to warm up, she cooked them a breakfast of rice. The hot rice would help Paul warm up from the inside. When she was done cooking it, Paul asked a short blessing over the food and thanked God for seeing them safely across the bay. By the time they were finished with their hot breakfast, Paul was warm again and the outside temperature had risen to the 60's. The sleeping bag was wet and they would need to dry it out, so Paul and Sally just loaded all their things on the bag. They each grabbed two corners of the sleeping bag and carried everything up to the Johnsen cabin. They had finally made it.

CHAPTER 16

The Rescue

Sally and Paul carried the sleeping bag and their belongings up to the porch of the cabin and laid it over the wood pile. They opened the front door and went inside. Their first task was to get a fire going in the stove. The air temperature was warm, but they had a lot of things that needed to dry out and the heat from the stove would be helpful. They got a fire going in the stove and hung up the wet sleeping bag and the wet clothing.

Then Sally jokingly started pretending they were a young married couple and they were looking to buy their first home. She pointed out the beautiful panoramic view from the picture window, the nice warm wood stove and then pointing to the recliner, she said, "It even comes partially furnished." "Can we buy it, Sweetheart, pretty please?"

Paul took up the role of a new husband and answered, "Honey, we need to be careful buying our first house. This one may work out for us but I am afraid that there is a slight possibility that the roof may leak." he said pointing to the caved in roof. Then they both burst out laughing.

Sally then walked close to Paul and embraced him. She said, "You're the husband and I will abide by your decision. If you think we should keep looking for a house, we will just keep looking" This left Paul wondering if by any chance the embrace was something more than just silly role playing.

When Sally embraced Paul, she looked over his shoulder and noticed a moose antler hanging on the wall. The sight of the moose antler instantly brought Sally back to reality. "Oh, Paul, look, a moose antler. Is that the one that Susan brought here for a Christmas present for the Johnsen's?" They walked over to examine it more closely. Sure enough, there was a scene carved on it of a couple of people fishing from a canoe.

"Why didn't you tell me this was here when I read to you about it in Susan's diary?" Sally asked.

"I had not noticed it." Paul replied. "You must remember, it was dark most of the time I was here before. Also, everything was covered in snow.

They looked closely at the carved figures on the antler. They were beautifully and realistically carved. Sally said, "Look at the guy in the back of the canoe. He looks so handsome!"

Paul looked closely, and replied, "Sally, I think you are pulling my leg." The figure carved into the antler looked almost exactly like Paul, flowing beard and all. Sally just giggled.

They went back outside to examine the reason for their trip. When they walked around the corner of the cabin, Sally exclaimed, "Oh no, the canoe is locked." The canoe was in fact chained and locked to the cedar post rack it was on. Because of all the snow, Paul had not noticed the chain and lock when he was here months ago.

"That was not very neighborly." Paul said. "I wounder why anyone would bother to lock a canoe up here. I mean just how likely were we to happen upon it and take it, and just how did they expect that chain to stop me." Paul then went back into the cabin and came back out with the ax. One blow of the back of the ax head knocked one of the log posts loose from the horizontal cross bar and the chain slid off the cross bar.

Sally just looked at him in surprise and said, "Paul, if you ever need a new job you sure have talent as a canoe thief."

Even though it was still morning, both Paul and Sally knew they would not be returning to the Le Forest cabin that day. The north bay still had ice but it was melting fast. There was still ice on some of the main lake, but if the weather held it would all be gone in a day or two. So Sally and Paul went about looking through the ruins of the cabin for anything that might be of use to them. Paul told Sally about the new sleeping bag in the closet. Now he was really glad that he had left it here, because he guessed that his sleeping bag would still be moist at bed time. They really did not find much. It looked like the owners of the cabin had taken most everything of value, either before or after the roof caved in.

Sally squeezed herself between the caved in roof and the kitchen cabinets. "Hand me the ax." she called out. Paul did and she used it to pry the door off an upper cabinet that Paul could not reach. Sally found a mason jar of pancake mix and another of white sugar. There was also a can of shortening. In another upper cabinet, she found plates and passed them out under the caved in roof to Paul. Sally called out, "Paul, I will make anything you want for lunch, just as long as it is pancakes."

"Sounds good to me. On that list, I think I will take pancakes, if it is alright with you." Paul replied.

So Sally made pancakes using one of the pans that Paul had melted snow in months before. They took the white sugar and spread it on the pancakes and had a pancake feast for lunch. After lunch Paul went and finished the job of getting the pipe curtain rod down from the bedroom. This time, he was not interrupted by a wolverine. With the pipe he was able to knock the canoe paddles from the gable. Then he turned to Sally and asked, "It never occurred to me to ask before now, but have you ever done any canoeing?"

"Yes, I have. I went canoeing several times as a teenager, but I have not been canoeing in years." came her reply.

"Good, what do you say, want to go get those tarps?"

The answer came, "Just lead the way, boss." They carried the canoe down to the north bay. There was still plenty of ice in the bay, but there was a clear enough path for them to canoe through. They lacked seat cushions or life preservers, but it did not matter. They would not last long in that icy water, if they were to tip over, anyway. They canoed across the bay, retrieved the tarps and were back in just a few minutes. When they got back, they put up the tarps inside the cabin to block any wind coming in from the caved-in roof and to help contain the heat from the stove.

As Sally made more pancakes for dinner, Paul retrieved the new sleeping bag from the closet in the bedroom. After dinner, they sat on the wood pile on the porch and watched the sunset. As it was growing dark, Paul assessed the possible ways for them to spend the night. His sleeping bag was still moist but the two blankets were dry. He decided that Sally would sleep in the recliner in the new sleeping bag and he would sleep on the floor on his moist sleeping bag wrapped up in the two blankets. The wood stove was putting out a lot of heat and they had protection by three walls of the cabin with the tarps acting as a fourth wall. It should not be too uncomfortable for him. Sally, however, had different ideas.

"I am not going to sleep on the recliner in the new sleeping bag, you are." Sally had said.

Each of them wanted the other to be comfortable and sleep in the new sleeping bag on the recliner. In the end, neither would agree to be the comfortable one. So, Sally just said, "Fine we will both sleep on the floor." They laid the moist sleeping bag out on the floor with the two dry blankets on top. Then they unzipped the new sleeping bag and used it as a comforter. Paul filled the stove with wood and they both went to bed. As soon as they laid down, they both went to sleep. The night proved to be the warmest one so far, and by the time the sun had been up for a couple of hours the next day, all the ice was gone from the north bay.

Paul and Sally took this as a sign that the ice was likely gone from the rest of the lake also, so they began packing for the return trip to the Le Forest cabin. They packed up most everything they brought with them in the two sleeping bags and put the sleeping bags into the garbage bags that had contained their extra clothes. They had decided that they would take the new sleeping bag with them for use on their planned trip down the river to civilization. They would leave the larger one that Paul had been using at the Le Forest cabin. The new sleeping bag and the one Sally had been using back at the cabin would make for a lighter load in the canoe for their trip out. Paul left out the fishing tackle and poles, because he wanted them to try some fishing on the way back. He tied a Rapala fishing lure to the line of both fishing poles. Sally brought a couple of the pans from the Johnsen cabin plus the can of shortening, some silverware, and two plates and packed them into the canoe.

The wind had come up from the north, and there were a few small whitecap waves on the north bay. Paul knew that once they cleared the north bay the rock escarpment would protect them from the wind as long as they hugged the north shoreline. "Sally, we could wait until the wind dies down to leave, if the bay is too rough for you." Paul stated.

"I am good to go now, if you think it is OK, I trust your judgment." came her reply. So Paul had Sally step into the front of the canoe and set down, then he launched it. They canoed with the waves at an angle to them, until they reached the calm waters that were protected by the escarpment, then they turned parallel to the north shore. They had canoed a couple miles when Paul's empty stomach started giving him orders.

Paul called out, "Let's see if we can catch a fish for lunch. You know, we were in such a hurry to leave; we did not have breakfast." So they put down their paddles and picked up the fishing poles and started casting.

Sally said, "Now we must look just like the people carved on the moose antler."

After they had been casting for a few minutes, Paul set the hook on what he had thought was a fish strike. Sally had turned around and was facing him. When she saw him set the hook, she asked if he had a fish on.

Paul replied that he had thought so, but he guessed he had just hooked into a submerged log. He had no sooner said that, than the "log" took off peeling off line from the reel's drag.

"Doesn't look like a log to me." Sally shouted with excitement.

Paul fought the fish for fifteen minutes before it showed any signs of tiring. Paul said, "This is a really big fish and I think that my best chance to land it would be to beach it on the shore." So Sally picked up her paddle and started slowly paddling towards the shore. Steering a canoe from the front is not as easy as steering from the aft. Fifteen minutes later, they reached the shore and after Paul had fought the fish for half an hour, it was finally tiring. Still, it was another ten minutes before Paul was able to guide the fish up onto the beach. It was a forty inch Northern and the biggest one Paul had ever caught. Paul had a big smile as he carried the fish back from the water to make certain that it did not escape. Part of his smile was because he knew that he would soon have a full stomach.

In the area they were in there was a twenty to fifty foot wide stone beach between the water's edge and the rock escarpment. This was a stroke of luck because much of the north shore there was no beach between the water and the escarpment. Paul and Sally each went in different directions, picking up driftwood for a fire. Paul used the last of his birch bark to get the fire going. They were not worried about that because Sally still had one pocket full of birch bark and they expected to make it back to the Le Forest cabin by nightfall or a little later. Once the fire had burned down to a nice bed of coals, Sally put the frying pan on the coals with some shortening in it to heat up. Paul filleted the fish and cut it up in a number of equally sized pieces. They had a lot more than they could eat now, but Paul said it would be best if they cooked it all and saved what they could not eat now for dinner.

"Usually it is impossible to fillet out all the bones on a northern pike, but I know a special trick and I think I got them all, or at least most of them. However, I am making no guarantees, so be careful when you eat it." Paul advised. There was a big boulder with a flat top and a couple of smaller rocks that would act as stools. It was almost like God had provided a picnic table for them and Sally set the plates on it. Paul asked a blessing over the meal and they began to eat. After Sally had made three batches of fish they were both full and could eat no more. There was a lot left over and Sally cooked up several more batches until she had cooked it all and placed it in a garbage bag to save until later.

Then she asked, "Do you mind if we wait here for a while before we start up again? I am too stuffed to move."

Paul answered "So am I."

So they just sat there with their backs against the picnic table rock looking out at the beautiful lake. After awhile, Paul expressed his opinion that catching the northern pike was another act of divine Providence. Northern pike have a mouth full of sharp teeth and it is almost unheard of to land one that size without a wire leader and on light line.

Then Sally said, "When we crashed, I did not believe in God, but I now see how wrong I was. Time after time he has provided for us. At first, I thought the things that happened were just by chance, but now I know that He has been watching over us."

This was the opportunity Paul had been waiting for, and he asked. "Sally, have you asked Jesus to be your Lord and Savior?"

Instantly Sally's eyes flooded with tears and she began sobbing, "Oh Paul, I do not deserve salvation."

Paul tried to comfort her, "Sally, the Bible says that the Lord is not willing for anyone to perish."

"You don't understand." Sally said between sobs. "I never told anyone this. I am so ashamed. When I was at University, I dated a guy named Vince. We had dated for almost a year and I thought he was going to ask me to marry him. One night, in my apartment he forced himself on me. I did not know what to do, I was in love with him and I thought it was perhaps my fault for somehow leading him on. I did not call the police and report the rape and I even dated him a few more times, but made sure we were never alone."

Sally was crying quite hard now and it was making it difficult for Paul to understand her. She continued, "Then I discovered I was pregnant and I called him on the phone and told him. He told me that he would pick me up in front of my apartment building in an hour and hung up. When I got into his car I thought he was taking us to get a marriage license. Instead he drove me to an abortion clinic and handed me $350, and told me to get out. He said that he did not love me and that I had tricked him into having sex with me, then he demanded that I go into the clinic and take care of our problem."

Paul wrapped his arms around the sobbing Sally and said, "Sally I am so sorry for the pain and guilt that man put you through."

Sally said, "Paul you still do not understand, there is more. My friend who had an abortion that I told you about was also raped by Vince. What I did not tell you about was that she killed herself. I do not know for sure, but I believe her rape and abortion had a big part in her failed marriages and suicide. If I had turned in Vince, none of that would have happened. God could not possibly want me."

Paul just held her, until her sobbing subsided and then he said, "When I was young there was a hymn in the hymn book of my church that had a line in it that said "There is nothing my God can not do." That is a nice thought and mostly it is true but it is not completely correct. God tells us in the Bible that there are things that He can not do. He can not lie, He can not change, He can not sin and most importantly He can not remember our sins once we repent and ask for forgiveness. He will forgive us for all our sins, if we humble ourselves and ask him to, and the best part is that he will remember our sins no more."

Sally was on the brink of accepting Christ when something intervened. Suddenly, they heard the sound of a plane. They looked back to where they just came from and saw a small float plane coming in for a landing. The plane landed on the water and went out of their sight in the north bay. Without saying a thing Paul and Sally had thrown everything back in the canoe and were on their way back to the Johnsen cabin.

Matt Johnsen had seen the canoe and people on the shore line and was surprised to see anyone on such a remote lake, especially this early in the season, but he had not thought much about it other than to wonder which one of his bush pilot competitors had flown them in. He had taken over flying his father's bush plane and was having a hard time earning a living because there were not nearly enough clients to go around. Because of the recession, there were very few people being flown into remote Canadian lakes. The stress from lack of business and lack of money was wearing on him. His father had turned the plane over to him the spring before when he finished getting all the endorsements on his pilot's license allowing him to fly paying customers.

The pressure was on Matt, because not only did he need to support himself, but also his parents. His father had retired to take care of his mother, because she had Alzheimer's. Matt needed to come up with some money fast to pay his outstanding fuel bill. He soon would not be flying anyone anywhere if he did not raise some money. That is why he was here on this remote lake. He came to retrieve his father's canoe so he could sell it. The canoe had not been used since the roof caved in on his father's cabin. The reason it was still there was that his father had problems flying it in originally and had warned him to only fly it out when the rest of the plane was empty. The lake was so remote that making a special trip to get it was not financially practical. By the time he paid for the aviation gas, the profit from selling the canoe would have been eaten up. Today, however, he had flown two fishermen into a lake twenty five kilometers away. So this was his chance to retrieve the canoe on his way back, sell it and at least partly catch up on his gas bill.

Matt landed the plane and taxied up in front of the cabin. He tied the plane off to a tree at the edge of the lake. The last time Matt had lived here was the winter when he was twelve. He was in a hurry to get back to Wawa but decided to look around in the cabin anyway for sentimental reasons. He opened the door and went inside. Matt stood in the living room and looked around then he thought about the blackboard hanging in what once was his room. He was overcome by the thought of the possibility that one of the lessons his mother had written on the blackboard so many years ago might still be there.

Matt climbed over the downed roof and went into his old room. When he saw the blackboard instead of a lesson written by his mother he saw the message written months ago by Paul but it looked like a $100,000 dollar bill to him and the answer to his financial problems. Then he thought, wait, this must be someone's idea of a sick joke. He knew all about the $100,000 reward that Sally's father had offered for information on what had happened to her. Every bush pilot in eastern Canada did. Still this had to be some type of joke. Sally McPhearson had went missing way back in December. There was no way she was still alive. One of his bush pilot buddies was surely pulling a joke on him. Still, it might be worth investigating on the off chance it was legitimate.

Matt climbed back over the roof and went out the front door of the cabin. He walked across the porch and around the corner of the cabin. Then he saw it. The canoe was gone. Suddenly, everything clicked in his mind. The canoe he saw from the air was his. He stood there staring at the broken empty rack where the canoe had been, then he found himself running down to the beach and to his plane. Matt normally was not a praying man but he was praying now. This could be the answer to all his money problems.

Matt Johnsen had only attained a height of a few feet above the waves when he set his plane back down and taxied the plane up towards the canoe that was heading in his direction. While he was still a ways off, he cut the engine and got out of the plane and stood on the pontoon. He called out, "Are you folks Sally McPhearson and Paul Sinhuna?" By this time Paul and Sally had moved the canoe closer to the plane and Matt threw them a rope. "Yes, we are." Sally excitedly yelled back . "In that case, my name is Matt Johnsen and you can call me Rich." Paul thought that Matt was talking about a nick name but Sally guessed that he was talking about a reward that she was sure that her father had offered for finding her. "Are you the only survivors?" Matt asked. Paul replied, "Yes, I am afraid we are the only ones."

"You folks are lucky. I came all the way up here just to bring back the canoe you are in so I could sell it. I need to raise some money in a hurry."

Sally asked, "How much are you asking for the canoe?"

"I was going to ask $200 but I will not be able to take it back with me if you folks want a ride."

Sally said, "Yes, we do want a ride, and I will pay you $500 for this canoe and we can leave it here."

"Well, Miss McPhearson, it looks like you have bought yourself a canoe." Matt said with a big smile on his face.

"Not only that, but I will pay you twice your normal fare, if you can fly us to Sault Ste Marie." Sally replied.

"I think that can be arranged, but we will need to land at Wawa and gas up and we will have to hurry to get there before the gal at the pump leaves for the day. Tie the canoe off to the side of the pontoon and I will tow it back to the cabin." Matt ordered.

Sally got into the plane and Paul handed the things in the canoe in to her and she stowed them in the back of the plane. Matt taxied across the north bay with the canoe tied to the pontoon and Paul still in the canoe. When they reached the shore at the cabin, Matt and Paul carried the canoe up and put it back on the broken rack. Soon they were back in the plane and in the air. Sally was in the back seat of the plane and Paul sat in the right front seat. Paul wanted Matt to land at the Le Forest cabin so they could return the things that belonged there but Matt just said that they did not have time and asked where their plane had crashed. Paul told him it was in the marsh at the east end of the lake.

When they flew over the Le Forest cabin Sally said a silent prayer thanking the Lord for it. They flew over the marsh at only a thousand feet and even at that low altitude the wreckage of the plane was hard to spot. The tail portion of the plane in the river looked like a sand bar and the cabin of the plane looked like one of the many boulders that surrounded the marsh.

When they reached an altitude of 3000 feet Matt reached for the mike of the plane's radio. "Matt Johnsen calling the Wawa sea plane base. Are you listening, Mable?"

"What can I do for you, Matt" came the answer.

"Mable, I am just leaving Starvation Lake and ETA at Wawa is three hours. That will put me at your dock about 5:30 and I need you to fill up my gas tank tonight because I have to fly to the Sault.

Mable answered, "Matt I would really like to help you out, I don't mind staying late, but I can't extend you any more credit. I can't wait until you sell your canoe, I need the money now."

"I have already sold that canoe and did not even have to fly it back, I will just need to wait a while to be paid. Plus, I picked up a couple of paying passengers at Starvation Lake and one of them is Sally McPhearson." Matt replied.

Mable radioed back, "Matt do you expect me to believe that story, or are you just joking?"

Matt answered, "No joke," and handed the mike back to Sally. She keyed the mike and said, "This is Sally McPhearson speaking."

There was no response for a few seconds, then Mable came back on the radio and said. "Matt, I will be happy to extend you all the credit you want."

Matt replied, "Good, now, Mable, would you please contact Search and Rescue for me and tell them the plane wreckage they are looking for is in the marsh and river on the east end of Starvation Lake. Also, tell them, I am flying the only two survivors Sally McPhearson and Paul Sinhuna, to the Sault and will be landing on the St. Mary's River."

The voice on the other end of the radio came back, "Will do Matt, just remember I knew you when you weren't famous." Paul wondered about the radio conversation but just figured it was some type of inside joke.

On the flight to Wawa, Matt asked Paul how they were able to survive the winter and Paul just said Divine Providence. Then Paul told Matt about how they were planning to take the canoe downstream on the river and find their way to civilization.

Matt got a horrified look on his face and said, "In that case it looks like I just saved your lives. You could never have made it down that river in that canoe. There are two dangerous rapids and almost every year some kayaker dies on the lower section. Even if you lined the canoe down those rapids, what would you do when you reached the mouth of the river? Which way would you go and depending on the tides and the weather, even if you chose the right direction, it would be an almost impossible trip."

"What do you mean about tides?" Paul asked. "The tide on Lake Superior is only a few inches and is hardly noticeable." Paul stated. "That is true." Matt replied, but that river would not take you to Lake Superior. It takes you to James Bay and you would have over a hundred miles of open ocean to reach civilization."

With Matt's statement, Sally just let out an "Oh, my!" She now knew why God had allowed Paul to fall from the cliff and break his leg. If Paul had not broken his leg they would have dragged the canoe back across the ice. They would have missed Matt and his plane and they would have died on their canoe trip out. God had really meant the accident for their good. However, now Sally was really worried about what had happened to Susan. Sally knew finding out if Susan made it safely out would be one of her top priorities when they got back.

Sally asked, "Matt, do you know Susan Smith?"

"Susan Smith, no, I can't say I have ever known anyone with that name."

Sally stated, "Perhaps you knew her by her maiden name, do you recognize the name Susan Le Forest?"

"Oh yeah, I remember Susan Le Forest from when I was a kid. I think she was four or five years older than me. I have not thought about her in years. I know that first her mother died and then her father died back when I was a kid but I don't know what became of Susan. I have not seen her in years."was Matt's reply. "This caused Sally's heart to sink even further.

Matt landed the plane and taxied over to the seaplane dock. They tied the plane up and Mable began filling the wing tanks. Paul excused himself to find a bathroom and Sally asked to use a phone. Sally called her father collect. He answered the phone and she said, "Daddy this is your little girl."

Her father yelled out at her mother, "Honey it is true she is alive! Praise God!" Sally's mother picked up the other phone and they were both talking at once.

"We have been praying that the rumors we heard on the radio, that you had been rescued, were true. We had almost given up hope." Sally's father said. Sally's parents and Sally were all crying for joy. Sally thought, news travels fast and "Praying?" Perhaps her parents had changed also. The "Praise God" was sure out of character for her dad.

Then Sally said, "I am sorry I am going to have to hang up shortly because we are about to leave and I really need to find a bathroom before we do. I will call you from the hotel. Dad, we will be landing near the Bush Plane Museum on the St. Mary's River. Could you have one of our news crews meet me there?"

"I sure can, that is my girl, always thinking, what better publicity than to do this in front of the Bush Plane Museum? What is the pilot's name who rescued you? I will have the reward check waiting for him." Sally told him and closed by promising to see them in a few days and that she loved them. Then she hung up and hurried off to find a bathroom.

When Sally came back, she pulled Matt aside and asked for his card. She wanted to be able to call him, because she would have more work for him. The flight to the Sault was just a flash for both Sally and Paul. The news conference when they reached the Sault went by in a flash also. Matt got his check and Sally's planning had paid off. Her news team scooped all the other news media. Her news team had paid for hotel rooms for them and another news conference with all the other news media was planned for the next day. Soon Sally and Paul found themselves alone in their own rooms.

Sally called her parents back, as she had promised and told them about the last months of trials. Her father told her that her cousin Beth had been instated as CEO and he would call an emergency board meeting to get Sally her job back. At that Sally said, "No, Dad, don't do that, at least not yet, I need to take care of some things before I can even think about whether I even want to take over as CEO again. I am sure that Beth has been doing a good job, hasn't she?" Sally's Dad was surprised by her response but told her in fact, Beth had been doing a very good job. Then Sally told her parents that she had to let them go, because she had something very important to do and told them again that she loved them.

After she hung up, Sally found the hotel room's Bible. She did not go to bed that night. Instead, she sat up all night reading the Bible. She read the four Gospels and then skipped around and read other parts that Paul had talked about. Sometime near morning she finally prayed and asked the Lord into her heart. Suddenly, she was filled with the joy of her salvation and could feel her Savior's forgiveness. Then she thought for being so happy she had sure been doing a lot of crying. Sally knew she still had something missing. She looked out the window and saw that the sun was coming up. Paul would be awake and she had to talk to him. She had to tell him that she had finally accepted Christ and something else. Sally had thrown a lot of hints at Paul but he had not picked up any of them, so now it was time to take matters into her own hands. She called the front desk to find out Paul's room number and was out the door.

When Paul had reached his room the night of the rescue he called his daughter Katherine, in Florida and had a tearful phone reunion with her. He asked her for her sister Gayle's number, because she had been moving and he did not have her new number. She gave him Gayle's number but Katherine said, "Dad, I am sorry, her number will not do you any good, half of Oregon's phone system is out, but I will Email her for you. She has satellite Internet." Tentative plans were made for them all to get together and the call was over.

Paul was feeling like he did back in December on the plane. He was wondering now what he was going to do with the rest of his life. He knew he was already missing Sally but he was sure there was no room in her life for him. Paul still had ten Canadian dollars in his wallet and a loony in his pocket, left over from his hunting trip. He went down to the hotel's store and bought a tooth brush, tooth paste, shaving cream and a razor. Paul went back to his room, brushed his teeth, then shaved his beard and his head. He took a long shower and went to bed. True to his mode of operation, when the sun got up the next morning, so did he.

Paul had just dressed, when there was a knock at his door. He opened it and found Sally standing there. For a few seconds Sally thought the man standing inside the room must be Paul's younger brother. She could see the family resemblance, and she wondered how his brother had gotten there already. Then she remembered Paul did not have a brother. Paul said, "What is the matter Sally."

"I did not recognize you without your beard." Sally answered. "You look much younger."

"Oh I only grow one for hunting season but I did not have any way to shave it off in the cabin. Come in." Paul said.

Sally stepped in and shut the door behind her. Paul inquired, "Did you sleep well?"

"No, I did not sleep at all! There was no snoring to lull me to sleep. Paul I wanted you to be the first to know, I accepted Christ an hour ago."

Paul said, "That is wonderful Sally. I have been praying for your salvation for a long time." and he embraced her."

When he released her from his embrace, Sally made her play. With her heart beating hard, she said, "Paul, I perceive that you are a man of your word."

The statement surprised Paul and he answered, "Well, I would like to think so."

"Do you remember that when you returned from the Johnsen cabin on the ice, that you promised me you would never leave me again?"

"Yes, I remember." Paul replied.

"Well then, if you are not going to leave me, don't you think you had better marry me?" Sally pleadingly asked.

"You would marry me?" Paul asked in shock. It was not really a proposal but it was good enough for Sally.

"Yes, I will marry you." she said and rushed to embrace him and give him their first kiss. They were now engaged and Paul did not even know how it had happened, but he sure was not complaining!

Paul asked, "When do you want to get married?"

"Just as soon as possible." came Sally's reply.

"Are you sure you want to marry me? I am ten years older than you." Paul asked.

"My father is eleven years older that my mother and that seems to have worked out OK." Sally answered.

Then Paul said. "Sally I love you and I want you to marry me but I have to warn you that my business has failed and I do not have very much money and no job."

Sally laughed, and said, "Paul, you don't have to worry about that. I just spent the winter with you in a one room cabin and if marrying you meant I had to do it again in a tent, I would. Haven't you figured out yet that I am crazy mad in love with you? I am hungry, so let's go to breakfast."

Chapter 17

Vows

At breakfast, they both had eggs, toast, hash browns and orange juice. Sally joked that eagle eggs are much bigger and she could only have eaten one instead of three.

"Paul, if it is alright with you, could we be married in your church. Because I am a new Christian, I don't have one yet?" Sally asked.

"My church is just a small country church so it depends on how many people you are going to invite." Paul answered.

"That will be fine with me, I am just planning on inviting my parents, so they can meet you, and my cousin Beth. She might bring her three boys and her husband. So that is seven on my side. Is that too many?"

"I believe that many will fit just fine." Paul replied. He was greatly relieved that Sally did not want a big wedding.

"Who are you going to invite?" Sally asked. Paul answered, "Just your future step daughters and their families. Oh, and also my friend Randy and his family. He is sort of responsible for all this, because he talked me into the hunting trip. So that is at the most eleven people. I do not think that they will all be able to afford to come."

"Paul, sweetie I have some connections. I am sure that I can arrange for them all to fly in for free if you want." Sally stated. Her connections were, of course, to her check book but she did not want to reveal her wealth to Paul yet, because she thought it might still scare him away.

"That would be great." Paul said.

"Paul I know that the husband usually takes care of arranging the honeymoon, but I would like to do it and surprise you with where we are going. So can I have your permission to, pretty, pretty, please, with sugar on top?"

Paul laughed and said. "Sally we have been engaged for less than an hour and I can already tell I am never going to be able to say no to you."

After breakfast they parted with another kiss and both went back to their own rooms with plans to meet for lunch before the news conference. Sally called her lawyer and told him to get started right away on researching the law so he could advise her of any legal things she needed to know about marrying an American. He advised her that she needed a prenuptial agreement signed. Sally just laughed, and told him, in no uncertain terms, that NO she did not!

Sally made some other phone calls and then she called Matt Johnsen. "Matt this is Sally McPhearson, I told you I would pay you double your going rate but you never told me how much that was." Matt had not even thought about that. He had already deposited his $100,000 reward check and really was not expecting anything else.

"Sally you don't have to worry about that, the $100,000 reward for finding you was more than enough." Matt stated.

Sally replied, "Nonsense, a deal is a deal, don't try weaseling out of selling me that canoe. I just arranged to have a check sent to you for payment for my canoe and the plane ride. I did not know for sure how much to send so I had it made out for $5,500 that is $500 for my canoe and $5000 for the plane ride. Is that enough?"

"Sally I don't know what to say. That is way more than enough." Matt replied.

Sally just said, "Good. Now Matt I have some more work for you. We left everything in the back of your plane yesterday. I need you to store it for us. Some of the things are wet and you will need to dry them out. Please take special care of the large snowshoes, you would never believe how much work they were to make. There is a .22 rifle in the sleeping bag and I need you to unload the magazine and clean it. Can you do that and save everything for me.?"

"Yes, Ma'am, it will be done." Matt replied.

"Good," Sally said again. "I also will be requiring your services as a pilot again soon, but I do not know when yet."

"Sally, I am at your beck and call." Matt replied, and that ended their phone conversation.

Now, Matt's business was booming, at least temporarily. Already that morning, Canadian Search and Rescue and the FAA had him scheduled to make two flights a day back and forth to the crash site for at least a week. There was already another big change in his life. Flying back from the Sault he had been thinking that his father's plane just was not big enough for his business. He had been limited to flying no more than two people at a time and very little gear. Sometimes, a small plane came in handy for landing on a small lake but Matt realized that the small plane limited him. He could make more money with a larger plane, as he would not miss out on flying in larger groups. He had returned to Wawa just as the sun came up. Matt called and woke up one of his dad's friends who had a de Havilland Otter seaplane for sale. Because of the recession Matt struck a bargain with him and agreed to a $50,000 down payment. He bought the plane for far less than it had been worth the year before.

Sally was not done with the phone yet. She called her cousin Beth.

Beth said "I saw that you were rescued and I want you to know I never stopped praying for you. I am so happy for you and I have just been keeping your CEO chair warm for you.".

Sally said, "Beth, thank you for praying for me. Your prayers have done a lot of good. I want you to be the first, ah second to know that I have accepted Christ as my Savior."

"Oh, Sally that is wonderful! Did you know that after you went missing I was able to lead both your parents to Christ, so now your whole family are Christians?" Beth replied with true happiness in her voice.

"Thank you Beth for leading my mother and father to Christ. and telling me about it." Sally then said. "Dad told me you have been doing a great job as CEO so I am giving you the chair you have been keeping warm for me." Beth was speechless and Sally continued. "I may be open to a board seat in a couple of months but I will need to discuss the possibility with my husband."

That brought Beth's speech back and she said, "Husband?"

"Perhaps, I should have said future husband. We just became engaged this morning but we plan to be married as soon as we can work out the details. I want you to attend the wedding. It will be in Michigan and I will call you soon with the details. Please do not print anything about the wedding in the newspaper."

"Now I need a favor. I need you to put a couple of your best investigative reporters on something for me. Write this down. I think that Harry Solon would be my choice for one, but don't let either of them know that the other one is working on this. I want all the information they can dig up on a girl named Susan Smith. She was married to James Smith who lost his life on a ship in Lake Superior. Her parents were Pierre and Mary Le Forest. I want to know if she is still alive and if she is, where she is. I do not want her to know anyone is checking up on her and I do not want any stories written let alone filed without my knowledge or permission. Give them both a big expense account and send me the bill. Do you understand and can you do this for me?" Sally asked.

"Yes, I will get them right on it." Beth replied. Then they said good bye. After the call Beth said to herself, "Who says miracles no longer happen? There are four miracles right here. My cousin has come back from the dead, accepted Christ, is getting married and is giving me her job!"

Sally was feeling a little proud of herself. With great dispatch, she had managed to tie a bunch of things up that morning in neat little packages. Then she thought, pride goeth before a fall. Was that a Bible verse? She did not know for sure. So she prayed, "Jesus, I have been on my own path for far too long. Please guide and direct my ways and keep me on the path you have for me." Sally concluded her prayer and remembered something else she needed to do before she met Paul for lunch. She did not have much time and needed to hurry. Out the door she went.

Paul had been working the phones also. First he called his pastor. His pastor said it was like getting a call from the dead. He had not been listening to the news and did not know that Paul had been rescued. Paul told him that he would need his help and asked if the church was tied up anytime in the next week.

"Just for Wednesday night and Sunday morning services." the pastor replied. "Why do you ask?" Well, I need you to perform a little wedding service." Paul said. "Who is getting married?" the pastor inquired. "I am!" Paul declared.

Next Paul called his credit card company. Paul did not realize that his hotel room had already been paid for and he figured he was going to need his credit card. He had always managed to pay his credit card off each month regardless of his lack of money. He knew he could not afford the high interest rate of the card so he only used it when he had the money to pay the bill. However, he had used the card before his trip and because of the crash he had not paid off the card in six months.

Once he had fed his credit card number to the animated phone answering system, he got a real live person on the phone. "Yes, Mr.

Sinhuna, what can I do for you today?" the voice on the other end of the phone asked. Paul explained his situation to the representative.

"Really", the representative said, "I saw you on the news last night. Let me see what I can do for you. Mr. Sinhuna, I see from your records that you always pay your bill off every month, but you are six months past due on a small amount. Your account has been flagged as possibly deceased. Let me put you on hold for a minute or so while I speak to a supervisor." When the man came back on the line, he said. "My supervisor asked me to keep you on the line as he checks into your situation. Mr. Sinhuna, would you mind if I asked you some questions that have nothing to do with this call while we are waiting?"

Paul said, "Ask away."

"How were you able to survive in the wilderness all winter?" the man on the other end of the phone asked. Paul told him how God had provided for all their needs. "Mr. Sinhuna, my life is so messed up right now, I wish I could have a belief in God like you do."

Paul said, "You can." and laid out the plan of salvation for the man right over the phone. Paul could hear the tears in the man's voice as he accepted Christ. Paul thought that even if he had never met Sally, all the suffering he had gone through over the last months would have been worth it, just for that one moment, and Paul silently thanked God for the blessing.

Soon the supervisor came on the line. "Mr. Sinhuna, I am happy to report that your account has been reinstated and we have even removed all interest and late charges. All you need to do is make the minimum payment on your next bill. Thank you for selecting us to be your credit card provider and welcome back from the wilderness."

Paul was relieved. Now he knew he would not have to wash dishes in the hotel restaurant to pay for his room.

Just then, there was a knock at the door. Paul opened it and found Sally was standing there with some packages. When she saw the tears on Paul's cheeks she asked, "Paul what is wrong, you haven't changed your mind about marrying me, have you?"

Paul replied. "Not a chance. Why, you have not changed your mind about becoming Mrs. Sinhuna, have you?"

Sally answered. "No way!"

Paul kissed her, and explained how he had just led the credit card representative to Christ over the phone. Now there were tears in Sally's eyes also. Then she explained how Beth had led her parents to Christ, after the crash. "Paul, you were right. God did mean everything we went through for our good.

"Yes, in the plane crash He planted the seeds for a bountiful harvest." Paul agreed.

"What is in the bags?" Paul asked.

"I got us some new clothes and shoes for our news conference. I hope yours are the right size and that you like them. I was just guessing on both counts and if you don't like them we can take them back. I will change in the bathroom and you can change out here OK?"

"That is fine with me." Paul answered.

They parted, with another kiss, to change their clothes. When Sally finished changing, she called out from the bathroom, "Paul are you decent?"

"As decent as I ever am." was Paul's reply. "Did anything fit?" Sally asked when she walked into the room.

"Everything fit just find, even the shoes. Thanks." Paul answered.

"Well those clothes are not free, I expect you to pay me back for them in kisses and I must warn you I charge high interest rates. Before long, you will owe me so many kisses, it will take the rest of your life to pay me off." Sally exclaimed.

"I tried to stay out of debt my whole life but this one time I will have fun trying to pay you off." Paul replied.

Paul asked Sally if she wanted him to announce their engagement at the news conference.

"No, please do not do that, I have not told my parents yet." Sally said. That was true she had not told her parents her good news, but mainly, she didn't want Paul to announce their engagement to keep their wedding from turning into a media circus.

"Do you think I have to ask your father for your hand in marriage? Paul asked.

"No," Sally laughed. "Don't do that He might say no. Then I would have to start looking for a husband all over again." Sally teased.

The news conference was just a blur to both Paul and Sally. During the interview, Paul expressed his firm belief that the only reason they were able to survive their time in the wilderness was the help and providence of the Lord. Paul and Sally answered a couple of dozen questions from a number of interviewers, only a couple of which made the evening news. Then the news conference was over and they were free to go back to planning their marriage and their life together.

At dinner that evening, Sally asked Paul what he thought about having kids.

"Sally I love kids. I am a little on the old side for starting over with a new family. However, I will not deny you the opportunity to be a mother if you want. Remember, I already told you that I am never going to be able to say no to you."

"I was hoping you would say something like that." Sally said. "I would love to have kids, but my Doctor told me years ago that there is only a slight chance I could become pregnant again. So I was hoping you did not have your heart set on having more kids. What would you say about adopting, Paul?"

"Adopting would be fine with me. Who knows what God has in store for us? Perhaps we will have a few and adopt a few." Paul answered.

Plans were made to rent a car the next morning and to drive to Paul's home in Michigan. Once there, Sally would stay in a hotel room until their wedding. Paul walked her back to her room and they parted with a kiss. Sally was really tired but she still managed to find enough energy to call her parents and tell them her good news, about her salvation and her up coming wedding. After that she wrote Matt Johnsen a note and faxed it to him from the hotel desk . This is how the note read. Matt: I know you are busy, but I need to impose upon you. I hope I can count on you, please do not let me down. I need you to procure the following items and have them waiting for me. A check is on its way to you to cover the cost of the goods and your time. Then came the following list. Propane camp stove and extra bottles of gas, large tent, satellite phone, life preservers and seat cushions, new fishing poles and assorted tackle, chainsaw and gas, double air mattresses and double sleeping bag, toilet paper (5 cases) , bug repellent, 250 pounds of rice, 150 pounds of flour and some yeast, 25 boxes of pancake mix and three gallons of maple syrup In one gallon tins, 20 pounds of table salt, granite head stone with the names Pierre and Mary Le Forest. assorted tools (for cabin maintenance), flash lights, ice chest with food and anything else you can think of for a two week camping trip.

The next morning at the Wawa Sea Plane Base, when Matt picked up two FAA investigators to fly them to the crash site, Mable handed him the fax. Matt looked at it and said, "If Sally is really serious, it is a good thing I just closed a deal on the Otter sea plane." This was because he would have needed to make a number of flights to haul all that with his old plane. That evening, Mable gave Matt, Sally's check. It had arrived by special courier and was made out for $25,000. When Matt looked at it he said "Well, it looks like she is serious". Mable knew Matt was busy so she offered to fly to the Sault and do the shopping if Matt was willing to share some of his loot. Matt took her up on the offer.

When Sally awoke the next morning she knew that God wanted her to do something. She had never experienced anything like that before. It was something she did not want to do. She knew God had laid something on her heart and wanted her to confess something to Paul. She had never really deceived Paul but she had been hiding her wealth and power from him. She greatly feared that her wealth would drive Paul away from her if he found out about it before their marriage. However, she had committed herself to Christ and she knew she had to listen to his voice in her heart.

That morning, she knocked on Paul's hotel room door and he let her in. Paul noticed right away that there was something wrong and asked what it was.

"Paul the Lord laid something on my heart and he wants me to confess something to you. I was going to wait until we were married, because I was afraid that you wouldn't marry me if you found out before. Paul embraced her to reassure her and asked what it was.

"Paul, I am wealthy," Sally stated.

"How wealthy?" Paul asked

She just said "Very wealthy."

"I see." Paul said This suddenly explained some things to Paul, and had taken him by total surprise. Paul asked, "Sally, if I asked you to, could you give all your wealth away?"

Sally thought for just a moment and then answered, "Yes."

"Well then, I don't think your wealth will be a problem for me." This was a big relief for Sally and she could see how much better the Lord's way was than her own. Then Sally asked if Paul was going to ask her to give her wealth away. He said he would not, but someday the Lord might.

On their trip down to Michigan, Sally stated "Paul I just had a terrible thought. Do you think all the plumbing in your house may have frozen up last winter?"

Paul replied, "I hope not. Fortunately, a month before my hunting trip, I set it up so my utility payments would be taken directly from the bank account I have from the proceeds of the sale of my parents house. So the gas, electric, and phone should still be working. I suppose, the furnace could have quit, but I also turned off the water before I left, so if it did, there shouldn't be too much damage." Sally's worries would prove unfounded.

Just after they crossed the Mackinaw Bridge, Sally asked Paul what his daughters had said when he told them about the up coming marriage.

"I have not told them yet." Paul answered.

"Oh, Paul why not?" Sally asked with alarm.

"Half of Oregon's phone system is out so I have not even been able to call Gayle since we were rescued. I called Katherine and she emailed Gayle for me, but I wasn't about to inform Gayle by email that I was getting married. I heard on the news that the phone system should be repaired by this afternoon. So we can call and tell them both."

"Paul, I am nervous about meeting your daughters."Sally stated.

"Do not be. Katherine will love you from the first minute you meet her, that is just the way she is. Gayle, on the other hand will be a littler harder to win over but I am sure you will."

Paul's predictions proved correct. Paul called Gayle first, and after their tearful phone reunion, he told her about the marriage plans. This took Gayle by surprise but she did quickly warm to the idea, and talked privately with Sally for an hour on the phone. Then Paul came back on the phone and told her that because of Sally's "connections" a travel agency would be calling her so she and her husband could fly for free to Michigan for the wedding. It was planned for Thursday, so the two pastor son-in-laws could return to their home churches in time to preach on Sunday.

Then they called Katherine and when she was told about the up coming marriage, she began crying and said this was an answer to her prayers. Katherine ended up talking to Sally privately for three hours. Near the end of the phone call Katherine asked Sally if it would be OK with her if she called her " Mother". With tears in her eyes, Sally told her she would be honored. Then Paul came back on the phone and told her that the travel agency would be calling her to make arrangements so that Katherine her husband and two boys could fly to Michigan for free.

After the call, Sally said, "I knew I was going to be a step mother, but Paul, you never told me, I was also going be a Grandmother." So Paul teased her by calling her Grandma the rest of the day.

Paul's family flew in on Tuesday. They could have stayed in a hotel for "free" but they all chose to stay at Paul's log home on the lake. It was a little crowded but everything worked out fine. There was however, just a little tension between Gayle and Sally. Gayle noticed that Katherine was calling Sally, "Mother", and it bothered her. So Gayle confronted Sally about it. Sally told Gayle that Katherine had asked her if it was OK and she had said it was. "Gayle, I know that I can never replace your real mother and just because your sister has chosen to call me Mother doesn't mean you have to. You can just call me Sally if you wish. This defused Gayle's affront, and before too long Gayle chose to call Sally "Mother" also. By the day of the wedding Sally already felt like part of the family.

Paul was worried about meeting Sally's parents but he really need not have been. They told him that the Lord had abundantly answered their prayers by sending Paul to their daughter. When Paul met Beth she gave him a big hug and thanked him for saving her cousin's life. Paul said that he only saved her once and Sally had saved him twice. Sally broke in and said that that wasn't totally true, because Paul had led her to the Lord, so they had both saved each other twice. Paul really hit it off with Beth's three boys and promised to one day take them fishing.

The wedding was not anything like Sally had envisioned when she was a young girl. She had envisioned a costly affair with several hundred guests. This wedding was small and intimate and she could not have been happier with the ceremony. She was also happy she was able to hide it from the media. Paul gave her a ring that had belonged to his Grandmother. It had a small and insignificant diamond but she treasured it more than she would have the largest diamond. She had learned it is not the size of the diamond that counts but the love behind it.

When Paul and Sally said goodbye to everyone and went to leave for their honeymoon Paul handed her the keys to his truck. "Why are you handing me your keys?" Sally asked. "I want you to drive." Sally stated.

"Have you forgotten? I don't know where we are going." Paul said.

Sally just replied. "Drive north."

As they drove north, Sally said, "Paul I am feeling a little unsure of myself on my chosen destination for our honeymoon."

"You need not be, as long as I am with you, I will be happy." came Paul's reply.

"Are you sure?" Sally asked, "What if I were planning to camp in a tent?" "I would be fine with a tent, as long as you were in the tent with me. However, if your planning to stay in a tent we had better stop and buy one because there isn't one in the back of the truck," Paul stated.

"We might end up staying in a tent for a few days if my other plans don't work out, but if we do, don't worry, I have already taken care of it." Sally answered.

They drove around Michigan's Upper Peninsular for a few days, staying in motels and looking at waterfalls. Sally said looking at waterfalls was a mandatory thing to do on a honeymoon, but part of the reason was to give Matt time to make all the arrangements. Then Sally directed Paul to drive across the bridge from Sault Ste. Marie, Michigan to Sault Ste. Marie, Canada. Sally made Paul stop and they bought fishing licenses. That had Paul really curious, because there were no fishing poles in the back of the truck. Then Sally asked Paul to guess where they were going. By this time Paul had an idea where their destination was but he did not let on. "Are we taking the circle tour around Lake Superior?" Paul guessed.

"No, but that is a good idea and we could do that, on the way home." Sally replied.

When they stopped to get gas as they followed the shore of Lake Superior, Sally called Matt Johnsen again while Paul was in the bathroom. He confirmed that he had the items she had requested packed in his plane and was waiting for her arrival. Then Matt said, "Miss McPhearson, I really appreciate everything you have done for me."

"That's OK, Matt. If you had not rescued me I would likely be dead now, but there is just one thing. You are pronouncing my name wrong."

"Oh, I am sorry, but I was sure that is the way they pronounced it on television. How do you pronounce it?" Matt asked.

"My name is pronounced Mrs. Sinhuna." Sally replied.

"You mean that you and Paul got married, congratulations!" Matt said.

"Thank you, Matt, just don't tell any news people, please. We will be in Wawa in about an hour and half." Sally said.

"I will be waiting for you." Matt answered, and they said good by.

As they pulled into Wawa Sally explained to Paul her plan to fly back to Starvation Lake and resupply the Le Forest cabin for the owner. Paul was genuinely happy about her plan. He had been bothered that they had used up a lot of supplies and had not replaced them. Matt had removed all but the pilot and co-pilot seats and one other in the Otter seaplane to make room for all the cargo. When they boarded the plane Sally sat in the spare seat and Paul took the co-pilot's seat. Matt had just finished his preflight check list when Paul asked him if he had an instructor rating.

Matt said, "Yes, I have, do you want to take lessons?"

" I might like to. I used to have a license but flying was so expensive, I let it lapse." Paul said.

In surprise, Sally said, "Paul, you were a pilot? Why didn't you tell me?"

"It just never came up." Paul replied.

"What ratings do you hold?" Matt asked.

Paul replied, "Single and multi engine land and instrument, but I have never flown a sea plane." Paul replied.

Then Matt asked if Paul would like to fly them to Starvation Lake. Paul said that he had never flown a plane this large before but he sure would like to give it a try, if it was OK with Sally.

They both looked at her and Sally said, "It is fine with me."

Matt said it was fine with him, but there were just two things. He wasn't allowed to have passengers while he was instructing so they had to keep quiet about it because he could lose his license and if Paul broke his plane they would have to pay for it.

Paul said he needed permission from his wife, because she was the one with the money bags.

Sally just said, "Go for it."

So Matt taxied the plane away from the dock, as Paul looked at Matt's aviation charts. When they were far enough out in the lake that no one could see, Matt turned the controls over to Paul. So for the first time in over twenty five years Paul was flying a plane when it took off. When they reached Starvation Lake, Matt asked Paul if he wanted him to take over the controls, but Paul said he would like to land the plane if Matt would let him, and Matt said he could. Paul made a picture perfect landing. A more experienced pilot would have landed closer to the Le Forest cabin at the very East end of the lake, but Paul wanted to make sure he left himself enough room. Consequently, after they landed they had to taxi over a mile. Still, Matt was impressed, and said that maybe he should be asking for lessons from Paul.

While they were taxiing to the Le Forest cabin Sally said, "Paul I still can't believe that we spent all that time together and you never told me you were a pilot."

"It was a long time ago, Sally. When I first married Joan we were planning to be missionaries to New Guinea but by the time I had my pilot's license God had closed the door." Paul stated.

Sally said, "Well, I think you should take some lessons and renew you license."

"Sally, does that mean that you would consider being a missionary with me in New Guinea?" Paul asked.

Sally laughed, "Oh, oh, I guess I did not know what I was getting myself into when I suggested that but if the Lord leads my husband to New Guinea, I will be going also." "Now, my love, is there anything about you besides the fact you can fly a plane I should know about?" Sally asked.

Paul thought for a moment and said, "I can't think of anything right now except that I can speak, read and write Japanese." The way Paul delivered that line made both Matt and Sally burst out laughing.

"Oh, Paul quit joking around." Sally stated. Of course, Paul was not joking, but it would be a long time until Sally found that out.

Then Paul asked Matt, "Do you know why they named this Starvation Lake?"

Matt replied. "My, father always told me that it was because this lake has the worst fishing of any lake in Canada."

They pulled the plane up to the beach in front of the Le Forest cabin and tied it to a tree. Matt had already flown Sally's canoe to the Le Forest cabin at her request. When Paul and Sally had last been at the cabin, winter was just releasing its grip, and the area had looked lifeless. Now, green leaves and grass had appeared and the change was remarkable. The area around the cabin was bursting with life. The desolate landscape had been transformed. However, there was trash up by the cabin that could be seen from the beach. Matt apologized to them, because he knew that some of the crash investigators had left the Le Forest cabin in a mess.

The three of them unloaded the cargo from the plane and laid it all out on the beach. The last thing they removed from the plane was the granite headstone with the names Pierre and Mary Le Forest on it. The head stone was bungee corded to a hand cart and Matt helped Paul pull it up to the grave site. After Sally lead them in a brief prayer, Matt helped them haul things from the shore to the cabin's porch with the hand cart.

Matt said, "Goodbye. Remember, just call me on the satellite phone if you want anything." Paul and Sally walked with him back to the shore and Paul helped cast off the plane from the beach. Paul and Sally waved good by as the plane took off.

Paul turned to Sally and said. "Matt is a nice guy but I thought he would never leave. He took her by the hand and lead her back to the cabin. When they reached the porch they noticed that someone had broken in the door sometime in the three weeks since they had left the cabin. Paul frowned as he looked at the damage and said. "It is partly my fault that someone has broken in the door, because I removed the latch string note."

Still holding Sally's hand, Paul turned to her and thanked her for bringing him back so they could put the cabin back in the condition they found it, because it had been bothering him. Then Paul looked her in the eyes and said, "We must fulfill all traditions." The next thing Sally knew he had picked her up and carried her across the threshold.

"Oh, Paul, think about your back!" Sally exclaimed in surprise.

Paul replied, "Let me worry about my back my bride. I will also carry you across the threshold when we get back home after our honeymoon, but because this little cabin was our home for over five months, I thought it was appropriate."

"You are right my husband." Sally replied.

The next morning, Sally cooked breakfast on the camp stove inside the cabin. It was too warm to cook on the wood stove. At breakfast Sally said, "Paul, I have been praying and have come to peace with what I am about to tell you. If the Lord leads you to become a missionary to New Guinea, I am ready to go too. I just want you to do what the Lord leads you to do, and I want you to know that I was serious when I said I was willing to go."

"Thank you, Sally, I already knew you were serious. Right now, I do not feel that God is leading me to New Guinea, he closed that door for me long ago. However, if he were to open the door, it is nice to know that you would back my decision to go. Now, if you feel led to become a missionary to New Guinea, be sure to let me know. Perhaps the Lord will choose to lead me through my wife."

They were very disappointed to find that the crash investigators had not only trashed the place, but had also burned up the skin stretchers that Paul and Sally had saved under the bed for the owner. In three days with the chainsaw Paul was able to cut more firewood than he could in a month with the ax. Carrying the firewood back and staking it on the porch was more work than cutting it, but soon there was more firewood at the cabin than was there on the day of the crash.

Over the next few days, Paul and Sally filled all the mason jars in the cupboards and the cellar with rice, pancake mix, flour, and the other items that they had used. They cleaned the place and made repairs. Susan's snow shoes were hung from the ceiling by a shoe string over the bed as they had been when they found them. When Sally asked why they were stored that way Paul surmised that it was to keep mice from chewing on the webbing.

The door was beyond fixing, so Paul took measurements and Sally ordered Matt to have a new one made and fly it out to them when he flew out another ice chest of food. Paul also took measurements of the broken window pane and asked Sally to have Matt get some glass cut to size and bring some caulk. Matt helped Paul install the door. Now there would be no need to latch the door from the inside and leave by the window.

After they had finished fixing, cleaning and resupplying the cabin, Paul and Sally used her canoe to explore around their end of the lake. One day they even went far enough to have a picnic at the picnic table rock where they had eaten Paul's Northern Pike. That meant that it was after dark by the time they returned and they listened to loon calls all the way back. They also did a lot of fishing but caught nothing.

"I guess that is really why they called it Starvation Lake." Sally said. "Dear husband, I am sorry, I hoped that this would be a fishing vacation for you."

Paul replied, "Dear wife, don't be sorry, the Lord of the heavens provided the fish when we needed them."

All too soon their time at the cabin came to an end. They left a note for Susan or who ever owned the cabin, thanking them and telling how they, had resupplied the cabin. Paul oiled the .22 rifle and hung it back from the log floor joist, in the cellar. Then he nailed the trap door back down and also nailed down the rag rug. They tried to leave the cabin as close to the way they had found it as possible. Sally called Matt on satellite phone and requested to be picked up. As they stood on the shore waiting for the plane to return Sally hugged her husband and said, "This lake may be named Starvation Lake, but it will always be Salvation Lake to me.

CHAPTER 18

Full Circle

Paul and Sally finished out the circle tour of Lake Superior on their round about way home. When they arrived home, Paul fulfilled his pledge to carry his bride over the threshold a second time. Soon after arriving home from their honeymoon, Sally received a call from her cousin, Beth with important information. Paul was still unpacking the truck when Sally came out of the house and asked him to put everything back in.

Paul said, "OK but why?"

The answer was, "We need to go back to Canada."

Twenty four year old widow Susan Smith was waiting tables in a restaurant while soon to be five year old Lilly was playing in the back room. She was living in the small resort cabin that her father had moved her to so she could finish her last two years of high school. That was seven years ago and things had changed. The saw mill and logging that had provided jobs in the area had moved on. The local school had been closed for lack of students. That meant Susan and Lilly would need to move soon so that Lilly could attend school. Susan had already received a letter from the Ministry of Education informing her that she needed to move somewhere that had a school or Social Workers would be notified and take custody of her child.

Susan was dreading the move. She did not know anyone in the city and lacked the finances she needed to move and make a new start. She had been praying for God's guidance and provision for the move, but so far it had not come. So she was just waiting on God. How had she let herself become trapped in this situation? It was her own foolishness she thought.

Five years before, she had left her father's Starvation Lake cabin with a thousand dollars worth of furs she had trapped. The trip would have given any two outdoors men pause. It was down three hundred miles of lake and river systems and it required lining the 24 foot birch bark freight canoe down several miles on two different dangerous rapids, over a hundred miles of open ocean and a few miles upstream on another river. Susan had done all of this alone, while six months pregnant and had thought nothing unusual about it. After all she knew she was not really alone, her Heavenly Father was with her.

She had arrived at the small bush town on the same appointed day that the wealthy collector had flown in. The collector had promised to buy the canoe sight unseen from her father for $7,000. Susan had told him that her father had died while the collector inspected the canoe. The collector had taken out his check book and started writing out a check, as he explained that his deal had been with her father and since he was no longer alive, he was under no obligation to honor it. As he handed her the check Susan realized he had her over a barrel and would have to accept what ever he offered for the canoe. The check was made out for $10,000.

The collector told Susan that he was very pleased to purchase such a fine birch bark canoe and that he planned to hang the canoe from the ceiling of the great room of his home. After he died, the canoe would be left to a museum to be put on display. The canoe would never again see the water.

Susan had sold her furs and her father's traps for $1150 and in November of that year, had collected $10,000 from her late husband James life insurance. The people that owned the resort felt sorry for her and let her continue to stay in the cabin in exchange for some care taking duties. The bank had never repossessed her husband's truck. No one at the bank knew where the former town of Sunrise was, and they had somehow figured how to "unfreeze" her late husband's bank account to take the payments out. The owners of the restaurant had continued to let Susan work in the summers when they were open.

So Susan did have a nice little bank account. However, the Starvation Lake cabin was on leased Crown land. The lease had come up for renewal. Susan knew she was being foolish to spend all her money renewing the lease, but what else could she do? Her parents grave was on the property. At the time, she did not know that she would need to move and would need the money. Now, she was between a rock and a hard place, because of her sentimental foolishness. She knew the Starvation Lake cabin was so remote that she was likely never to be able to afford to visit it ever again. Did she really have a right to expect God to bail her out? Why had she been so foolish?

Susan was happy seven o'clock had finally arrived and she could close the restaurant. Now, all she needed to do was clean up the kitchen before she could bring Lilly back to their cabin. The owners of the restaurant had left her alone and in charge early that morning. It had been a busy day with lots of customers and she had to wait the tables and cook all the food herself. All the customers were gone now and she was about to hang the closed sign on the door when a tall man and a woman entered. "Sorry, we are closing." Susan said with a smile.

The tall man said, "Please, my wife and I have been driving all day and we have had nothing to eat. It is miles to the next town and I promise to make it worth your while, if you could just give us something to eat."

"I don't have much left to feed you, our specials are all gone." Susan said.

The tall man said, "Please, my wife and I would be happy with just some fried eggs and toast."

Susan said, "I guess I can handle that." As she put the closed sign in the window to prevent any other late customers. Susan asked, "How many eggs would you like?

"Four." said the man and "two." said the woman.

"Please seat yourselves anywhere you like." Susan said as she made her way to the kitchen to prepare the meal.

As Susan fried the eggs she noticed little Lilly had left the back room and was talking to her customers. She heard the man ask her if her name was Lilly. This did not alarm Susan. Lilly was a big hit with the customers of the restaurant. The cute, friendly and precocious little girl brightened everyone's day. She just figured that the man had been there before and remembered her daughter.

When Susan brought out the plates of eggs and toast she said, "Lilly, honey, what has mother told you about bothering the customers."

The tall man said, "Susan, she has not bothered us one bit." Susan was surprised he knew her name, she usually recognized repeat customers, but did not remember the two now sitting at her table.

"Mommy, Mommy, I have to go to the potty." little Lilly said, as she tugged on Susan's arm.

Susan said, "Please excuse us." and hurried her little girl off the the bathroom.

When Susan came back from taking Lilly to the bathroom, her customers were gone. At first she thought they had stiffed her for the price of the meal, but then she thought they did not seem like that kind of people. They were probably in a hurry and left payment on the table. Looking across the room she could see that indeed they had left some money. She walked to the table without giving the matter any more thought. When she reached the table she looked down and in amazement found a ten dollar bill and two, one hundred dollar bills. One of the hundred dollar bills was U.S. and the other Canadian. She thanked God for the tip but wondered why anyone would leave so much money for less than a ten dollar meal.

As Susan picked up the money, she noticed the money was covering something else neatly stacked . It was a letter, paper clipped to an envelope. For a second she thought that the couple must had left this here by mistake, but then she noticed SUSAN SMITH on both the letter and the envelope. "How odd." she said as she sat down at the table to read the letter, with little Lilly playing at her feet. Somehow, Susan knew that this was going to be the answer to her prayers.

The letter was intentionally vague, because Sally was still embarrassed that she had read Susan's diary. It started, Dear Susan: I must apologize for my hand writing. I am writing this in a moving car. I am afraid that this letter will not make much sense to you now, but it may someday, only God knows.

If not for you and your father, I would have died alone in my sins many months ago. Our Heavenly Father used you and your father to provide for me and my future husband in our hour of true need. Thanks to you, I am now married and for the first time in my life truly happy. Most importantly, I have now accepted Jesus Christ as my Lord and Savior. The letter then quoted the book of Matthew, ...for I was hungry and you gave me food; I was thirsty and you gave me drink; I was a stranger and you took me in; I was naked and you clothed Me... Susan, I know you can not possibly understand, but the Lord used you to do that for me and more. I will have to wait until I reach heaven to thank your father for what he did for me, but I am thanking you now.

Before you had Lilly, you knew the Lord would provide for you. The Lord used you to provide for me in my desperation. Now I am very honored that he is using me to provide for you and Lilly. Please let the money in this envelope be a blessing to you and Lilly. May the Lord always bless and keep you. Yours in Christ, Sally Sinhuna.

Susan did not know what to think. She could not comprehend how this letter could be true; however, there was a small voice in her head confirming that it was. But how? Her father had died five years ago and it sounded like this stranger knew that. So how had Susan's father provided for this woman? There was so much of the letter she just could not understand.

With trembling hands and tears in her eyes she opened the envelope. A cashiers check fell out onto the table. Susan gasped when she saw the amount. At first she thought it said $500. That, along with the tip they had left, would help her move to the city and she praised God for answering her prayers. However, when she blinked her eyes she thought it said $5000.! She stared at the check for a full minute before she could bring herself to comprehend that the check was, in reality, made out for $500,000.00.

THE END

AFTER WORD

This book is a work of fiction, any resemblance between the charters in this book and real people living or dead is purely coincidental. However, some portions of this book are true.

The mention of a place in Texas where dinosaur and human tracks can be found in the same rock strata is true. They can be seen during the dry season in the bedrock of the Paluxy River. However, there are a number of other areas that dinosaur tracks and human tracks can be found side by side. Just check the Internet for more information and photos.

The information about man made artifacts found in coal seams is true. Again more information and photos can be found on the Internet.

The missionary and elephant story was told many years ago to the author by a Sunday school teacher and is thought to be true.

The story of the reformed bank robber turned pastor is similar to a true story. However, the name, locations, and details have been changed to protect the identity and privacy of the people involved.

The 1925 discovery of a large rotting carcass of some kind of duck billed plesiosaur type creature in Santa Cruz is a true. As is the 1977 incident where a Japanese fishing ship pulled aboard a rotting carcass of what they still believe was a plesiosaur. Western scientists are convinced that the carcass was merely that of a basking shark that just looked like a plesiosaur because of the advanced decay. It however, is the author's understanding that the trained Japanese Zoologist who was on board the ship at the time is convinced that it was a plesiosaur or other unknown species. He has had vast experience with sharks and because the flesh did not smell of ammonia and because it had hard bone and not cartilage he believes that it could not possibility have been a carcass of a shark.

The area of the book that talks about Biblical Archeology is all true.

Most importantly, the part of the book where Sally accepted Christ is fiction but the part about feeling His peace and forgivingness is true, it has happened to untold millions of people. If you have never felt His peace and forgiveness, there is no reason to wait any longer. The Lord Jesus Christ stands ready to welcome you into his kingdom. Your past does not matter to him. He will forgive you and forget yours sins. All you have to do is humble yourself and invite him into your heart.

Jesus told the parable of the sower in Matthew 13:3-8 "Behold, a sower went out to sow. "And as he sowed, some seed fell by the wayside: and the birds came and devoured them. "Some fell on stony places, where they did not have much earth: and they immediately sprang up because they had no depth of earth. "But when the sun was up they were scorched, and they withered away. "And some fell among thorns and the thorns sprang up and choked them. "But others fell on good ground and yielded a crop: some a hundredfold, some sixty, some thirty.

If you have accepted Christ as your Lord and Saviour make sure your seeds have fallen on good ground so they do not wither and die. Read the Bible, it is full if treasures just waiting for you to find them. Also, find a good Bible believing church and regularly attend. A word of caution here, not all churches are Bible believing. Use prayer and your discretion to find a church that is right for you.

May the Lord bless and keep you.

CPSIA information can be obtained
at www.ICGtesting.com
Printed in the USA
LVOW12s0917110816

499824LV00001B/1/P